W9-AAC-140

MURDER IN A HURRY

**Books by Richard and Frances Lockridge
In Thorndike Large Print**

MURDER WITHIN MURDER
MURDER IS SUGGESTED
MURDER IS SERVED

Murder in a Hurry

A MR. AND MRS. NORTH MYSTERY

Frances and Richard Lockridge

Thorndike Press • Thorndike, Maine

Library of Congress Cataloging in Publication Data:

Lockridge, Frances Louise Davis.
    Murder in a hurry : a Mr. and Mrs. North mystery /
Frances and Richard Lockridge.
        p.   cm.
    In large print.
    ISBN 0-89621-195-9 (lg. print : alk. paper)
    1. Large type books.   I. Lockridge, Richard 1898–
II. Title.
    [PS3523.0243M76   1988]
    813'.54—dc19   88-28605
                                                              CIP

Large Print edition available in North America by arrangement
with Harper & Row Publishers.

Cover design by James B. Murray.

MURDER IN A HURRY

I

It is an inconsiderable street neither long nor wide, and it is appropriately modest. As if even further to shorten its length, it bends in the middle, abandoning a course which is roughly west by south to pursue one which is by a degree or two north of west. This sort of behavior on the part of streets is familiar enough to those who live in downtown New York, but many feel that West Kepp Street somewhat overdoes it. Those who live in West Kepp Street — there is no East Kepp Street, and so far as anyone knows there never was — speak of it with an odd mixture of fondness and apology; it is, they say, the funniest little street, and the hardest to find.

It is, certainly, hard enough to find. Taxi-cab drivers who can go unerringly, and by one of the shorter routes, to the always somewhat preposterous intersection of West Fourth and West Twelfth Streets, are baffled when Kepp is mentioned. Taking strangers there, they pause to enquire the way of other hackers and even, as a last resort, of traffic patrolmen. Such enquiries are seldom satisfactorily answered, nor are residents of the neighborhood often much more helpful. They have heard of it; it is surely around here somewhere. It is over that way, probably; but perhaps, on the other hand, it is over this way. But then more often than not, they decide they probably are thinking of Gay Street, which also has a crook in it and runs from nowhere in particular to nowhere of importance.

Homing Kepp Streeters do not, therefore, precisely reveal their destination to cab drivers or to friends who have agreed to drop them off. They assign a more comprehensible objective, a nearby landmark, and promise to guide from there; expecting valued guests, they commonly arrange to meet them at the nearest subway station and lead on by hand, as one living in the trackless suburbs will meet visitors at the white barn which cannot be missed (but often is) and is on your right just before you come to that series of forks which can in no manner be described.

And having finally been led to West Kepp Street, visitors are unimpressed and, not wishing too much to offend local pride — there is nothing, not even West Kepp Street, of which someone cannot be proud — are apt to say hesitantly that it is a very quaint little street. But even this term, unaffirmative as it is, is not particularly applicable. West Kepp Street is not lined by crooked little houses, with window boxes and red doors. Patchin Place is much more quaint; Macdougal Alley has it all over West Kepp Street for oddity. The buildings on either side of West Kepp Street are four and five story tenements, most of them still with the indigenous stoops. They have, to be sure, been reconstructed internally, so that now instead of large inconvenient flats they contain, in most cases, small inconvenient apartments which are entered through a kitchenette.

The street itself is absurdly narrow; two cars could hardly pass, even were two-way traffic allowed. Car owners living in West Kepp Street park, habitually, half on the sidewalks, which is manifestly illegal. But the police seldom visit West Kepp Street, which is otherwise generally law abiding. Firemen assigned to the nearest company sometimes shudder when they think of West Kepp Street, knowing that no hook-and-ladder could be got around the corner and that the buildings, in spite of their new fire resistant staircases, are merely waiting to go up in flames. But, so far, none of them ever has.

All things considered, it would be difficult to find anywhere in New York a location less attractive to commercial enterprise than West Kepp Street. At both ends of it there are, to be sure, shops, but they front on streets which, by comparison, are thoroughfares and present their flanks only to West Kepp. Those one might expect. But halfway along West Kepp itself, and just where it bends (as an over-tall man stoops a little, to make himself less conspicuous) there is nevertheless a shop. It occupies the ground floor of one of the four story buildings, it is reached by going down three steps and in recent months it has been vacant. One may still see the sign it last bore: "J. K. Halder, Pets." Curious people wandering through (and generally lost in) West Kepp Street stop to peer through the shop's dusty front window, but they see nothing for their pains. There are no longer any pets in Mr. Halder's pet shop, nor is there any longer Mr. Halder. The pets are elsewhere and so, of course, may Mr. Halder be. But he is no longer alive.

He was alive at ten-fifteen on the night of May twenty-third. He left a cab at the eastern end of West Kepp Street and walked down the street to his shop. He was an erect, slim man and, although it was a warm evening, he wore a light topcoat over his dinner clothes and a suitable dark hat on his gray hair. He was seventy-two years old and recently had been feeling older than his years justified. He was not thinking about this at the moment; he was very annoyed about something else. He shook his head as he walked toward the shop and, once, said a few angry words. But there was nobody near enough to notice his shaking head, or to overhear his words, and this, as things turned out, was rather a pity.

Mr. Halder went down the three steps and two cocker puppies in a pen in the window hurled themselves delightedly at the window-pane, pawing at it with earnest, ridiculous feet, opening pink mouths widely, emitting high-pitched, happy barks. In the pen next them a long-haired black kitten, awakened by this nonsense, stood up, arched her back, relaxed it and, with forepaws extended and clutching the floor, stretched it the other way. Having thus established that she was in working order, she moved over to the window, looked up at Mr. Halder, and opened her mouth. If she said anything, it was not audible through the glass.

Mr. Halder unlocked the door and went into the shop, which at once became noisy. The black kitten pushed a paw between the wooden bars of her pen and attempted to reach Mr. Halder's coat, meanwhile calling attention to herself as loudly as a small cat could. The cockers tried to jump out of their pen, bouncing hopefully against the bars, now and then falling down and not minding. From the shadows of the shop, which was deep, a variety of other sounds emerged.

"Good evening," Mr. Halder said, gravely, and turned on a center light. The variegated clamor increased. "Now now," said Mr. Halder. "Now now." The sounds did not abate.

Without removing either hat or coat, Mr. Halder then began his rounds. He went first to the black kitten, in the pen nearest the door. He put down a hand and the kitten, hardly bothering to smell it, rubbed against the offered fingers and began to purr. "You're a very pretty girl," Mr. Halder assured her and went to the cockers in the next pen. The kitten walked along beside him until the mesh between the pens stopped her. She put her nose to the mesh and, thoughtfully, smelled dogs. Mr. Halder tumbled the puppies briefly and continued, followed by their barks, by their adoring brown eyes.

Other pens, half a dozen of them, ran down one wall. Three dachshunds, almost full grown, were in the pen nearest the front of the shop and they stood up against the bars, shaking their rear ends furiously, holding their heads to be stroked. Mr. Halder obliged and spoke friendly words; he continued to the next pen, which held a single Siamese cat. The cat was waiting, sitting straight, black tail curled to the circle of the haunches. He was a young male, he spoke to Mr. Halder peremptorily, in a harsh voice. But then he rose and rubbed against the bars, pressing closely against them. Mr. Halder scratched behind the pointed brown-black ears. The cat purred, much more resonantly than had the black long-hair.

The third cage was empty; the fourth held a baby boxer and she, curled in the back of the cage, only raised her head when Mr. Halder stopped in front of her. "Poor girl," he said, and she whimpered a little at his voice. "Nice girl, poor girl," Mr. Halder said, but he did not touch her. Whatever ailed her, and the veterinarian was not yet certain, Mr. Halder wanted to do nothing to spread it. By tomorrow they would be able to tell whether the penicillin was working. Mr. Halder shook his head again, but this time in commiseration, not in anger. The next pen also was empty; the baby boxer was in isolation.

Five kittens were piled in the last pen and these Mr. Halder very gently lifted, one by one, from the pen. He examined each in turn, stroking gently with a fore-finger. They were too young for all this; they should still be with their mother. But their mother, after several years of wariness in traffic, had the week before proved herself not quite wary enough. If he could bring the kittens to healthy semi-maturity, Mr. Halder thought, he might be able to find foster homes for them. So far they seemed to be doing as well as could be expected. He put the last one back in the pile; it crawled over the others and dug itself in, sleepily.

Mr. Halder then visited two small monkeys in a single cage in the rear of the shop and looked thoughtfully at a shrouded cage containing a parrot, but decided to let well enough alone. Now and then he almost wished somebody would buy the parrot. Mr. Halder took off his hat and coat and went out through the rear of the shop, entering the single room in which he lived. He tossed his hat and coat on the bed, went to a refrigerator for food and began to measure it out for the animals. Being young, they required bed-time snacks.

Watching Mr. Halder prepare the food, one might have thought him over-fussy about it, and indeed, the animals in the main room seemed to feel this and made audible protests, having recognized the clunk of the closing refrigerator door. Hurry, the dogs told him; hurry, we are starving. What are you doing out there? the young Siamese demanded, abrupt and harsh. The small black cat, high-voiced, was plaintive, and almost drowned out. Even some canaries, although not immediately concerned, piped small remarks. But Mr. Halder, working under a bright light which threw the remainder of his living quarters into shadow, heating milk for the youngest kittens, ground meat for the other cats, prepared food for the dogs, did not hurry. He washed the feeding dishes meticulously, measured food into them with precision; might, for the care he expended, the scrupulous cleanliness he exercised, have been preparing food in the diet kitchen of some most modern hospital. He would not, as old Felix often told him, go to half so much trouble for himself. But that was so obvious that Mr. Halder did not bother to think about it and was surprised to hear it mentioned, even by old Felix.

He took milk to the smallest kittens first; took milk warmed, in a broad, flat pan. The kittens were standing, wobbling slightly, making small sounds. He put the pan down carefully in the center of their pen and, when all of them tried to eat at the same segment of the pan's circumference, rearranged them with gentle care. The kittens made strange, bobbing motions at the milk, now and then putting up small, surprised heads and sneezing as milk entered their noses. But the progress generally was encouraging; watching them for a moment, Mr. Halder speculated as to where he would find homes for them, feeling that their chances of growing up were improving. He smiled down at the kittens and went back to set the sick boxer's broth. She lapped at it with little interest and then went again to the rear of her pen and lay down, now on her side. Mr. Halder shook his head and made sad sounds with tongue and teeth.

He fed the Siamese, the dachshunds and the excited cockers; he presented meat to the small black cat, who crouched in front of it, looked in all directions, waved her plumy tail, abandoned the dish to go to the window and survey the visible terrain for enemies and, returning to the dish, finally ate. Mr. Halder then collected the used dishes, beginning with that of the five small kittens, and washed them in very hot water. The black cat had finished by then, and Mr. Halder lifted her from her pen and carried her into the back room, switching off as he went all but a single dim bulb in the shop room. In his living quarters, Mr. Halder sat in a chair with the little black cat on his knee and began slowly, gently, to brush her long fur. The cat purred and Mr. Halder looked as if he would have purred if he could have.

He had almost finished when the bell rang. The cat jumped on his knee and put in her claws for stability and, if necessary, for a leaping start. Mr. Halder soothed her, but swore softly to himself. He carried the cat back through the shop, turning on the lights as he passed through it, and put her back in her window pen. Then he went to the door and looked out. He started to shake his head and then saw who it was. He swore again, under his breath, but partially opened the door.

"So it's you," he said. This did not appear to require an answer, and the visitor made none. "I should have expected it," Mr. Halder said, and there was a kind of contempt in his voice. "It won't do any good, you know." There was no response to this, either, and Mr. Halder did not seem to expect one. "Well," he said, "come in. What are you waiting for?"

The visitor went in.

II

Tuesday, 2 P.M.
to 4:25 P.M.

The trouble with the cat they called Gin was that, although she obligingly assumed all the characteristic positions, she remained in none of them. That was, of course, usually the trouble with cats; it was one of the things which made them so hard to do, but at the same time so much fun to try to do. "Gin!" Liza O'Brien said suddenly, her voice soft but insistent. Gin sat, looked at her and pricked up dark ears. Quickly, almost frantically, Liza O'Brien's pencil moved on her drawing pad. Gin stood up and came to help. "No," Liza said. "Oh, *damn* you, Gin!" Gin rubbed against the girl; Gin scratched her chin on a corner of the drawing pad; Gin purred furiously, charmed by the words of approval and affection. Liza sketched for a moment longer, from memory.

The sheet on which she was working was covered already with fragments of the cat they

18

called Gin — of Gin stretching, Gin scratching herself; one priceless one of Gin sitting straight up, like a rabbit, batting at something over her head which only Gin could see. All that morning, Liza had been making such quick, tantalizing sketches of the cat they called Gin; most of the evening before she had worked on the one they called Sherry. (The one they called Martini was still under a table, all round blue eyes and suspicion. But there was one rather promising picture note on blue eyes and suspicion.) Gin was much the hardest of the three, and on the whole the most fun. By using Gin's long body and pointed face, Martini's enormous eyes, by trying to add to them the evasive wistfulness of the one they called Sherry, she might have the composite they wanted. It would be wonderful if she did; it would be wonderful if, tonight at dinner, she could tell Brian that she had it — that really she was certain she had it, that it was going to come off. It was wonderful to have nice things to tell Brian.

Gin, ignored, left in disgust. She went to a chair, reared up to it, sank her claws in, and began to scratch with the full, lithe strength of her muscled body. The slip cover shredded satisfactorily and Gin, encouraged, took a new hold. Liza O'Brien, her dark hair falling about her face, leaned over the pad and sketched furiously. That, certainly, was characteristic; if she could only get that! A cat scratching her owner's slip covers was almost at her best; you got the muscles, then; could show them under the misleading softness, the encompassing fur, which was all so many cat artists seemed to get — softness and charm.

"Not that," Gerald North told her the Friday before, when he had told her to try it. "Not just the fluff of cat. You know what I mean? This — " he had waved at the drawings she had brought in to show him — "this makes me think you do. But they all tell me it's difficult."

She had known what he meant; she had said she would love to have a shot at it.

They had talked terms, then, and Gerald North had admitted they could not be generous. Not this time. Some day, he said, and was perhaps talking more to himself than to the slender young woman who sat in the chair beside his desk, he would really do a book. But this couldn't be it; this time, the costs mattered.

Terms didn't matter, she told him; it was grand to have a shot at it. She had been told to thank Dorian Weigand for that, and had said she did; had said indeed she did. And then

Gerald North had said that he supposed she had cats, or could get at cats.

"I'll find them," she said. "I know where —"

"If you like," Gerald North said, "you can use ours, for Siamese. Not that they're show cats. Still —" He paused. "God knows," he said, with sudden feeling, "they do everything cats do." He sighed. "At least," he added. "Sometimes I think —" He did not finish the sentence.

And so Liza O'Brien sat on the edge of a chair in the Norths' living room, bent over a drawing pad with her hair falling around her face and tried to get down enough of Gin to go on with. Gin finished the slip cover, for the moment; sat briefly in thought, uttered a deep, apparently angry, cry, and dashed across the room to claw her way enthusiastically up the curtains. Halfway up, she paused, clinging to the damask, and looked back over her shoulder to see whether she was being observed and admired. "Wonderful, Gin," the girl said, and started a new drawing as rapidly as she could. If she could only get the shoulder muscles, the cat's indescribable twisted neck, the cat's excited eyes; a hint of all that, in half a dozen sure lines! All she needed, she thought as her pencil moved, was a miracle.

21

Then, before the girl heard anything, Gin spoke sharply, on a different note, and began to come down the curtain, swinging perilously from hold to hold, evidently in a great hurry about something. Sherry appeared, loping, from another room; Martini, with a side-long glance at Liza, emerged from beneath the table. All three cats gathered at the door to the outer hall. They looked at it intently as a key rubbed metallically in the lock. Then they looked up, higher than the sound and Sherry, whose voice was lighter than that of the other cats, as her coloring was, spoke in a drawn-out tone of ineffable longing. The door opened and Pamela North came in.

"I had the most interesting taxi driver," Pam said. "Nice Gin, nice Sherry, nice Teeny. Nice babies." She crouched to the cat level and began to stroke. Gin arrived first, purring loudly, and was assured that she was the nicest cat. Sherry floated in reach, was touched, floated out again in a curve. Teeny spoke in a scolding tone. "The main cat," Mrs. North said. "The principal cat." Teeny said, "Yah!"

"Jealous," Pam North said. "The others first always makes her. But the others came first. He said he'd picked up a couple he didn't think had stopped drinking since the night before and that he drove them to pick

22

up her husband to explain why she hadn't been home. He was in a bar and when he got in the cab they had a bottle and everybody had a drink, although the taxi driver said all he wanted was to get them out before the shooting started. Nice Teeny, is the *major* cat."

"Oh," Liza O'Brien said.

"But they just went to another bar and all got out," Pam said. "An anti-climax, but still interesting. Of course, with taxi drivers, you never — Did you make out all right? They behave at all?"

"Bits and pieces," Liza O'Brien said. "Want to look?"

Pam looked. Several times, studying the small sketches — all line; all cat — she laughed. She pointed at the one of Gin sitting high, like a rabbit. "The only one I ever knew who did," she said. "Except in tall grass, of course. To see over it. Gin just *likes* it. Pretends there's something up there. These are perfect, you know. If I were Jerry — "

"I hope," Liza said. "It's swell of Mr. North to give me a chance."

"He likes the book," Pam said. "He liked the things of yours Dorian showed him. So why not?"

Liza flipped the rolled back pages flat on

the pad; found brown paper and string in the chair behind her; wrapped up the drawing pad with the assistance of Gin and Sherry. She said she might want to come back, but for the moment she had enough to go on with. She said it was wonderful of Mrs. North —

"Nonsense," Pam said. "Does the cats honor. You've got long hairs? I'd think they'd be harder. I mean, so *much* fur."

"They're easy to make pretty," Liza said. "Hard to make real. Yes, I know where a fine black kitten is."

Liza left the Norths' apartment then, walked a few blocks to have a sandwich at Bigelow's and then walked some further blocks. She was a small girl, and the drawing pad was large; people she passed turned back to look at her and smiled with a kind of contentment, as if something pleasant had just been proved. Liza found West Kepp Street with no difficulty, having been there before; she walked along to J. K. Halder's shop, and down the steps to the door of the shop. She paused, then, before she touched the door, and tapped her fingers lightly on the window-pane. The black kitten rose on hind legs and boxed with the fingers through the glass. Liza turned away and pushed at the door. The door did not open.

This was surprising. "Any time during the afternoon," the old man had said. "We're always here." But now it appeared he was not there.

"Well!" Liza said, and pushed at the door again, and again without result. I could have stayed and had another shot at the Norths' major cat, she thought. But Mr. Halder had seemed so cooperative, after she had shown him one or two sketches. "You like animals," he had told her, and she had said, "Of course."

"No of course about it," Mr. Halder had told her then, this the Saturday before. "Most of the people I know — " He had broken off, and there had been a look of dislike on his face; it was as if she had annoyed him. But then his face cleared. "Nothing to worry your head about," he said. He smiled at her.

But that — that sudden look of displeasure, almost of anger on his face — had for some reason prevented her from saying what she had planned to say, from explaining how she had happened to find a black long-haired cat in this particular, so securely hidden, shop in this secretive street. It could come out later; perhaps while she was sketching. "By the way," she could say, and she had planned the words in her mind, "by the way, I didn't just happen to come here. You see — " This decision to postpone had been made intuitively, with the idea that it might be better if he knew her first, approved of her, as herself. So arranged, it would seem unarranged, or she had hoped it would. But at the same time she was puzzled why it should be so important, why either arrangement or the absence of arrangement mattered. She supposed she was merely self-conscious about Mr. Halder, of whom she had heard a little, all of which had made him sound difficult.

She pushed at the door again and then looked into the shop. It was only dimly lighted; one hanging bulb, deep in the room, seemed to create rather than to disperse shadows. Then she saw why this was: the light was screened so that glare from it would not fall into the pens along the wall. But now, she thought, it's the middle of the afternoon. It's as if —

"Nonsense," a sharp voice said behind her. "Of course it'll open. Get out of the way."

She turned quickly, emerging from the preoccupation of her thoughts. A man was standing on the lowest step of the three leading down to the door level. Even so, her eyes were almost on a level with his; why, she thought, he's the *smallest* man. He was also, she thought next, one of the oldest men; he had a little, amazingly wrinkled face and very sharp blue eyes. The eyes stabbed at her, suspiciously, almost angrily.

"Women!" the little man said, and came down the last step. Now he was appreciably less tall than she, which meant he was under five feet. "Why should it be locked?" he demanded, looking up at her, somehow implying that she was attempting to deceive him.

"I don't know," she said. "It just seems to be."

"Crazy old fool," the little man said. "Afraid somebody'll want to *buy* one." He paused a moment. "*You* want to buy one?" he demanded.

"No," she said. "I — I just want to see Mr. Halder. But apparently he isn't here."

"Here?" the man said. "Nonsense, girl. Of course he's here. Where would he be?"

"Look," Liza O'Brien said, trying somehow to bridge a gap which must, she thought, have a width of more than fifty years. "I hardly know Mr. Halder. But he told me I could come around." The sharp blue eyes continued to bore at her. "To sketch a cat," she said, and for some reason almost added, "please."

"Absurd," the old man said. "Get out of the way."

She moved aside. The little old man pushed at the door. When it did not open he turned the knob and then, angrily, shook it. Then he turned to her. "Well," he said. "He's a crazy old fool. Tell him so to his face."

There did not seem to be an answer to this.

"Want to sketch a *cat?*" the old man said.

"Why?"

"For a book," she said. "A book about them."

"Books!" he said. "Nonsense. Ever hear of chess?"

"Yes," the girl said. She felt a little as if she were swimming under water.

"You're a pretty thing," he said, next. "Waste your time with books. Sketching cats. No boy?"

"Please," Liza said, surfacing. "Mr. Halder isn't in, obviously. It's very nice of you to be so interested, but I'll just — "

"Nonsense," the old man said. "Let you in. Not going to poison the animals, are you? Anyway — "

This time he did not finish. He began to slap the pockets of his dark suit. He found what he wanted and pulled a key from one of the pockets. He unlocked the door and at once went in.

"Well," he said, over his shoulder and without stopping, "come on in. What're you waiting for, girl?"

Liza O'Brien went in. The little old man was somewhere in the shadows; then lights came on. He came back to her, looked a little up at her and, suddenly, smiled.

"An old man, girl," he said. "Old enough for your grandfather. Great-grandfather. Don't mind me. Where *is* the old fool?"

He looked into the pen which was the home of the black kitten, almost as if he expected to find Mr. Halder sharing the pen. "Where is he, Electra?" he said, in a quite matter-of-fact voice. "Where's the old man? Sleeping it off?"

The little cat looked up at him, opened her pink mouth widely, made a very small sound. The cockers in the next pen began to clamor loudly. The little man listened, moved in front of their pen and looked at them.

"You've got no water," the man said. He spoke almost accusingly, as if it were the fault of the cockers. They spoke together, in a frenzy of assent.

The little man turned sharply to Liza O'Brien.

"Something's the matter," he said. "They

haven't got water."

He turned again and began to walk rapidly down the room toward a door at the end. He walked so rapidly it was almost as if he trotted.

The room in which Mr. Halder lived was empty. The bed had been made up, rather sketchily, since it was last slept in. The little old man went to the shelves by a refrigerator and looked at the dishes on them. The dishes shone.

Liza had gone to the door, had stood in it watching the little old man. Now, as he turned and started toward her, she moved aside to let him pass. All the wrinkles on the little face seemed even deeper than before; she saw that he was very disturbed, perhaps even frightened.

"J. K.!" he called into the shop, in a high, ancient voice. "J. K.!"

There was no answer. It took them only a few minutes to find out why. Mr. Halder, dressed in black and white, folded so that his knees were against his chest, lying on his side, was in one of the pens. A young boxer in the next pen was as far from him as she could get; she was curled up and she was shivering.

Even as, involuntarily, Liza O'Brien shrank back from the pen in which Mr. J. K.

Halder was so grotesquely folded, she heard the little old man beside her suddenly begin to cry. He cried gaspingly, like a child.

And Liza turned to him, involuntarily, as she would have turned to a child. She was shocked, and frightened, to see how the little wrinkled face had changed; how, between one moment and the next, life seemed to have gone out of it. The blue eyes which had been so sharp were now strangely vacant, seemed almost like blind eyes, as if the tears forming in them had washed away sight. The wrinkled cheeks, where color had been bright under the thin, aged skin, were now a kind of yellowish white. The little old man groped around him, uncertainly, as if he were indeed blind, and she reached out to steady him, but he made uncertain gestures which seemed to ward her off. Then, on the other side of the room, she saw a wooden chair and moved quickly and put it within his reach. He sat on it, still uncertainly and then turned in it, resting his arms on the back of the chair and his head on his arm.

"Are you all right?" she said, her voice hurried, carrying the message of her shock and fear. *Why*, she thought, *he's going to die right there, sitting there! Something terrible is happening to him!* And she felt, hopelessly, that there was something to do, some aid to give, and that she, in her terrible youth, her utter lack of knowledge, was uselessly letting him slip into death. She looked around the room in a kind of desperation, trying to see in it some means of helping the little man but not, in that first shocked uncertainty, knowing what she sought. Then it came to her — a stimulant, brandy, perhaps. She remembered the room in the rear and said, "Wait! I'll get something!" and thought the old head, still resting on the arm, moved in agreement. She went quickly into the room in which Mr. Halder had lived.

She found a glass quickly, in one of the cupboards, but it took her much longer, opening doors, pulling out drawers, in a desperate conviction of the need to hurry, to find the bottle she sought. Then it was whisky, not brandy, but she almost ran as she carried the bottle and the glass back toward the room in which it seemed the little man was dying. She pushed open the door and started to speak as she entered the show room and then, blankly, stopped. The chair was empty. *It's happened*, she thought, *oh* — But then she saw that the little man had not slumped from the chair to the floor; was not, indeed, anywhere in sight. Still carrying the bottle and the glass, she searched rapidly through the room, looked finally, when it could no longer be put off, in the pen in which the body of Mr. Halder was hideously folded. But there was no other body there and she turned away quickly, feeling, as her anxiety flowed away, almost indignant, almost angry. Why, she thought, I've been — fooled. He's just gone; he just got up and went away!

She put glass and bottle down on the chair in which the little old man had been sitting, and went to the door of the shop. It was closed, and she opened it and, holding it open behind her, looked up and down West Kepp Street. But the little man was not in sight. Then she went back into the shop, closing the door behind her. The little old man had, it was clear, merely got up and gone away; perhaps that was what he had all along planned to do. He had left her in this room with the animals; in the room with the grotesquely folded body of Mr. J. K. Halder. "Well!" Liza O'Brien said, aloud, in something approaching her normal voice.

Momentarily, she was tempted to follow the example of the little old man. It would be simple merely to pick up her wrapped sketching pad, go down the length of the shop and out the door into West Kepp Street and leave what was in the room to another's finding. But she shook her head instantly; even if it weren't for Brian — Her thoughts broke off. That was it. Before anything else, she must tell Brian. Poor dear, she thought; I was worrying about the little old man, when all the time I should have been thinking of Brian.

It took her only a moment to find the telephone, on a desk in a rear corner of the room. She dialed a number which, although she had used it infrequently, was familiar in her mind because, in a minor way, it was part of Brian. "Mr. Brian Halder, please," she said to the switchboard operator. "Is Mr. Halder in? Miss O'Brien," she said to someone else who was not Brian. And then the voice was Brian's, for the instant blank, a voice answering an office telephone; then, as he heard her voice, or as realization brushed away previous preoccupation, warm and gay. "Liza!" Brian said. "Hel-*lo!*"

"Brian," she said and, hearing his voice, she was suddenly close to crying. "Brian — something terrible. Something — "

"Liza," he said. "What's the matter?" His voice had changed now; held alarm and concern.

"It's — it's your father, Brian," she said. "I'm at the shop. He's — he — "

It was hard to say.

"What is it, dear?" Brian said. "Go on, Liza."

"He's dead, Brian," she said. "Something — oh, I'm afraid, Brian. It's — it's so strange. So awful. He's — he's sort of fallen in — in one of the pens and — "

"Wait," Brian Halder said. "You're there, you say? *There?*"

"I told you," she said. "I was going to sketch a cat. I — I *found* him, Brian."

"Wait," Brian said. "Who else is there? Have you — told anybody?"

"There was a little man," she said. "A strange little man. But he's gone, now."

"You're sure he's dead?" Brian asked.

"Oh. I'm sure," she said, "I'm — I'm afraid it's sure, Brian."

"Let me think," he said. "We'll have to — you say he was in one of the *pens?*" There was incredulity, and something else, in his voice.

"Yes," she said. "Sort of — sort of folded up. He must have fallen, somehow."

There was a moment's silence.

"I don't see — " Brian Halder began, then, slowly. But then he paused again.

"Wait there," he said. "I'll come. Can you — just wait? You say nobody's been in?"

"Only the little old man," she said.

35

"That's probably — " he began, and again paused. "Never mind," he said. "I'll be there in — oh, ten, fifteen minutes. Not more than twenty. Will you just wait until I get there? Can you do that, Liza?"

"Of course," she said.

"Sit down," he said. "Don't think about it — worry about it. He — Dad was an old man, Liza. I suppose — " Again he trailed off. "Wait," he said, "I'll hurry." Then he hung up.

She sat for a few minutes by the telephone, feeling relief because the hard thing was said to Brian, relief because he was coming. But then she found that she was too restless merely to sit, waiting, and she got up and began to walk around the room, looking at the animals. Then she remembered what the little old man had said about the cockers having no water and looked into their pen and the other pens, and found that none of the dogs had anything to drink, nor did the Siamese cat. There was still water in the bowl in the little black cat's pen. She walked back to the rear room, passing as far as she could from the body and found a pitcher and filled it with water. It was only when she tried to pour from the pitcher into the water bowl in the cockers' pen that she realized she was shaking, as if with a chill. She managed to pour water into that bowl, and into the others, but she spilled some in each pen because she could not stop her hand's shaking. Then, putting the pitcher down on the floor, she stood for what seemed a long time looking down at the black cat, trying (without too much success) to study the little animal with an artist's eye, to shut out all other thoughts. But stubbornly her mind kept re-creating another image: a thin old man grotesquely, mockingly, folded in a pen meant for a dog, a cat. Now that there was nothing else to do, nothing else to think of, she could think only of that, and she could feel her whole body trembling.

Yet it was really not much more than twenty minutes before Brian came. He came hurriedly, running down the three steps, but she was at the door, wrenching the knob, before he quite reached it. She stepped back and he came in, kicking the door behind him and at the same moment taking her in his arms.

"Oh Brian," she said, her face against his coat. "Oh Brian!" She was shivering uncontrollably, and he stroked her hair, then held her closer to him, pressing his right hand against her back. "There, baby," he said.

"It'll be all right, Liza. It'll be all right." She breathed deeply, and let her breath out in a sigh, and then her trembling lessened. But she wanted to stay there, held by him, hiding her face against him, shutting out the ugly thing deep in the room. He did not hurry her, but, almost imperceptibly, the pressure of his arms relaxed and, so signalled to, she freed herself and stood back and looked up at him.

He was tall; much taller than she. Actually, he was hardly older — twenty-two or twenty-three — and yet to her, and particularly when his face was serious, his manner intent, he seemed a great deal older. (Once she had said to him, surprising herself, and laughing in part because of her own surprise, that he looked like Abraham Lincoln. "Without the wart, without the beard," she said, hurriedly. "And much better looking. But still — " He had said, his wide mouth in a wide smile, "Now listen, baby!" and then had laughed with her.) Now as she looked up at him his face very grave, his wide mouth a line, his deep-set eyes darkly shadowed. Now he looked much older than twenty-two or twenty-three. Looking down at her, his hands still gently on her shoulders, he said, again, "It'll be all right, Liza." But now his voice was different. "Where?" he said, then.

She motioned, first; then led him back to the place. When they could see into the pen she began to tremble again, and he put his arm around her shoulders. But he did not speak at first; merely stood, looking down at the body. She did not try to see what was in his face. When he did speak it was, first, only to swear in a voice much harsher than any she had ever heard from him. And, she thought unconsciously, the pressure of his hand on her shoulder tightened until it was almost painful.

"What can we do?" she said. "Can we — it's awful for him to be there. Like that."

Instead of answering, he bent down and touched the body, taking his arm from her shoulders as he did so. Almost at once he withdrew his hand.

"He's dead," Brian Halder said, more to himself than to her. "It's happened. It's — " Then he broke off; then he spoke to her. "There's nothing we can do, Liza," he said. "Nothing at all. He's been dead a — quite a long time."

"But what do we *do?*" she said. "We can't — " She gestured at the body instead of finishing the sentence.

"We'll have to get the police in," he said slowly. "There's no way out I can see. He's — we couldn't move him easily even if — even if it wouldn't make things worse. You see, Liza, the — body's stiffened." He touched her shoulder again, gently.

"Then we — " she said, but he shook his head.

"Not we," he said. "We're going to get out of here; out of the whole thing. Then I'll — find Dad's body. You'll not be mixed up in it."

"But — " she began, and again he shook his head.

"It's the best way," he said. "The only way. I'll take you home. Then come back." He looked again at his father's body. "It doesn't make any difference," he said. "It's just better."

"But the little man," she said. "He knows I was here. And, anyway — "

"Very small?" Brian said. "Very wrinkled? Very blue eyes?" She nodded to each. "That'll be Felix," he said. "I'll take care of Felix. He's — odd, Liza." Again he looked at his father's body. "They both were," he said. "Dad was a strange man."

"But Brian," she said, "what happened to him?"

He shook his head slowly. It seemed to her that he had, somehow, suddenly, gone far away. "I don't know," he said. "That's why,

40

that's one reason, we have to have the police. I'm afraid — " But he did not say what he feared.

"Play it my way, darling," he said, and now he tried to come nearer her, tried to smile down at her. "It's the best way. There're reasons. I'll — we'll talk about it later. Tonight, some time. Now I'm going to take you home."

She did not understand; she shook her head, puzzled, and tried to find in his face, in his eyes, some explanation. But there was nothing there she could decipher. In his face she saw only distant stillness, and what seemed a kind of harshness. His face, she thought, rejected her, and then she wanted only to run out of the place, away from it all — away, for the moment, even from Brian himself, whose attitude now seemed so inexplicable. She turned and started toward the door and did not look back as she heard him following her.

Because he stopped at the outer door for some purpose, and she did not hesitate, she was some little distance down Kepp Street before he overtook her. And then she did not look at him, but merely walked beside him, numbly, to the end of the street.

"You don't understand," he said. "Don't

make up your mind about anything, Liza. I'll — I'll call you tonight."

She did speak, then. "You know something," she said. "You're shutting me out."

"No," Brian said, and then raised his voice and called to a passing cab. The cab stopped and they walked toward it. "I don't know anything," he said, as he held the door open. "There are certain things I've — got to find out. And it's only that I don't want you mixed up in it."

He started to get into the cab after her, but she shook her head.

"Go back," she said. "I'll go to the apartment. I'll wait."

"An hour or two," he said. "A few hours. It depends partly on the police." He did not repeat his effort to enter the cab.

"I'll wait," she said again, and then ended it by giving the cab driver her address. As the cab started she looked back. He was standing, unmoving, looking after the cab. Then he turned away and went back into West Kepp Street.

The cab had gone some blocks before she realized that she had left her sketch pad in Mr. Halder's shop.

III

Tuesday, 5:30 P.M.
to 7:20 P.M.

"Jerry!" Pam North said, putting down her
glass. "It's too strong. I can taste the vermouth." She paused, took another sip.
"Unless it's a different kind of gin," she
added, thoughtfully.

Jerry North tasted from his own glass.
Sometimes, he told his wife, she baffled him.
It was, he said, the same gin and the same
vermouth. The proportions were unchanged.

"Then it's me," Pam said, "but I still think
it's the vermouth. Anyway, it's too strong."

"Listen," Jerry said. "If that were true, it
would make it too *weak*. Too strong would be
gin."

"All I know is, it *tastes* strong," Pam said.
"Bitter. It could be the lemon peel, of course.
They're new lemons."

"What," Jerry said, and ran the fingers of
his right hand through his hair, "has the new-
ness of the lemons got to do with it?"

"For heaven's sake," Pam said, "I was merely looking for an explanation. If it isn't the vermouth or a new kind of gin, it's the lemon peel, because it's just the same ice and what else is there?" She paused. "Except me," she said. "And I'm just the same, far as I can tell." But she looked reflective, as if this were a point needing further consideration. She sipped again and tasted, thoughtfully. "It isn't me," she said, with more assurance. "You taste it."

Jerry crossed to his wife's chair and tasted his wife's drink.

"See?" she said.

"I think it's you," Jerry said. "It tastes just like mine."

Pam got up, went to Jerry's chair, and tasted his drink.

"You mean," she said, "you don't taste it?" She sounded entirely astonished. "It must be you, not me. Yours is just the same. Strong."

"Darling," Jerry said, sitting down in Pam's chair. "It isn't the vermouth makes them strong. Why do you keep on saying strong?"

"I think," Pam said, tasting Jerry's drink again, "they need more gin. Usually, they're so perfect. And it can't be me, because I don't want pickles, and anyway I'd know."

Jerry shook his head slightly to clear it, and finished Pam's drink. Then, cautiously, he said "Pickles?"

"Babies," Pam said. "If it would make you want pickles, it probably would make drinks taste funny."

"Oh," Jerry said. He looked at her suspiciously.

"No," Pam said. "Of course not. They just need more gin." She looked at the glass which had been Jerry's, and which now was empty. "Next time," she said. "Jerry, I've got your chair! I — "

Then the telephone rang. Because Pamela North was in Jerry's chair, she was nearest the telephone.

"It'll be for — " she said. But Jerry, grinning, shook his head.

"Goes with the chair," he told her, pleased.

Pam made a face at him and continued it into the telephone. Then she said, "Oh, Bill!" and then "What?"

"Look, Bill," she said then, "it must be a bad connection. He says he's in a pet." The last was to Jerry, who raised his eyebrows, who said, "How perfectly duck — " before Pam said. "Shhhh!"

"Oh," she said then. "*Shop*. A *pet shop*. What on — "

But then, listening to Lieutenant William Weigand of Homicide, Manhattan West, she sobered very suddenly. She said "Oh" in a different tone and then, after another moment of listening, "Of course we will. Right away." She listened again. "Of course not," she said. "We're not doing anything." She hesitated briefly. "Except martinis, of course." she said. "We were just talking about vermouth." She listened again. "Of course we can," she said. "We live here. Jerry'll know." And then she hung up, and stood up.

"You *do* know where West Kepp Street is, don't you?" she said to Jerry. "Because Bill's in a pet shop there and wants us to come to look at something. And the man who owns the shop was killed in a pen, or killed himself and got into a pen." She listened to herself. "I don't mean that the way it sounds," she said. "Do you, Jerry?"

"Approximately," Jerry North said. "Opens off Christopher, or maybe Green-wich. No — wait. Isn't it that funny little street over by Commerce?"

"That's Gay Street," Pam said.

But Jerry shook his head, because he was sure — almost sure — that Gay was the one off Christopher.

"Anyway," Pam said, deciding it for them,

46

"we won't find it here, and Bill doesn't want to leave because he's waiting for somebody, so come on."

They went. It was not the one off Greenwich. It was not — they were in a cab by this time — the one off Commerce. For a time it looked as if it were not off anything, but then another cab driver — a very old and somewhat battered cab driver — directed theirs.

But there was no getting into West Kepp Street in the cab, even after they had found it. The cab, which had started to enter the street, confronted a policeman and stopped abruptly. The driver knocked his flag up, turned, and looked back at the Norths. "Looks like something's going on in here," he told them.

It did. One sidewalk of West Kepp Street was almost filled with people, all looking in the same direction, looking across the narrow street. There were uniformed patrolmen in the middle of the street, and at both ends; along the curb opposite the people there were more cars than West Kepp could hold. Several of them were partly on the sidewalk. Small boys darted from the walk on which so many people stood, moved restlessly, and made for the cars, and policemen said, "Now, get back there. Get *back* there!"

47

The little boys got back, but did not stay back; the sight of so many police cars was irresistible. Privileged, on the same side of the street as the center of interest, but not wandering, standing in a restless group, were several men with press cards in the bands of their hats.

"Can't come in here 'less you live here," the patrolman who had stopped their cab said to the Norths, leaning in a window to look at them. "You live here?"

"Not exactly," Pam North said, before Jerry could speak.

"Then you'll have to move along, lady," the patrolman said. "Can't come in here 'less you live here." He looked at Pam, and was moved to further speech. "Been trouble here," he said.

"Look," Jerry said, and reached for the door handle on the side opposite the policeman. "We — "

"Lieutenant Weigand," Pam North said, at the same time, but more rapidly. "Sergeant Mullins. Inspector O'Malley."

"Listen, lady," the patrolman said. "I don't care who — "

"Look, officer," Jerry said, and closed his free hand firmly on Pam North's wrist, "Lieutenant Weigand called us and asked us

48

to come over. My name's North. Suppose you — "

"There he is!" Pam said. *"Mullins!"*

Everybody, Jerry thought — all the people on the sidewalk, all the men with press cards — looked at the cab from which Pam North's clear, bright voice emerged.

"Listen, Pam," Jerry said. But then he too saw Mullins, large, reassuring, coming down the sidewalk toward them. The patrolman stepped back from the cab window and looked around the cab at Mullins. Now, everybody looked at Mullins. Anything that made a sound, anything that moved, was good enough.

"Mr. *and* Mrs. North," Mullins said, when he was close enough. "O.K.," he said to the patrolman, "the Loot says it's all right. He wants to see them."

There was the faintest possible emphasis on the word "he."

"Really, Mullins," Pam said, as they got out, as she waited for Jerry to pay the cab driver, "you're so disassociative."

"What?" Mullins said.

"Never mind," Pam said. "But remember, we were asked."

"It's only when I think of the inspector," Mullins said. "You know how he acts, Mrs.

North." The three of them began to walk through West Kepp Street. "And it's already a screwy one," Mullins said. "As soon as I saw the set-up, I says to myself, it's a screwy one, so — " He broke off.

"So the Norths will be in it," Jerry said. "I know what you said."

"Look, Mr. North," Mullins said, earnestly, as they went down three steps to a shop door, as now, everybody looked at them, as there was a kind of expectant murmur from the crowd. "Look, it's just that the inspector — "

"You know," Pam said, more or less to Jerry, "they all think we've been arrested. That we're being taken in to see — to see — "

But then the realization of what they probably were being taken in to see overcame Pam North, and the excitement died in her voice. "Oh," she said, and went ahead of the two men into the shop and, as she entered it, looked around anxiously. Lieutenant William Weigand detached himself from a little group midway down the shop's length and came toward them, saying "hello," saying he was sorry to have dragged them out. Then he looked at Pam's face and smiled faintly and shook his head.

"It's been taken away, Pam," he said.

"Don't look so — frightened. All that part of it's over. It's something else I want you to see. And probably — " He shrugged. "I'm playing a hunch."

He started back toward the rear of the shop, and the Norths went with him.

"You see," Bill Weigand told them, over his shoulder, "we got an anonymous squeal; one of those telephone things. 'I want a policeman. I want to report a murder.' That sort of thing."

He opcned a door in the rear of the shop and motioned them into a smaller room, obviously a room in which somebody had lived — had slept, had eaten, had sat in a worn, deep old chair, to read by the light from a cheap bridge lamp.

"When the boys got here there was nobody," he said. "The door was locked. Question whether they should have come in at all, but they did. Nobody here — except dogs and cats and a man named Halder. He was dead; been dead for hours. Crammed in one of the pens. Led Mullins to decide it was a screwy one; that the Norths would be in it. Well — then we found this."

He picked up from the bed a loosely wrapped package, shucked off brown paper. And Pam North, faintly, gasped. Bill looked at her briefly and turned the blank first sheet of a drawing pad. He showed them the second sheet.

"I thought I recognized some friends," Bill Weigand said. From half the page, enormous round eyes looked out of a dark, suspicious, furry face. From the other half, a hind leg waved in air, as a cat contorted for ablutions. Bill flicked the page over. There were more cats. "Right?" Bill Weigand said.

Pam nodded slowly. "I guess Mullins was," she said. "Yes." She turned to Jerry. "Anyway, they're good, aren't they?" she asked. "What you wanted?"

Jerry took the pad from Bill Weigand and leafed through it. Then he nodded.

"She'll do," he said. "If — " He looked at Bill. "If she's available," he said.

Bill Weigand only shrugged.

Brian had called at a few minutes after six.

He had spoken rapidly, strain evident in his voice. For a moment, when she answered, the strain apparent when he spoke first in greeting seemed to lessen, then at once it returned. He had called, he said, to see if she got home all right; to tell her that he could not, as he had hoped, come around. "To explain this mess," he said. He had notified the police. "I

52

didn't identify myself," he said. "I — I haven't time now to answer a lot of questions. I've got to get things straightened out."

"Brian!" she had said. "You've got to tell me what all this is."

"Not yet," he said. "I don't know myself. I've got to see — someone. So far I haven't. Anyway, you're out of it."

"Darling!" she said. "Listen to me! I wasn't in it. I — I just happened to go there."

"Of course," he said. "All the same — "

"And anyway — " she began.

"Liza!" he said. "Please, dear!" His voice was roughened, almost impatient. "I'll call back as soon as I can." Then his voice, she thought by an effort, became softer, more his voice. "Wait for me, dear," he said. "Don't worry. It's nothing to do with you."

And then, while she was still saying, "All right," there had come the click as he cut the connection.

It would have been better if he had not called at all; better for her nerves, less rasping in her mind. He was strange, not Brian at all; what he had said was incomprehensible; his whole attitude told her that, beyond even his father's death, there was some strange thing, some enormity, of which he was a part and from which he was trying to shield her. She did not know, could not tell from anything he had said or done, whether he even felt grief at his father's death; he was excited, upset; it was as if the old man's death were not an ending, but the beginning of something more complex, more threatening. But they did not even know how the old man had come to die. Then Liza O'Brien thought: I mean *I* don't know; that's all I mean. *I don't know what Brian knows or doesn't know.*

It was a little before seven when someone knocked on the apartment door. She went quickly; although it was not Brian's usual knock, it might still be Brian on this evening when nothing was as usual, nothing serene and accustomed. But it was not Brian. It was a man almost as tall, a man with a dark, sensitive face. She put her hand up to her mouth, the knuckles against her lower lip and did so instinctively and, dimly, was aware of surprise at her own action.

"Miss O'Brien?" the man said. His voice was courteous, without emphasis. "I'm Detective Sergeant Stein. Lieutenant Weigand would like to see you, if you don't mind."

"Weigand," she said. "Why that's — " She broke off.

"He's a Homicide man, Miss O'Brien," Sergeant Stein said. "Just a couple of questions he wants to ask you." He looked down at her. "About West Kepp Street," he said. "Do you want to get a hat, or something, Miss O'Brien?"

She got a light coat while he waited. She went with him in the elevator to the street level, walked with him across the side-walk to a car parked in front of the building. They might have been a young man and a girl going out to dinner, going to the theater, going somewhere to dance. He opened a front door for her, closed it after her, went around the car and got in beside her, under the wheel. From the building, which was in the Murray Hill district, they went east, then up First Avenue.

The car, after slowing while Sergeant Stein peered out for street numbers, stopped in Sutton Place, in front of one in a row of houses which, Liza remembered, had rear gardens, rear windows, from which one could see the East River. The house in front of which they stopped was larger than most of them; several other cars were parked nearby, as if their occupants also were in the house.

"Guess this is it," Stein said. He paused after she had joined him on the sidewalk and looked up at the house. "Quite a place," he said. "Come on, Miss O'Brien."

"But you said — " she began.

He looked down at her, and his face was, momentarily, friendly.

"The lieutenant's inside," he said. "Talking to some other people." He took a police badge from his pocket and showed it to her. "See?" he said. "It's all right." Then, unexpectedly, he smiled. "But you should have asked sooner, Miss O'Brien. You shouldn't be so trusting."

Then they went up to the door of the house, which opened at once, as if someone had been expecting them, had seen the car stop. The man who opened the door was a large man, with a broad, weathered face and, rather unexpectedly, gentle brown eyes.

"Miss O'Brien," Stein said. "O.K., Al?"

"Go on in," the big man said. "Take her right along. We're getting quite a crowd." He paused. "*And* the Norths." Sergeant Aloysius Mullins added, more or less to himself.

There was an entrance hall, and, beside it, a small room which, as Liza glimpsed it through the open door, seemed to be lined with books. Two steps up from the little foyer brought them into a very long, rather narrow room which seemed to run the full length of the house, to tall windows looking out on the garden in the rear. Near the right wall, as Liza

56

looked towards the windows, a spiral staircase led up. And Pamela North came up the room toward them, walking quickly.

"I'm sorry," Pam said. "Bill knew the cats. There wasn't anything I could do. Why did you leave it?"

The drawing pad! That was it.

"I — I just forgot," Liza O'Brien said. "I was — scared, I guess."

She looked at Pam, who smiled at her, and suddenly, for no reason at all, except the friendliness, the interest, in a small, expressive face, Liza felt better. Then she looked beyond Pam North at a man of a little over middle height who was moving toward them, and moving rapidly although he did not seem to hurry.

"Pam," the man said. "Wait a minute." Then he spoke to Liza, saying, "You're Miss O'Brien?" She nodded. "My name's Weigand," the man said.

"I know," Liza said. "You're Dorian's husband."

He looked at her quickly, doubtfully; she felt she had said the wrong thing. But he said, "Yes, Miss O'Brien," his tone noncommittal.

"I'm sorry," she said. "I didn't mean to — to — "

"Right," Bill Weigand said. "I'm sorry to

57

have to bring you up here, Miss O'Brien. But you couldn't just walk out, you know. Walk out, then telephone the police and report. What made you think you could?"

"After all," Pam North said, "she forgot she'd forgotten. The drawings, I mean. Otherwise she could have. Probably she was just frightened."

Bill looked at Pam North for a moment; he checked the movement of his right hand toward his hair. All the men in Pam North's life, he thought momentarily, distractingly, acquired disarranged hair. It was also evident that Miss Liza O'Brien, little and pretty and with the freshness of a young animal just beginning, had acquired a partisan. As quickly as that, perhaps merely by looking like that.

"Let Miss O'Brien answer, Pamela," Bill Weigand said, mildly. He turned back to the girl. "You did find Mr. Halder's body, down at the pet shop?"

For a moment she hesitated. But it was no good now; whatever Brian planned was no good now.

She nodded.

"Tell me," he said. "No, wait. We don't have to stand here."

He turned away and looked down the room. Liza had been conscious that there were other people in the room, clustered at the far end of the room, near the tall windows. Now she looked at them. There were two men and two women, and, sitting detached from them, a third man. One of the women was full-bodied, with white hair piled high, very recently piled high by expert fingers. The other woman was younger; if the large woman was in her late forties, the slighter one, the blond one, was about thirty-five. The two men were nearer an age, roughly, like the older woman, in their middle or late forties. One of them was heavily built, wore a double-breasted suit with squared shoulders, stood solidly erect. The other was tall — why, Liza thought, he's as tall as Brian. Then she realized that she had thought this because, elusively, he looked like Brian Halder. Then it must be —

"Oh, Colonel," Weigand said, and the heavily built man turned from the window and gave attention. Then he walked toward them, his face full of gravity. The third man, as if this were a signal, stood up in front of the chair in which he had been sitting. Liza recognized him; he was Mr. Gerald North, to whom she was going to show her sketches of cats.

"This is Lieutenant Colonel Whiteside,

Miss O'Brien," Weigand said. The lieutenant colonel nodded gravely. "I have a few questions to ask her before we go on. I wonder if — "

"The library, by all means," Whiteside said. He nodded toward the small room off the foyer. "Have you — ?" His voice was anxious. Bill Weigand shook his head, absently. "I haven't heard anything as yet," he said. "Miss O'Brien?"

They went to the small room. She preceded him into it; then he hesitated, looked back. "Pam," he said. "You and Jerry. Will you come in for a minute or two?" The Norths came. The room was comfortable for four; it would hardly have been for six. The books, Liza thought — and was puzzled that her mind was now, of all times, capable of the irrelevancy — the books in the shelves were impassive, as if for a long time they had not been disturbed and no longer expected to be. At Weigand's indication, the three of them sat down. Weigand himself remained standing.

"Go ahead, Miss O'Brien," he said.

She had made up her mind, by then. To a point, she would tell it just the way it was, the little old man and everything. She did; Weigand did not interrupt. She told of the little old man's disappearance while she was getting him a drink. Then she paused, involuntarily.

"Go on," Bill Weigand said.

"Well," she said, "all at once I — I just got scared. I knew he was dead and there wasn't any way to help. And — well, I'm afraid I just sort of — of panicked. All at once I had to get out of there."

"And you did?" Weigand asked. "Just like that."

"Yes."

"And you locked the door after you?"

She had not thought of that; apparently the door had been locked when the police came. If she could remember about the lock. But she had no time to remember, to speculate.

"I don't think so," she said. "I was — very worked up. But I think I just pulled the door behind me. Of course, if it's a snap lock, it would have — "

"Right," Bill Weigand said. He did not say whether the catch on the pet shop door could be set to lock automatically. "And then? You thought better of it, decided to report what you had found, used a telephone?"

She nodded, not hesitating this time. If it couldn't be the way Brian wanted it, maybe this way would do. (But why? her mind asked. What's happening to us?)

"At about what time?" Weigand asked her.

And now again she had to hesitate. What time had Brian telephoned the police? Would there be a record? She could only guess, guess vaguely.

"I don't know, exactly," she said. "Probably — oh, a little after four." But then she realized that didn't fit. "No," she said. "It must have been nearer five."

"And said it was murder?" Weigand asked.

Again she had to guess, to temporize.

"Did I?" she said. "I don't remember. I — I suppose I did."

Weigand said, "You did. If you made the call, Miss O'Brien. And you made it — "

And then the door of the little library opened suddenly, and Brian Halder stood in it, his height making it seem small.

"All right, Liza," he said. He looked down at her. He managed to smile. "I guess it's no go, darling," he said, and then he spoke to Weigand.

"She telephoned me," he said. "I don't know quite what she's said. I suppose she's been keeping me out of it. She telephoned me, I went down, got her out of it, telephoned the police myself after I put her in a cab. About four-thirty, I'd guess. Does that fit?"

"Better," Bill Weigand said. "And you said it was murder?"

"Yes," Brian Halder said. "I guess I did."

Bill Weigand looked at the tall young man slowly, carefully.

"How did you know, Mr. Halder?" he said. "You are Brian Halder?" Brian nodded. "How did you know it was murder?" Weigand asked, again, and his voice was oddly soft. "So long before we did? Because, you see — *we don't know that yet.* As far as we can tell, it could have been suicide. *How did you know?*"

They all looked at Brian Halder then, and to Liza, hoping desperately for an answer which would be simple, would wipe away the uneasy trouble in her mind, it seemed that his eyes grew blank. But, after a second, he seemed surprised and startled, and then almost angry.

"My God," he said. "Didn't you see him?"

"Oh yes," Weigand said. "We saw him. The medical examiner saw him. The medical examiner assumes poison. But — there's nothing to indicate how administered."

"You saw where his body was?" Brian Halder demanded.

"I saw where it was," Weigand said. "But — your father was eccentric, Mr. Halder. Very eccentric."

"That's what they say," Brian Halder said, and moved his head toward the door of the

63

library, indicating (Liza realized) the others in the house. Weigand shook his head.

"What everybody will say," he told Brian Halder. "What they said even in the old days, you know. And now — he had millions, owned this house. He kept a pet shop in the Village, on an out-of-the-way street; I doubt if he ever encouraged anybody to buy one of the animals; he lived in a little room behind the shop. You've seen the room? But of course you have. You saw it today, didn't you? Your brother — "

"Half-brother," Halder said.

"Half-brother," Weigand said. "He says your father liked animals so much that — well, that he would have seen all of you die if that would have saved — well, that sick boxer pup at the shop."

"That's absurd," Brian said. Now he seemed more convinced, was more convincing. "The old man didn't have to mean all he said. He didn't mean half of it."

"Even half," Weigand said. "Your father was eccentric. Perhaps bitter; perhaps more. He may have been ill, decided to kill himself, arranged these bizarre circumstances — to point up, somehow, his feeling about animals and people. And — to make the family ridiculous."

"You've got quite an imagination, Lieutenant," Brian Halder said.

"Is it easier to imagine somebody killing him and putting him in the pen to die?"

"It cer— " Halder began, and stopped abruptly. Liza could almost see his mind working. "Maybe you're right," he said. But didn't he realize Weigand would see what she saw?

Weigand merely looked at the tall young man for a moment. Then he spoke mildly. "It may be that — yes, Sergeant?"

Sergeant Mullins was at the door. He moved his head back, summoning Weigand. Weigand went out of the room and closed the door behind him. Then Halder looked at the Norths, seemed to see them for the first time. Quickly, Liza introduced him. He narrowed his eyes, then opened them. "Don't you — ?" he said. "Aren't you often involved in — ?"

"Too often," Jerry North said. He shook his head. "Ever since — " He looked at Pam North.

"We had one of our own, or sort of," Pam said. "And met Bill. But I don't think involved's the word. It's just that — " But now she stopped and looked at Jerry, who told her the word would do. But then Weigand returned. He looked at Brian Halder for a moment.

65

"Your father died of strychnine," he said. "Hypodermically injected. Presumably from a syringe which he must have kept in his shop to destroy hopelessly sick animals. And — only his prints are on the syringe." And then Weigand stopped, and waited for Brian Halder; waited obviously for the tall young man to speak.

Halder shook his head slowly, his expression shocked.

"But isn't that horrible — painful?" he asked. "Would anyone — ?"

"A good many have," Weigand told him. "It's much more frequently used by suicides than by murderers. I agree it's odd. But there it is. Unless you can think of some better reason, Mr. Halder? Had you some better reason for deciding it was murder?"

"But Bill —" Pam North said, and he shook his head at her and waited for Halder.

"I guess I just — just jumped at it," Brian Halder said, slowly. "It just — seemed likely. I —"

"Bill," Pam North said. "Listen to me. You say Mr. Halder had the hypodermic there? Did he have strychnine, too?" Bill Weigand nodded, and now he did not try to stop her. "And you think he had it to destroy sick animals?"

"Well?" Bill said.

"Then he was murdered, of course," Pam said. "Because he liked animals. Don't you see?"

"Go on, Pam," Bill said.

"He never would have used strychnine," Pam said. "Not for the animals. It's — they say it's horrible. He would have used — what is it, Jerry?"

"A barbiturate," Jerry said. "Injected, probably. A shot to put the animal to sleep. Then another, stronger, to — well, to finish the job."

"Of course," Pam said. "But never strychnine. Don't you see, Bill? Never anything so cruel"*

And now Bill Weigand nodded, and said, slowly, "Right." And then he smiled faintly.

"But there's a better reason," he said. "If he got into the pen, injected strychnine — well, death from strychnine isn't easy. They're spasms, you know; convulsions. He — well, probably he would have kicked the pen apart."

*Pam is only partly right. Some veterinarians use strychnine to destroy animals, but only by injecting directly into the heart. So used, it causes almost instantaneous death, and is thought to be relatively painless. Administered by a layman, such as Halder was, strychnine would almost inevitably bring about slow and agonized death.

67

Then, quickly, he turned on Brian Halder. "Is that what you knew?" he demanded.

Now Halder shook his head quickly, without hesitation; now the expression of shock, of horror, was unmistakable on his face. Weigand saw it; Liza saw him see it.

"Didn't you know about strychnine, Mr. Halder?" Weigand asked, and now his voice was quiet again. "Didn't you know how a man dies from it?"

IV

Brian Halder had never answered Weigand's question; he had had little chance to answer it. He had been, not too abruptly, yet with finality, dismissed. He would be talked to later. But Liza had not been dismissed. She had been given the chance to revise her own story, confirm Brian's and, flushing a little, had taken it.

"Now," Weigand said, "you knew who Mr. Halder was?"

She opened her eyes wider.

"Brian's father," she said, surprised. Then Weigand smiled faintly.

"More than that," he said. "You never heard of J. K. Halder?" He looked at her. "No," he said, "that would have been about the time you were born."

"For God's sake!" Jerry North said. "*That* Halder."

"Right," Bill said. "That Halder." He

turned back to Liza. "He was quite famous, once," he said. "Quite spectacular. Did you ever hear of Industrial United?"

She shook her head.

"An investment trust," he said. "In the middle twenties, one of the biggest. Halder was Industrial United — almost all of it. He started with a few hundred thousand; small change in that league. He built up to — well, nobody ever knew exactly how many millions. There were yelps along the way from — well, call them the building materials. The people, the organizations, which in one way or another made Halder's millions out of his few hundred thousands. And then, at the right time, very suddenly, in 1928, he cashed in on the whole business."

"My," Pam North said.

"Not quietly," Weigand said. "He'd not been in the limelight before, not much in the newspapers. After he sold out, and for no reason anybody could understand, he held a big press conference. Talked for almost the only time in his life; talked to a bunch of financial reporters and editors. And told them, in effect, that the whole thing was a racket — all he had done, all they were doing. Except, as he pointed out, he had made money out of it; made it, he told them, out of even bigger fools than they were. 'If possible,' he told them. I knew a man who was there. Halder said that the only reason he had been able to do it was because everybody — apparently he made no exceptions — was like himself, out for what he could get. The difference was, he told them, that he had got it. Then he said, 'Frankly, gentlemen, people make me sick' and told them where the bar was."

"Well," Pam said. "All that. And he died in a pet shop. What happened to the money?"

As far as Weigand knew, nothing had happened to the money. The money was still around. The house they were in was part of the money. On that, they were still working and for some time would be. But so far as they had discovered, J. K. Halder had leased an obscure shop, filled it with animals, gone to live in it merely because he was, as he said, "sick of people."

"Now," Weigand said, "you are going to marry Mr. Brian Halder, Miss O'Brien."

She nodded.

"Did his father object?"

"No," she said. "I — I don't think he knew. Brian said — "

"Yes?"

"I didn't know all this," she said. "All this you say about him, about Mr. Halder. But

Brian said he was difficult that — that you had to put things to him in the right way. That he didn't — " she flushed again and swallowed. "Well," she said, "that he thought there were too many people around already, and didn't think there ought to be any more marriages and — "

"That," Pam North said, "is the silliest thing I ever heard of. Seriously?"

"I don't know," Liza said. "No — not literally, I guess. Brian maybe said that more to show how — how odd his father was. But that's what he said. He may have been half joking. Exaggerating."

"But you say Halder didn't know about your and his son's plans?" Weigand asked.

She shook her head. "Unless Brian told him in the last day or two," she said. "I don't think he did."

Weigand stood for a moment, then, looking down at her. She could not tell what he was thinking; could not, although she wanted to, feel him, understand him, as a person.

"Right," he said. "I think that's all for the moment." He shook his head. "Don't try to mix things up after this, Miss O'Brien." Again he paused, looking down at her. "One other thing," he said. "Where were you last night?"

She looked at him, her eyes wide.

"Last night?" she repeated.

"Until about eleven-thirty," Pam North said, "she was at our apartment, trying to get Martini to come out from behind a sofa."

Weigand nodded. "And after that?" he asked.

"I went home," Liza said. "Straight home. And went to bed. Was it — was it last night?"

"It might have been," Bill Weigand said. "All right, Miss O'Brien. That's all for now."

"Must I go home?"

He hesitated. Then he smiled, and then, fleetingly, he became a person to Liza; someone she could almost understand.

"Go find him," Weigand said. "Talk it over. Get it straightened out — if you can. You'll have some time. But don't try to cook up anything else between you."

"Oh no," she said, and went out through the door he opened for her, went to find Brian, but went frightened and uneasy, fearing as much as she hoped.

Brian came to meet her up the long room and put both hands on her shoulders and looked, gravely, into her eyes.

"I'm sorry," he said. "I guess I made a mess of it. You were swell, Liza. Very swell."

Then he put an arm around her shoulders, and walked with her down the room toward the windows, where the two men and the two women were sitting, now were looking at Brian and at her, and waiting. There seemed to her a kind of uneasiness, almost suspicion, in the way they all looked at her. But both of the men stood up as she and Brian approached, and the heavier man — lieutenant colonel what? — smiled in a friendly enough fashion. Then Brian introduced them and she tried to concentrate on their names, associate them finally with the way their faces were.

Whiteside, that was the lieutenant colonel, although Brian called him colonel. The older woman was his wife, Barbara. "My sister," Brian said. "My half-sister."

"How do you do, Miss O'Brien?" Mrs. Whiteside said, enunciating so distinctly that it seemed she really asked the question, expected an answer.

The tall man was Brian's half-brother. Jasper, Brian said. "But everybody calls him 'Junior.' Or J. K. As they do — " he paused. "As they did Dad," he said.

"Skip the 'Junior,' for God's sake," Brian's half-brother said. It was odd, Liza thought, that he could so remind her of Brian and yet be, in all but height, physically so different. It's more, she thought, than his being so much older, although he must be twice as old as

Brian; more than twice.

And the blond woman, slight, not a great deal taller than Liza herself, she was Jennifer Halder, Jasper Halder's, "Junior's," wife. Seen close, she was well-groomed, her features regular; seen close she was much younger than her husband, or than either of the Whitesides. She smiled at Liza; looked from her to Brian and back to her again, smiled and nodded. "But such a dreadful time," she said. "So awful about Father Halder."

"*Father* Halder," Mrs. Whiteside said. "Really, Jennifer! You never called him that, you know. Why start now?"

"Dear Barbs," Jennifer Halder said sweetly. "Poor dear Father Halder."

"Anyway," Mrs. Whiteside said, "I didn't truckle. Didn't get down on my hands and —"

"Now," Colonel Whiteside said. "Now my dears. We're all on edge."

"Truckle," Jennifer said, still sweetly. "When did I ever hear 'truckle'?"

"Please, Jennifer," the colonel said, his voice low, persuasive. "Barbara. We're all very much upset, Miss O'Brien."

"Much more, Raymond," Jennifer said. "Broken hearted. All broken hearted."

"Really!" Barbara Whiteside said. "*Really*, Raymond!" Impatiently, she gestured with strong, square hands, carefully cared for, newly manicured.

It was embarrassing; they rasped at one another, indifferent to anything but the need to rasp. Liza wished, anxiously, there were some way to escape from the group, from the sharp words, the cutting meanings, they were throwing at one another, over her head, around her, as if she were not there. She looked up at Brian.

For a moment he looked down at her, for that moment it seemed that something — assurance, confidence — was to be reestablished. But then there was a sound from the other end of the long room and Brian's head turned toward the sound.

Weigand and the Norths had come out of the library, but it was not at them Brian Halder looked. A slim, dark woman was coming up the steps from the foyer, with a tall, very fair, very scrubbed-looking, man behind her. And Brian seemed to forget Liza; to forget her even before he withdrew his arm from her shoulders as if it were misplaced there, and started down the room toward the newcomers.

"Mary!" Brian Halder said. "Mary! Where on earth?"

The dark woman came toward Brian in a little rush.

"My dear!" she said. "Brian! We just heard. Oh — Brian!"

Then he put his arms around her and she put her face against his coat and he held her there, close, and patted her shoulders. He said something to her, but now he spoke softly, for her ears only — And Liza stood, her eyes wide, looking up the room at them, feeling all security crumble around her.

Then the woman, this Mary, stepped back out of Brian's arms and looked up at him, and spoke in an odd, carrying voice.

"But why?" she said. "You're so — excited, my dear. It wouldn't have brought him back to life. Why was it so — ?" He was looking down at her and there was, apparently, something in his eyes which answered her question. Because now she stepped still farther back and said, "Brian! You can't! Why you — "

Then Weigand, who had been watching the two, stepped forward and interrupted.

"Now," he said, and allowed his voice to carry, as the woman's had done, "now I think we're all here, at last. Your son's been anxious to find you, Mrs. Halder. So have we."

"But — " she said. "Who are you?"

Weigand told her; his identity seemed to astonish her.

"Yes, Mrs. Halder," Weigand said. "We're

investigating your husband's death. Because he was murdered, Mrs. Halder."

But then, Liza thought, and something which had been like an iron band around her chest relaxed, was suddenly gone — but then, *she's Brian's mother! Not somebody else!*

It was easier to realize this as, with Weigand and the Norths, with Brian Halder's arm around his mother's shoulders (but it didn't matter, now; it was all right, now) they came down toward the others by the tall windows. Mrs. Mary Halder was young to be Brian's mother; she was slender and quick as a girl. But she wasn't a girl; she must, Liza thought, be about forty. As old as that!

Then Brian was introducing them. "Liza, this is my mother. Mary, Liza." Mary Halder was looking at her, looking at her slowly, carefully — at her body, her dress, most of all at her face. The gaze was not hostile; it was not even, or did not quite seem to be, appraising. And yet, Liza thought, it must be that only it's so — so impersonal. But then Mary Halder smiled and held out her hand.

"She's sweet, Brian," she said. "And so pretty, isn't she?"

Yet even the praise was somehow impersonal.

"She — " Brian began, and Liza found she

was waiting, waiting anxiously, to hear what Brian would say. But he was not allowed to finish.

"Mary," Jennifer Halder said. "My dear. It's all so dreadful! They say he was — was killed!" Then she said, and this was to the scrubbed blond man, "Isn't it awful, Piney?"

"Tragic," the man called Piney said, as if he had been rehearsing the word in his mind. He shook his head, seemingly to give emphasis to the word. Then he repeated it, in a slightly deeper tone. "Tragic." Then he turned to Liza and said, again as if he had formed the words earlier in his mind, "Nobody will remember to introduce us, Miss O'Brien. I'm Sherman Pine." He held out a well-shaped, well-cared-for, hand. Liza looked quickly to Brian as she took Pine's hand, but Brian was not looking at her, not looking at Pine. He was looking around at the others — at his brother, his brother's Jennifer; at the Whitesides, lieutenant colonel and lady.

"Now that you're all here," Lieutenant Weigand said, "I wish you'd sit down. I want to talk to you for a moment — to all of you. About what has happened."

He waited, expectantly; the others found chairs, the Norths outside the circle; Mr. North, she thought, hesitantly, after some

passage of the eyes between him and Weigand, between both of them and Mrs. North.
Liza herself stood for some seconds uncertainly, feeling more than ever strange among
these people — these people of Brian's — and
yet, because they were Brian's, and he was
one of them, feeling included among them.
Then Brian's hand was on her arm, he was
guiding her to a chair, he was sitting beside
her on the arm of the chair. Weigand looked
from one to another of the group.

"I think I have you straight," he said. "Let
me see. Mr. Halder — J. K. Halder, Junior?"
He nodded to Halder, who mirrored Weigand's nod. "And Mrs. Halder, Junior? Mrs.
Whiteside — you're Mr. Halder's daughter,
this Mr. Halder is your brother?"

"Certainly," Mrs. Whiteside said.

"Right," Weigand said, and he was unper-
turbed although, Liza thought, he was supposed to have been perturbed, put somehow
in his place.

"Colonel Whiteside? That's right?"

"Well," Whiteside said, "lieutenant colonel,
actually."·

Weigand nodded. He went on. But he did
not speak Mary Halder's name, or Brian's
or, finally, Liza's own. He merely nodded at
them. But his eyes stopped on Sherman Pine.

"Mr. Pine's a friend of mine," Mary Halder said. "We've been — we were going on to dinner. But we heard the news." She paused momentarily. "On the radio," she said.

Bill Weigand nodded.

"Some time last night," Weigand said, then, "Mr. Halder died in his shop, of strychnine poisoning. The poison had been administered hypodermically. Although it means a very painful death, and not as quick as is generally supposed, strychnine is often used by suicides. We may have been supposed to think that Mr. Halder was a suicide — that he had decided to end his life in a bizarre fashion. His reputation for eccentricity — the very fact that, as a rich man, he chose to live in this out-of-the-way shop, change all his normal habits — that reputation was supposed to make the suicide theory attractive to the police. And — the theory cannot be dismissed. The hypodermic used may have been his; so may the poison. He could have injected the poison, put the hypodermic back in the cupboard where we found it, in a box with the poison, walked to the pen in which he died and — well, merely waited to die. It would have been fifteen minutes to half an hour before the symptoms began. It could have been that way."

He looked around at them, slowly.

"But," he said, "I may as well tell you I don't think it was that way. I think someone stronger than he held him, just long enough to inject the poison, kept him — again by superior strength — from summoning help, watched him die, put him in the pen before the body began to stiffen. I think somebody did this last night — say between eleven and two o'clock. And — I don't think that person needed to be very strong, because Mr. Halder was a fairly old man, and not a particularly strong man." He looked around at them, giving them a chance to comment.

"Dreadful," Jennifer Halder said, and the others slowly, speculatively, looked at her, then looked back at Weigand.

"Now — " Weigand began, and then stopped and looked at the spiral staircase. Everybody looked at the staircase, down which a black Scottie was scrambling, scratching, making noise enough for a great Dane. The Scottie reached the bottom of the stairs and stopped abruptly, looked around in surprise. The number of people in the room seemed momentarily to baffle the Scottie, and he considered sitting down. But he abandoned this intention even before he started to put it into effect. He walked to Jennifer Halder, who was nearest, and smelled her briefly; he ignored Jasper Halder, greeted Colonel Whiteside, but only in passing and made a slight detour around Mrs. Whiteside.

"Aegisthus!" Mary Halder said. "Here I am, Aegisthus."

The little black Scottie, who had hesitated to sniff Brian's shoes, to look up with interest — and with apparent surprise — into Brian's face, turned toward the voice and barked briefly. Then, a sudden scurry of Scottie, he rushed toward Brian's mother, did not pause for the enquiry of smell, put forepaws on her knees and barked in welcome and relief.

"Good boy," Mary said. "Good boy."

"Really, Mary," Barbara Whiteside said. "That dog!"

"He's not doing any harm," Mary Halder said. "Anyway — anyway, J. K. gave him to me. He was mine and — and his. Don't you remember?" As she said this, for the first time, Liza thought, she seemed moved by something other than surprise, than shock. "Aegisthus," Mary Halder said, and bent toward the little dog. "He's dead, Aegisthus. The man's dead."

"Really, Mary!" Barbara Whiteside said again. "Really!"

Whiteside, like the others, had been watching the slight, pretty woman and the little black dog. Now he turned to his wife; now, as she repeated, but almost to herself, her deprecatory "really!" he shook his head at her. She did not appear to pay any attention.

"I'm sorry," Mary Halder said to Weigand, looking up from the little dog. "My husband gave him to me. He was — was something we both loved. But — I suppose I'm silly."

The black Scottie with the tragic name tried to lick Mary Halder's face, but now she pushed him, gently. He got down, stood for a moment looking up at her, seeming to study her, and then continued investigation. He was especially interested in Mrs. North, who required, who got, a thorough smelling.

"Cats, boy," Pam North said. The black Scottie looked up at her, doubtfully. He barked. "I'm very sorry," Pam told him, speaking with all seriousness. "But that's the way it is. Remember — " She broke off and looked at Mary Halder. "Did he come from the shop?" she asked. Brian's mother nodded. "Then of course you remember," Pam told the black Scottie. "Cats? That's what I smell of."

The Scottie's gaze into Pam's face was as grave, as serious, as hers. He barked briefly.

"I knew you would," Pam said. "I — " she

broke off. "Aegisthus?" she said, asking confirmation of Mary Halder; who nodded.

"My husband named him that," she said. "It's — oh it's out of literature, isn't it? A Greek play, or something? So many of them are — the animals, I mean, at the shop."

"Oh," Liza said, before she thought, speaking freely for the first time in, it seemed, many hours. "The little black cat. She was named Electra he — he told me."

"Poor dear Father," Barbara Whiteside said, with detachment, as if her father had been dead for years, rather than hours. "So — fanciful. So — odd."

"Well," Pam North said, "our cat's named Martini. Our chief cat. And Gin and Sherry, the ingredients." She paused. "Of course," she said, "I always feel it ought to have been the other way around. I mean, Gin and Sherry first, *then* Martini. But it wasn't practical."

She continued to look at the little Scottie. It was almost, Liza thought, as if Mrs. North had, for the moment, decided to keep their thoughts on the little Scottie.

"Smell Jerry," she advised him.

He did; it was an agreeable coincidence.

"Hello," Jerry said. "Yes, boy, the same cats."

Now they were all watching the little dog.

Aegisthus left Jerry North, smelled Sherman Pine, without comment; regarded Weigand, apparently with favor, came to Liza herself, and was again entranced.

"Same cats," Liza told him. He looked up at her and barked.

"Really, Mary," Barbara Whiteside said, once more. "Don't you think we've had enough of — this?" She pointed at the dog, who turned suddenly and faced her, and seemed to understand the disapproval in her voice, because he barked again, this time on a different tone. Then, Liza thought, he almost growled, but Mary Halder spoke his name quickly, and he relaxed and went to her. "I'll take him downstairs," Mary Halder said, and looked briefly to Weigand for his approval. He nodded. She picked the little dog up in her arms, then, and went toward the spiral staircase. But she went behind it and to another flight leading down. She was gone several minutes, and during those minutes, Weigand merely waited; during those minutes no one spoke. Then Mary Halder came back up the stairs, without the dog, and went back to her chair.

Liza looked at her and then, for some reason, at Pam and Jerry North. She was just in time to see some unspoken communication between them — a communication of eyes, of the slow movement of Mr. North's head. Again she felt, as she had felt in regard to Brian's family, that she was alien, left out. The feeling was only momentary; it was ridiculous to have such a feeling; the Norths were as she and Brian would be. *Oh please, as we will be,* she thought, and felt lost again at the need for thinking it, for praying it, like a child. Until now, until today, it had been as inevitable, as beyond the need of praying for, as her next breath.

Now, with the little, curiously named, dog put away "downstairs," with Mary Halder back, the group turned again to Lieutenant Weigand who stood, more or less facing the windows, with the windows forming a background for the men and women who faced him. He waited a moment, seemed about to speak, and then turned away again, seeing the attention of the others go to something behind him. Sergeant Mullins was coming down the room. When he saw Weigand's attention, he made a motion with his head, and Weigand went up the room to join him. They talked for a moment, and then walked back toward the door, where two other men in civilian clothes were waiting. The four of them walked together, then, and it was several minutes before Weigand turned back toward the group at the end of the room, regarded it for a moment, and then walked back. Their eyes, which had followed him as he left, were on him now as he approached.

"Miss O'Brien," Weigand said, and he spoke crisply, "this man who was with you when you found Mr. Halder's body. Will you describe him again, please?"

Now all of them looked at her.

"A little man," she said. "A very little, old man with a wrinkled face, with blue eyes, with — " She went on, doing as well as she could, trying to make words do what a pencil could so much better have done. She finished.

"Does any of you know such a man?" Weigand asked now, and he spoke more curtly than he had done before, as if now there were a need for haste.

For a moment no one answered and Liza, looking at the faces of the Halders, could not tell at once whether the description had meaning for any of them. But then, as if he had waited merely to give the others a chance, after looking briefly at the woman who now, again, seemed almost too young to be his mother, Brian spoke.

"Sure," he said. "A crony of Dad's. His name's Felix. I'm not sure of his last name —

Stedman, something like that. He and Dad played chess together; when Dad was away — he usually fed the animals. He had a little shop around there somewhere. A second hand store, something like that." He stopped.

Weigand nodded. He looked around at the others. "Any of the rest of you — ?" he asked.

"I heard of him; my husband mentioned him," Mary Halder said. "Just about that much, but I don't think his name is Stedman."

For a moment longer Weigand waited. Nobody else contributed anything.

"Not Stedman," Bill said. "Sneddiger. Felix Sneddiger. He's an upholsterer; has a little shop around there as you say, Mr. Halder. He was with Miss O'Brien when — when she went into the shop this afternoon. She found Mr. Halder's body, you know." This, Liza realized, was for the benefit of anyone who did not know. "Mr. Sneddiger was with her only part of the time. He was very much affected by — by what they found. According to Miss O'Brien, he more or less collapsed." He looked at Liza. "Right?" he said. She nodded. "She went to get him something and he disappeared," Weigand said. "We've been trying to find him."

He looked around at them.

89

"None of you has seen him, of course?" he asked.

Nobody answered.

"That's strange," Weigand said. "Because — *he apparently came here. To this house.*"

He tossed this, let it explode. And then, Liza saw, the members of the family — Mr. Halder's daughter and her husband the colonel; Jasper Halder and his wife; Brian and Brian's mother — looked at one another quickly, uneasily; looked each of them at one face, then at another, the glances intercepting, racing (she thought) away from such interceptions; each of them, it seemed to Liza, at once doubtful of the others and unsure of what they might find in his own face; each of them wary and each alone. The detective lieutenant, his own face expressionless, watched them, waited for them, gave them time. It was Mrs. Whiteside who finally spoke.

"But that's ridiculous," she said. "This — this odd little man Miss O'Brien says she saw. Why would he come here?"

"I saw him, Mrs. Whiteside," Liza heard herself say.

Mrs. Whiteside ignored this; ignored it pointedly.

"Why should he come here?" she repeated, asking it of Weigand.

Weigand shrugged. He said that, nevertheless, there was every indication he had come
there. He told them what the indications were.
Precinct men, with Liza O'Brien's description to work on, had had no trouble finding
out the little man's identity. Everybody knew
him, apparently, for blocks around. They had
had no trouble finding his shop. But they
had not found Felix Sneddiger himself; only
by rather amazing luck had they found trace
of him, but they had had the luck and found
the trace within minutes of finding his empty
shop.

There was a hack stand on a nearby corner
and, on the chance, one of the precinct men
asked the driver, reading a pocket mystery
behind the wheel, if he had seen a little old
man around, and described the man, named
him. And the driver, gnarled, almost as old,
from his appearance, as the man they sought,
said, at once, "Felix? Sure."

He had not only seen him around; he had
taken him away. His records showed when —
ten minutes of five — and where. The where
was Sutton Place.

"I was settin' here reading," the hacker told
the precinct man. "Felix comes along, sorta
trotting. He says to me, Joe, he says, you
know where Sutton Place is and I says to him,

I've been driving a hack in this town for twenty-five, thirty years, whatta you think? Kidding, like, account of I know Felix maybe ten, fifteen years. So he gets in and I drives him — "

He had driven him to the Halder house; the precinct man had taken Joe on the trip again, Joe had stopped in front of the house and said, "Yeah, this is it."

"And," Weigand said, "he waited long enough to see Mr. Sneddiger come up to the door, apparently ring the bell, stand there for a minute and then, when someone opened the door, go in. The driver didn't see who opened the door. But he'll swear Mr. Sneddiger came here, was let into the house. Now — there isn't any of you remembers anything about this? It would have been about — five-fifteen, five-twenty."

"*I*," Mrs. Whiteside said, "wasn't home at that hour. I had been shopping and — oh, it must have been almost six."

Weigand waited; he got statements from the others. Colonel Whiteside had got in about that time, he thought, he hadn't noticed, he had not seen Sneddiger. Mrs. Mary Halder had, on the other hand, gone out at about that time, to meet Sherman Pine. "For cocktails," she said. She had not seen Sneddiger.

"I was home," Jennifer Halder said. "We don't live here, you know, Lieutenant. We live — " she gave an address in the East Sixties. "I was just — oh, dawdling around, waiting for J. K. to come." She paused. "My husband," she said. "We call him J. K., mostly or — well, we used to call him 'Junior' a good deal. then I — I heard the awful news on the radio and — well, I came here. Oh — my husband called and said he had heard it too and suggested we come here."

"Junior" it appeared, it was said by "Junior," had stopped off for a drink, heard the news on the radio in a bar, telephoned his wife. But where, precisely, he was at five-fifteen or five-twenty he wouldn't try to say. He conveyed that he wouldn't take the trouble to decide, even if it were very little trouble.

And Brian was not much more definite.

"After — after I put Liza in a cab," he said, "after I called the police — I decided I needed a drink. I was — well, I was pretty much shot, I guess. After all — " He did not amplify, he let it trail off. "I had a couple of drinks," he said. "Then I decided to come here, to — to tell the others. I should have done it right away but — well, as I said, I was pretty well shot by — by everything. It was around six when I got here, probably."

It didn't sound like Brian, Liza thought. *Oh please, Brian, can't you tell it doesn't sound right?*

But the detective lieutenant had merely listened, not shown on his face whether it sounded right or not, not hurried Brian Halder. When Brian finished, he even nodded.

"By the way," he said. "You don't live here either, Mr. Halder? But you have a key?"

Brian didn't live in the house. He had a key.

"And you, Mrs. Halder? Mr. Halder?"

Jennifer Halder had a key; her husband had a key.

"Of course," Whiteside said, "if this man — this Sneddiger — really came here, one of the servants may have — "

They would see, Weigand told him. A man was talking to the servants; he was downstairs now, talking to the servants.

"Really!" Mrs. Whiteside said. "We might at least have been told!"

Weigand looked at her, did not answer, looked away; looked back up the room toward the door and then went to where Sergeant Mullins stood, with one of the other detectives. Weigand talked to them for several minutes, and then returned.

"Three servants," he said. "Right? Burns,

his wife. A girl named Grace" — he looked at a slip of paper in his hand — "Grace Forward? Is that right?"

"Farwood," Mrs. Whiteside said. "Really, Lieutenant!"

"None of them admits to seeing Sneddiger," Weigand said, ignoring it. "Nor to hearing the bell ring. And all of them were here, they say."

"Of course," Mrs. Whiteside said. "You see how ridiculous it is, Lieutenant."

But now Weigand shook his head.

"I'm afraid not," he said. "We'll have to find out, of course. We'll have to go over the house."

"Really!" Mrs. Whiteside said. "That's perfectly ridi — "

"Of course," Mary Halder said. She looked at Mrs. Whiteside. "My house," she said. "Now. Or didn't you realize, Barbara?"

"Well!" Mrs. Whiteside said. But she did not deny it was Mary Halder's house.

The search took some little time. It began in the downstairs kitchen, the servants' quarters there; it was cursory on the main floor, where there was so little place for concealment. It lasted longer on the second, third and fourth floors of the tall, narrow house. It ended in a closet on the third floor; a closet of the big, rear bedroom, a bedroom with a view of the river, which was Mary Halder's.

The closet, like the room, was large. Felix Sneddiger's body was in a far corner of it, concealed by hanging clothes. The little man with the wrinkled face had been strangled; merciless hands had squeezed his life out. It hadn't, the detective thought, been much trouble to kill the little, aged man, nor had it taken very long.

V

Tuesday, 9:10 P.M.
to 11:25 P.M.

She had fainted; that was it. Now, in the cab, sitting between Pam and Jerry North, memory was merciless; now the numbness which had supervened was gone and she had to remember. Someone had called to Weigand from the top of the spiral staircase, and Weigand had gone up the stairs, very quickly. And all of them had looked up, their eyes following after him. After a few minutes, Weigand had come down again, not so quickly, had stood for a moment looking at all of them, at one and then at another. His gaze stopped at her and then he said, slowly, that he was sorry. He was sorry, but he would have to ask her to do something for them. And, at his indication, she had gone up the spiral staircase and then, from the second floor to the third, up another, but straight, stair flight and into a big room in the rear of the house, with windows opening toward the east, toward the lights on the river, on the island in the river, on the shore beyond. Each step she took, she thought, she could remember now.

It had been in a closet, and Weigand, standing behind her, reaching over her shoulder, had held back a long dress — a black lace dress. And he had said, "Is that the man, Miss O'Brien?"

The little old face was hideous, now; the blue eyes were wide open, sightless and horrible. There were the marks of fingers on the thin corded neck. The face itself —

She had never fainted before; never known that blackness comes in, swirls in, from either side, so that the visible world narrows, until there is only a shrinking tunnel of fading light, until — Backing away, feeling herself sinking into the blackness, surrounded by it, she had said, "Yes. That's the — " She could remember saying that.

"It's all right, now," Pam North said, and Pam North's hand, pressing her arm, tightening on it, brought Liza back. "Good girl," Pam said. "It's all right, now."

Liza tried to smile; she could feel herself shaking.

"A drink is what you need," Jerry North said. "A drink and another drink and then some food. Did you have any dinner?"

She shook her head; she was afraid her voice, if she used it, would tremble as her body did.

"Neither did we," Pam said. "Now I come to think of it. Only one martini with too much vermouth, terribly strong. And then all that." She paused. "Including Aegisthus," she said. "Is it too late for Charles?"

"Almost," Jerry said. "We can try."

"I — I don't want to eat," Liza heard herself say.

"Well," Pam said, "I do. Jerry does. You can sit with us."

"I ought to go home," Liza said.

"Why?" Pam said. "Anyway, we told Bill. He's very sorry. Because of Dorian, partly, I suppose. But he would be anyway. Only, of course, he had to."

"Listen, Pam," Jerry North said, "the child's been through enough." His tone was light, almost laughing.

"She knows what I mean," Pam said. "So do you, as a matter of fact. It's just because you read Fowler."

"Now," Jerry said, "you've really got me."

She's got me, too, Liza thought. But I'm listening; I'm almost forgetting.

"English usage," Pam North said. "You really expect people to, but nobody ever does.

99

Perhaps I don't more than some people, of course. It's — here's Charles."

The cab was U-turning in Sixth Avenue, stopping in front of the restaurant. They were, it turned out, just not too late. "One thing," Pam North said, "there's room at the bar, now. Hello, Gus."

"I don't think — " Liza began.

"The only question," Pam told her, "is whether a martini or something else. There's no basic question."

There were three martinis, softly sharp, very cold, with tiny dots of oil from the peel of a lemon slowly spreading on their surfaces. They were full; Pam leaned forward and sipped at hers without raising it from the bar. "Easier," she explained. Then she raised it and drank.

Liza's stomach was surprised; then it was pleased. She was no longer, she found, shivering. She sat between the Norths, drank, said she was being a lot of trouble. She was told not to be absurd.

"By the way," Jerry said, "about the sketches. They're fine. I'll send you something to sign."

That was good, too; that helped; that pushed back, momentarily, the recurring memories. She finished her drink and there was another one before her. Now she did not hesitate.

After the second round, they went to a corner table in the café section and now Liza was hungry; it was surprising, it was incontrovertible. She was still between the Norths, they still talked, including her, not requiring anything of her. She felt strangely at home, as if she had known them for a long time, instead of for days only.

"Better, now?" Pam asked her, finally, over coffee.

"Oh," Liza said, "so much. I'm all right now."

"Eating's good for people," Pam told her. "Does things for them." She looked quickly at Jerry. "Well," she said, "it does."

"Always," Jerry said.

Then there was another pause. Then it was Liza herself who returned to it. It was time to return to it.

"You've been good to do this," she said. "I needed this. It was — it's so dreadful. But you two oughtn't to have to — "

Pamela North shook her head, shook off that aspect.

"Obviously," she said, "the little man knew something. Mr. Sneddiger. Knew too much. But — didn't you think he was surprised when he saw Mr. Halder's body? It sounded as if he were."

"Oh yes," Liza said. "I'm certain he was."

"But then — " Pam said, and shook her head. "There was so little time afterward and — " She sounded puzzled, as if things were refusing to work out. "And you had gone and Mr. Halder — your Mr. Halder — had — " This time she stopped as if a new idea had presented itself. She looked quickly at Liza.

"You mean he could have seen Brian do something?" Liza said. "After Brian put me in the cab? You mean Brian could have — have gone back and — oh, *no!*" she shook her head. "Anyway, Mr. Halder was already dead. He'd been dead for hours, hadn't he? So what could there have been?"

"I don't see it either, Pam," Jerry North said.

"Neither do I, I guess," Pam said. "All the same, Mr. Sneddiger did go to the house. And — got killed."

"Presumably," Jerry said, "he saw something last night. Something which meant more today than it did then. So — he went to check. And — it meant a great deal more."

"Listen," Pam said, "let's go to the apartment. It may be that — " And again she did not complete her sentence.

Liza demurred, but she wanted to be persuaded. She did not want to be alone, be shut out; did not want to think alone, with thoughts going endlessly in a circle of fears. She was persuaded. A cab took them to the Norths' apartment and the three cats, in a circle, greeted them inside the door. But Martini, seeing Liza O'Brien, made a low sound of indignation and retreated under a chair. The other cats seemed to recognize her, smelled to make sure. But then Gin growled, mildly.

"A dog," Pam told Gin. "Just a little black dog with — with an odd name. Nothing to worry about." Gin looked up at Mrs. North and spoke, seeming to express doubt that it was anything like so simple. "Small enough for you to chase," Pam assured the little cat. "Particularly as he probably wouldn't know what you were, with that funny face and — "

"Yah," Gin said, with more emphasis.

" — voice," Pam said. "Probably used to soprano cats, Aegisthus is. Such an odd name. I sounded as if I were lisping."

"You were," Jerry said. "Aegisthus."

"So were you," Pam told him. "What happens is that the end of your tongue gets all over-loaded and — well, things kind of slip off. Esses. I should think Clytemnestra would have found it a — a little handicapping. He could have called her Clytie, I suppose, but when she wanted to — " And she stopped. She stopped as if, approaching a precipice, she had dug in her heels, leaned back against the wind.

"Aegisthus?" Liza O'Brien said. "I don't remember." But then she did remember.

"Yes," Jerry said. "Agamemnon came from the wars. Aegisthus had taken his throne, and his wife, who was Clytemnestra. And — they killed him. A way the Greeks had. It was long ago, a legend."

"And," Pam North said, "a little black dog. So — so unpleasantly named. Perhaps, though, Mr. Halder named all the animals out of the tragedies."

Liza spoke slowly.

"I think he did," she said. "The black cat, the one in the window. He called her Electra."

"Of course," Pam said. "So there doesn't need to be any — significance. Probably there's another cat, or a dog, or a monkey, named Orestes. Perhaps — "

"I remember now," Liza said, and spoke even more slowly. "Orestes and Electra, who was his sister, killed Aegisthus and Clytemnestra. And — and were pursued by Furies. Orestes was Clytemnestra's son, and Agamemnon's."

"Yes," Jerry said.

"Actually," Pam said, "we're making a lot out of a little black dog."

"Mr. Halder gave his wife the dog," Liza said. "Why would he give her a dog named — named that? Unless he meant something by it? Unless — " She paused. "It's so dreadful," she said. "So — so frightening." Her eyes were wide; she was trembling again.

"Damn the little dog," Pam North said. But Jerry shook his head. He said it was no good. He said, whether they liked it or not, it was there. The implication was there.

"But she, Mrs. Halder, didn't even know," Pam said. "The name — what did she say? — 'It's out of literature, isn't it? A Greek play?' But not as if it had any significance to her."

"Which he might have enjoyed more," Jerry pointed out. "A jest, and, in a way, a challenge. But private, to be enjoyed by him and, perhaps, a few others. His sons, perhaps. While she didn't know, missed the point of it."

"Cruel," Pam said. "Even if — if she was."

"Oh yes," Jerry agreed. "Cruel. But *he* died, you know. It's possible that — " he stopped and looked, involuntarily, at Liza O'Brien.

"The challenge was taken up?" she said. "Is that what you mean? By — by Brian's mother and — and who?"

Neither of them answered.

"You mean this man who was with her?" Liza said. "This — Sherman Pine, wasn't it?"

"We're only guessing," Jerry said, but now Pam shook her head.

"Partly guessing," she said. "They heard the news on the radio, remember? But — in a cocktail lounge, somewhere? In the kind of bar the other brother stopped in, maybe. At the tail end of a ball game, or something. But Mrs. Halder and Pine wouldn't have been in that kind of a bar. Where they were, there'd have been music, if anything, or even television. If — if they were in a cocktail lounge at all. But if they were in an apartment, say, in — Mr. Pine's apartment. Then — "

"Listen, Pam," Jerry said. "You sound like your maiden aunt."

"My aunt is no maiden," Pam said. "She's been married four or five times. Don't you remember? *And* wears a wig."

"Listen," Jerry said again, and now he ran the fingers of his right hand through his hair. "Listen, Pam. Keep your aunt out of it."

"All right," Pam said, "only don't call her a maiden. How did she get in, anyway?" She sounded honestly puzzled.

"She was an abstraction," Jerry said. "I'm very sorry."

He was told he should be. He was told to leave out the abstractions. "Particularly wigged," Pam added. "An abstraction with a wig."

"All right," Jerry said. "You implied, way back there when we were on the subject, that if Mrs. Halder went to Pine's apartment for a drink, instead of to a cocktail lounge, he was — well, Aegisthus to her Clytemnestra. Which is an idea which would occur to — all right, *my* maiden aunt."

"I didn't know," Pam said. "Oh, all right, Jerry. Not that I don't sometimes think maiden aunts weren't pretty smart. I mean, weren't sometimes pretty smart. There's no point in saying that merely because there's smoke there *isn't* any fire."

But then Pam looked at Liza O'Brien, who was looking at nothing.

"We forgot," Pam said, and now her voice was soft, unhappy. "We do, sometimes."

But Liza shook her head. It didn't matter; it was not what anybody said, or could say. It was Brian, always it was Brian; now it was, it might be, Brian pursued by Furies, Brian running for the rest of his life down a hated corridor of memory, Brian never the same again — never hers again. If a man's mother killed his father, because there was another man for her, what would be left of the son's life, if he were a man like Brian? If —

"Remember," Pam said, "there's nothing to go on. Agamemnon was killed because he came home, you know. Mr. Halder — well, there's nothing to indicate he was coming home. Nothing to indicate he wasn't merely — well, amused. So then, why?"

But there was an answer to that, and Liza faced the answer, and spoke it slowly.

"He had a lot of money," she said. "Maybe they — maybe somebody — wanted the money."

There was nothing to say to that. Its inescapable truth was given a brief tribute of silence. Then Pam North spoke.

"Sometimes," Pam said, "It's easier not to begin at the beginning. I keep thinking of Mr. Sneddiger. Because there are several reasons for killing Mr. Halder, and only one for killing Mr. Sneddiger. Of course, most of the reasons for killing Mr. Halder probably are money, one way or another. Because, if you've got money, that's what happens."

"Listen, Pam," Jerry said, "lots of people with money die perfectly natural — "

"Obviously," Pam said. "Especially when they haven't got relatives. But you aren't arguing that strychnine is natural, are you?"

"No," Jerry said.

"Sometimes, Jerry," his wife told him, "you do wander from the subject."

"Which is?"

"Mr. Sneddiger. For whom there was only one reason. He knew too much."

And then Pam made a small sound which was almost a gasp, and looked at Liza O'Brien with an expression of concern, almost of alarm. Then she looked at Jerry.

"Jerry!" Pam said. "Won't whoever did it think, wonder, whether Mr. Sneddiger didn't tell — " She did not finish, but looked toward Liza. And then both of the Norths looked at Liza gravely, and watched her shake her head.

"He didn't tell me anything," she said. "I know he didn't. I've — I've been thinking back. He was just surprised, and shocked, and — and there wasn't anything to make me feel that he knew more than I did, than we could see." She looked first at Pam and then at Jerry. "I'm sure," she said. "I've thought and thought."

"Only — " Pam North began, and the door buzzer rasped sharply, interrupting her. It rasped twice, then three time quickly.

"Let Bill in, Jerry," Pam said. "I wondered."

And Liza O'Brien realized then that all of this had, to some degree at least, been planned; been planned, as it were, around her, over her; that her being there was part of some plan and that now Bill — Dorian's Bill; the police department's Bill, also — was coming as part of the plan. For an instant she felt oddly defrauded, as if counterfeit had been offered, and the most nefarious of counterfeits — spurious friendship. But then Pam said, "Liza," gently, and the girl looked at Pam, at Pam's small intensely alive face and thought, no, it isn't false, isn't a fake, they're not against me, or against Brian. Then Bill Weigand was in the room, not surprised to find her there, half smiling at her.

"So," he said, "you're all right, I see."

"Oh, yes," the girl said. "I'm all right now."

"We have to ask unpleasant things," Weigand said. "It can't be helped. We're in an unpleasant business."

"I realize that," Liza said. "It was — I'm sorry I couldn't take it."

She was, Weigand told her, taking it fine. Better, he said, than a lot would.

"Bill," Pam North said. "Did you realize about Aegisthus? The little dog?"

"Yes," Weigand said. "Why yes, Pam."

"That Aegisthus was — ?"

"Right," Weigand said, and looked quickly, seemingly with doubt, at Liza O'Brien.

"Oh, we've been all over it," Pam said.

"And got?" Bill asked her.

"Oh," Pam said, "in the air. So — what about Mr. Sneddiger?"

Bill Weigand sat down. He looked again at Liza O'Brien. He spoke slowly, to her. He said that, first, he wanted to make her position clear, and his own. "Pam and Jerry hear a good deal," he said. "More than they should, from time to time. My superiors — " He paused, and suddenly grinned at Pamela North. "O'Malley doesn't know, yet," he said, in an aside. He sobered. "Won't approve," he finished, to Liza again. "In theory, you should be kept completely in the dark, Miss O'Brien. Because, in theory, you're involved. But, I think in this case you'd better — well, know the general situation. Because — "

He paused and looked at her. She waited; felt, once more, growing uneasiness.

"Felix Sneddiger was killed because he knew something," Weigand said. "I don't know what; perhaps only the person who killed him knows what. Unless, Miss O'Brien, Sneddiger said something to you. At the shop."

He paused; she shook her head.

111

"Nothing," she said. "We've been talking about it. There was nothing."

"Tell it to me again," Weigand said, and listened as she told him again. He asked questions — small, probing questions; questions which were hard to answer; questions which required that she try to inject her mind, thus retrospectively, into the mind of the little, wrinkled man she had met so briefly, who so uglily had died. Again, more vividly than before, she saw the little shop and herself and the little old man in it; saw the animals, the black cat Electra, the sick boxer; the hideously folded body of J. K. Halder. Weigand was patient; Liza tried to make her patience match his own; tried not to let her nerves rebel under the cross-examination.

"Bill," Pam said, finally, "can't you see?"

Then he nodded, slowly; then he said, "Right." He had, he told them, and now Liza felt herself again on an equal footing with the others, included with them, to find out.

"Because," Weigand said, "somebody is wondering just what I was wondering. You may as well realize that, Miss O'Brien. And that person who is wondering most, cares most, is the person who killed Halder and then killed Sneddiger. Did Sneddiger tell you what he knew?"

"He didn't," Liza said. "You can see he didn't."

Now Bill Weigand nodded again. He repeated that he had had to be sure.

"So," he said, "for your own — safety, I think you ought to know how things stand, so far as we can tell how they stand. Because, Miss O'Brien — you're going to have to be careful for a while. Do you realize that?"

He spoke very seriously, very slowly, as if each word were important. And his tone, his gravity, made real to Liza what had been before a theory, a possibility. *Why*, she thought, *I might be killed! I might die!* The idea was suddenly too large, too overwhelming, for her mind; it filled her mind, forcing everything else out of it; it was a strange and terrible, and entirely new, idea and then she thought, why, I'll never be so young again; never so young as before I thought of death as real.

Bill Weigand said, "I see you do." Then she thought there was concern in his face. "I'm sorry," he said. "Don't be too frightened." He spoke gently.

"What we all need is a drink," Pam North said. "Wait." She got ice and whisky. Liza shook her head at first, but then said, "Yes, please." Jerry North and Weigand let their glasses be filled with Scotch and water;

Pamela North put approximately a teaspoonful of Scotch in her glass, added ice, filled with water, drank and said, "Ah!" Jerry grinned at her.

"I don't," Weigand said then, "know how much you know of the Halder family, Miss O'Brien?"

"Almost nothing," she said. "Except — except Brian, of course. We met at a — a sort of party. Why — " and her voice was surprised — "it was only about a month ago, really."

"Right," Weigand said. She might as well, then, hear what they knew; most of it would be in the newspapers in the morning, in any event. "As background to the picture," he said. He pointed out that she, that all of them, knew about J. K. Halder himself. It must be evident to all of them that he had married twice.

Barbara and J. K. Halder, Junior, had been born, in that order, to Halder and his first wife. The first wife had died in 1915. Halder had settled down, apparently, to life as a widower, and to making his first few hundred thousands. Then, unexpectedly, in 1926, he had married a girl of eighteen — Mary Callan, or calling herself that, and then the very appealing girl of a boy-meets-girl play which was having an unexpected success. "She came out of nowhere in particular," Weigand said. "A lovely child named, originally Mary Gallagher. Everybody thought she was wonderful; would do wonderful things. She married Halder, and left the cast of the play. And, a little later, the play left Broadway."

Mary Gallagher Halder was, the next year, the mother of a boy. "Your Brian," Weigand told Liza. They were living in the Sutton Place house; everything seemed to be working out well, despite the disparity in age between Halder and his wife. And then, when Brian was a year old, Halder dramatically "retired" and, a few months later, left the Sutton Place house and went to live in the room back of the shop in West Kepp Street. "Just like that," Weigand said. "Mrs. Halder says 'he just decided that was what he wanted.'"

He had kept the Sutton Place house, given his wife and son a very ample allowance and, when his daughter, Barbara, and her husband lost most of what money they had in 1929, agreed willingly enough (as Mrs. Halder had) that they move into the house.

"He supported them too, largely," Weigand said. "Whatever he was, he wasn't a miser. He — well, he just didn't like people. Didn't want to live with them; preferred his animals. Obviously, I suppose, he was what, if you have a sufficient amount of money, is called 'eccentric.' "

"Brian told me once," Liza said, "that his father lost all interest in him after he quit crawling around on all fours. He — Brian and I laughed about it."

Weigand smiled. He said that Halder certainly seemed to have shifted his interest to quadrupeds.

Brian had, of course, been far too young for the war; had been in school and had remained in school. Then he had studied architecture at Columbia, but quit before he was graduated and gone into an architect's office, where he still was. Liza shook her head, slightly. He was still attending classes at Columbia, evenings and Saturdays, in the School of General Studies. He had merely — "well," she said. "I suppose in a way he resented his father's attitude. This 'take what you want so long as you don't bother me' business. Wanted to make his own way." She paused. "He never phrased it so," she said. "I'm guessing mostly."

Weigand nodded; said it sounded reasonable. When Brian went to work, he had found a small apartment of his own and left the Sutton Place house, so that only the Whitesides and Brian's mother remained in it. Whiteside, incidentally, was a National Guard lieutenant colonel, perfectly willing to be called "Colonel." So far as Weigand had determined, that was his chief occupation although now and then he bestirred himself to lose a little money in the market. "He has some money left, apparently," Weigand said. "And his wife has — had — a good allowance from her father."

J. K. Halder, Junior, and his wife, Jennifer, had an apartment of their own; the younger Halder was trying to follow in his father's financial footsteps; the police didn't yet know with what success, although he and Jennifer lived well enough, in a comfortable apartment at a good address. They were often at the Sutton Place house, as was Brian. "He's devoted to his mother, apparently," Weigand said, and looked at Liza for comment. But she had none to make.

"As to the characters of all these people," Weigand said, "you've all seen them; seen about as much of them as I have."

"And you think — " Pam North began.

Weigand, apparently ahead of her, shrugged.

" — one of them did it?" he finished, for Pam. "I don't know, of course. It's a place to start. You heard them as to where they were when Sneddiger was killed. They're not much more definite about last night; they all seem to have been out and around. Brian was working, he said — working at home. Whiteside says that, after dinner, which ended earlier than they expected, he'd gone to his club for a rubber of bridge. Mrs. Whiteside stayed at home, alone. Mrs. Halder was 'with friends.' She didn't want to go further; we haven't required her to, as yet. Jennifer Halder — "

"Mrs. Junior," Pam said. "Isn't that simpler?"

Mrs. Junior, if Pam preferred, was at home in her apartment, also alone. Junior himself had, unexpectedly to her — "and not very convincingly to me," Weigand said — gone downtown to his office. But his wife supported him when he said that he had had to leave some work unfinished to get to dinner and, when the dinner ended early, had seized the opportunity to return to his office and get on with it.

"You keep talking about the dinner," Pam said. "As if it were special. Was it?"

"Well," Bill Weigand said, "the old man was there. As a matter of fact, he seems to have arranged it."

"Not," Pam said, "not to tell them he'd changed his will? *Not that!*"

"Why no," Bill said. There was amusement in his voice, momentarily. "Whatever made you think of that, Pamela?"

Pamela North made a small, quick face at him.

"It could be," Jerry North said, with detachment, "something she's read."

But Lieutenant Weigand was sober again. Actually, he said, all of the members of the family — and they had all dutifully shown up — denied knowing why Halder had arranged the dinner. He had asked — "asked" was as good a word as any other — his wife to invite the others. She had done so. They had arrived at the Sutton Place house around seven, Halder himself a few minutes later than the others; they had had a drink or two and had sat down to dinner at a quarter of eight. They had finished, had coffee; the old man had seemed more relaxed than usual, to have nothing on his mind — "actually," Weigand said, "there seems to have been nothing particularly eccentric in his normal social behavior" — and, until about nine o'clock it had been an uneventful, apparently not too interesting, family gathering.

"And then, unexpectedly, the old man got up and left," Weigand said. "They all agree on that. One minute he was talking, or listening; the next minute he stood up, said, in effect, 'Well, good night' and went away. All of them say they haven't the faintest idea why

119

and admit they wondered at the time, since abruptness of that sort wasn't the form his eccentricity usually took."

"And he never said why he had arranged the party?" Pam said. "After — after going to all that trouble?"

The trouble Halder had gone to apparently amounted to sending a telegram to his wife, Bill Weigand told them. However — that was the way it had been. "The way they all agree it was," he qualified.

"But look," Pam said. "Somebody must have *done* something. Said something."

Bill agreed that one would suppose so.

"But," he said, "none of the others admits to having seen anything, or heard anything."

"Admits," Pam repeated.

"Admits is the word, of course," Bill Weigand said.

"What was the matter with the telephone?" Jerry asked, and they all looked at him for a moment before Pam said: "Of course! What was? Temporarily disconnected, or something?"

"Oh, that," Weigand said. "Why did Halder send his wife a telegram instead of telephoning her? Well, apparently he usually did. I suppose because it was more impersonal, avoided — lessened — contact. Anyway, he did. Mrs. Halder gave me the wire. Wait a minute." He took a yellow Western Union form from his pocket and read aloud from it. " 'Please arrange all family to dinner seven Monday,' " he read. " 'J. K. Halder.' "

"Succinct," Pam said, and Bill Weigand, putting the telegram back in his pocket, said, "Right."

"And, of course, it proves Mr. Halder really did make the arrangement," Pam said. "If somebody wanted to prove it. Only, of course, it doesn't really, does it? Because usually they merely count and don't even look up."

There was the slight pause which was, Liza was beginning to realize, the customary tribute to Pam North's syntax. And yet it was not difficult: the actuality of the telegram might be supposed to prove the validity of the arrangement; it need not because someone other than Mr. Halder might readily have sent it and signed Halder's name; it would be difficult to identify the person, Halder or another, who had handed in the message, if it had been handed in, since Western Union clerks usually counted, without looking up at the sender, the words in a message. It wasn't, Liza decided, really clearer phrased so; it was merely longer.

"Anyway, there's always the telephone," Liza heard herself saying. "To, I mean — "

"Of course," Pam said. "Much more likely. Only, easier to trace, wouldn't it be, Bill? A record so they could charge?"

"Right," Bill said. "We're checking. I think we'll find Mr. Halder actually sent the wire. We may not."

"Nobody admits knowing why?" Pam asked.

"Nobody," Bill said. "After all, he may merely have wanted to see them about nothing in particular."

They seemed to come to dead end. There was a pause.

"And nobody admits to knowing Sneddiger?" Jerry North was saying.

"Except Brian Halder," Weigand said. "He met him once. As a matter of fact, he seems to have kept a little more in contact with his father than the others did. But Brian denies having seen Sneddiger for a couple of weeks. And the others say they never saw him before, although Mrs. Halder — Brian's mother, I mean — admits she had heard of him."

"They all — looked?" Pam said.

"Right," Weigand said. "After Miss O'Brien made the identification they all — looked. All normally upset, so far as one could tell. Nobody more than that."

"All the same," Pam said, "one of them

should have been."

"Oh yes," Weigand said. "Yes, I think so. It's hard to see it any other way."

VI

Tuesday, 11:40 P.M.
to Wednesday, 1:35 A.M.

Lieutenant Weigand drove Liza home, in a convertible Buick which looked like any other convertible Buick, except that there were red-lensed lights where fog lights might have been. During the short drive through comparatively uncrowded streets, Weigand did not talk of the murder. He asked how long she had known Dorian, how they had met, in the casual tones of acquaintanceship. "Dorian's wonderful, she's tops," Liza said and, without taking his eyes from the way ahead, Bill Weigand smiled and said that sort of remark was one for which he had never found an answer. "Except," he added, " 'Right,' which never seems particularly responsive. I do agree, of course."

"She put me on to this chance with the cat book," Liza said. "With Mr. North. He says he likes the sketches, incidentally. Do you — do you suppose he does?"

"Of course," Weigand said. "Otherwise he'd hardly have — also, I saw them. I like them myself. I even recognized the cats, you know. Whereas, in life, I'm constantly confusing Martini and Gin."

"Oh, there's lots of difference," Liza told him. "The eyes, the expression, to say nothing of Gin's being so much longer and having a tail like a whip."

He could see it in the drawings, Weigand told her. That's why he thought they were good. And, while he remembered it, here they were. He gave her the wrapped drawing pad as he stopped the car in front of the apartment building. He started to get out to open the door for her, but she had it open and smiled and shook her head. "Good night," she said, and Weigand said, "Good night. Take care of yourself." She smiled and nodded and went into the building, carrying the package.

Weigand watched her for a moment, and then put the Buick in gear. She'll be all right, he decided, particularly as eyes were being kept on the others. He did, he thought, letting the clutch in, wish there were more eyes available. But he did not think anything would happen tonight. The pressure wasn't on yet. He thought it wasn't on.

Liza went up in the elevator, down the corridor to the door of her small apartment. She tried to keep her thoughts at the level they had reached in the car. There was no good brooding about it, hitting herself in the head with it. There was nothing she could do; there was — She opened the door and went in and flicked on the lights. Then she found that, anxiously, almost fearfully, she was looking around the little living room. But it was empty, as it should have been; undisturbed, as it should have been. So was the kitchenette in its closet; so the bedroom, into which she and a chest and a three-quarters bed fitted with such nice precision. She got herself a glass of milk from the refrigerator and sat down to drink it, pushing off her shoes. She unwrapped the pad and began to look at the drawings. They are good, she thought; pretty good, anyway. I can make them —

But she still had to make studies of ordinary cats — of grocery store cats, and drug store cats and cats with only back fences to their names — and of long-hairs, like the little black cat at the shop. Like Electra. (Electra, Aegisthus, Electra — she forced her mind away.) She hoped the little cat, all the animals, were being taken care of, being fed. She took a sip of milk. Particularly the tiny kittens, Mr. Halder had shown her, because kit-

126

tens, she thought, had to be fed — And then, in an odd way, she recognized her own thoughts and sat up suddenly. She hoped the animals were being fed. But were they?

For heaven's sake Liza, she told herself, what a thing to get upset about! Of course somebody's feeding them. And the responsibility isn't yours. The responsibility is — But she could not finish that, she found. Who had the responsibility? The police? She doubted it. The members of the Halder family, of course; in a sense the animals had, now, become their property. But with all this — with grief, fear, shock, whatever it was they felt, together and as individuals — which of them would remember a few very small kittens, a black long-haired young cat with a pink mouth, a half-grown Siamese with a strident voice? And, actually, wouldn't everybody just assume that the responsibility was that of someone else; wouldn't everybody merely hope, idly, as she had hoped, that somebody else would remember? Whereas, Liza thought, uncomfortably, I *have* remembered.

It was five minutes before she gave up to the compulsion which she considered, with all the logic she could summon, to be entirely ridiculous, and which was none the less compulsive. (Why, the little kittens might die!

127

Just lie there in that funny little pile of kittens and starve to death. They might cry their funny, quavering little cries, and never understand —) *Oh, for God's sake,* Liza told herself, go down and do it, then. If you're going to be so utterly silly, keep yourself awake about a bunch of animals, probably fed hours ago at that, go down and see. Whereupon she put her shoes back on, put the empty glass which had held milk in the sink, and went down to look for a taxicab. She found one quickly, which was lucky or not, as you looked at it. She gave the cab driver a point of reference near West Kepp Street. You *are* a fool, she thought and leaned back in the cab and lighted a cigarette. And then she sat up again and repeated the accusation with increased vehemence. And, she thought, whatever makes you think you can get into the shop? Don't you know it will be locked up?

She almost abandoned it then; almost told the cab driver to take her back to Murray Hill. But they had gone so rapidly through the almost traffic-free streets, were so clearly only a few blocks from her destination, that to go back seemed more foolish than to go on. After all, she thought, there probably will be a policeman guarding the place, and he will let me in when I tell him why. He can come in with me, to see — to see that it's only for that.

The cab slowed and the driver looked around.

"The next corner's all right," she said.

"There was some trouble down here to-day," he said. "Somebody got knocked off."

"Did they?" she said. "This will do, thanks."

It did. She left the cab, watched it drive away, walked another short block and turned into West Kepp Street. She could see to the crook in the middle of West Kepp, and for a distance beyond, before the angle cut the sight line. It was empty as far as she could see. But then — was it? Wasn't that a man — or was it only a shadow? — in front of the shop, standing on the sidewalk, bent a little and seeming to peer in? Of course, Liza thought, there is a policeman; there would be. She went on, feeling that she had been right, after all, to come, because there was a policeman to let her in. She went more quickly, her heels clicking on the pavement.

But when she was nearer the shop, there was not really any man in front of it. There was a shadow, thrown by the standard of the street lamp, which might have seemed, from a distance, to be a man. There were other shadows in the inadequately lighted street; between the shop and the house next door there was, she now saw, a narrow area-way. She hesitated, momentarily, and went on, more slowly. It was to be a fool's errand, after all.

But having come so far, so foolishly far, she might as well try the door, Liza thought. It would, of course, be locked; it was absurd to think it would not be. But it was even more absurd to come a couple of miles downtown to do something and to stop, in the last twenty feet — fifteen feet now; five, now — without even trying to do it. Liza O'Brien, small and quick (and inwardly very contemptuous of herself), went down the three steps to the shop level and tried the door. It opened at once.

This was so surprising, and at the same time so disquieting, that Liza stopped with the door ajar and looked carefully into the shop. It was dimly lighted by a single bulb near the rear of the room and, at the instant, the animals were quiet. But then the cockers in the window barked together and then the room was full of sound, and this was cheering. What's happened, actually (she thought), is that the policeman was standing in front of the shop, looking into it, and now for some reason has gone in, leaving the door unlocked behind him. Probably the policeman is in the

130

rear room, in which Mr. Halder had lived — and might, if Lieutenant Weigand was right, have died. Perhaps the policeman has even —

But that thought died as she looked into the pen which held Electra. The little cat's water bowl was empty and there was no sign of food; Electra looked up and, wistfully, hopefully, complained about this. The cockers, when Liza went to their pen, were less wistful, more emphatic, equally unprovided for. And the Siamese cat in the first of the pens arranged down the right wall spoke his grievance with harsh, almost jungle fury. "You poor things," Liza O'Brien said, generally, to the occupants of the room and, on her way to the rear room, walked down the row of pens against the wall. None of the animals had been fed. The sick boxer was gone, so that now there were, one after another, three empty pens. Liza passed the last of these pens quickly, not looking at it.

The five tiny kittens got up as she stopped in front of them, got up out of their defensive pile, and wabbled to the front of the pen, and their complaints were tiny, worried squeaks. Liza squatted until her face was level with the faces of the kittens and said, "Now just wait. I'll fix things." One of the kittens made a tiny gesture toward her face with a forepaw, the fumbling suggestion of a cat's quick jab. Unbalanced by the effort, the tiny cat fell down. Then it squeaked more loudly than the others.

The little kittens first, Liza decided, and went to the door leading to the back room and opened it. The room was unlighted; with the door open, some of what little light the larger room had to spare seeped into the back room. It was enough to help Liza find a wall switch and then the back room was brighter, gave back with interest the light it had borrowed from the shop. But the shop still was dim.

The room was as she had seen it before, except that someone had opened the barred window. Liza found milk in the refrigerator, tasted it and found it sweet, warmed what she thought might be enough and put it in a flat dish she thought might do. This she carried in to the small kittens; around this they gathered, tails in the air, snuffling, getting milk in their noses, getting some — she hoped — into their stomachs. Then she filled a pitcher of water and, from it — as she had done those hours before while she waited for Brian, done then because it was something to do — filled the drinking vessels in the pens. Then she went back to the refrigerator, found meat for the cats, hoped the dogs would be content for the time with prepared food, filled pans with each and turned back toward the shop. She was busy, now; preoccupied with the task, thinking of nothing else. She stepped quickly into the shop room, stepped confidently; had stepped too far before she realized that the single bulb which had grudgingly illuminated the room had gone out.

She half turned to retreat, the movement involuntarily, too quickly, made for more than the beginning of fear to rise. But the movement was not completed. There was, with no warning, a great, numbing pain in the back of her head, a great swirling of darkness and she felt herself falling. As she fell she thought, dazedly, *Why, I've fainted again! I've* — Then the blackness surged over her thoughts. . . .

"Liza," a voice said. It was a faint voice; it came from an immeasurable distance, whispered across stretching darkness. "Liza!" It was stronger, now. *"Liza!"*

She was lying on her back on the floor, on the hardness of the floor. But there was a pillow under her head. She moved, resenting the hardness, the discomfort. *"Liza!"* she opened her eyes; a face was near her own, looking down at her.

"Hello, Brian," she said, and smiled. "Where did you — " Then she remembered, partly remembered, and tried to sit up. "Lie still," Brian said. "You're in the shop."

"Of course," she said. "Nobody fed the animals. But I fainted." But then there was a pain surging in her head. She half raised herself and, this time, Brian did not object. Instead, he helped her to a sitting posture. Her hand went to her head, to the place where the hurt was. It was much worse, incredibly worse, when she touched it. "I bumped myself," she said, and now was conscious that she was speaking like a child.

"Liza!" Brian said. "What were you doing here? What did you come for?"

The concern which had been in the voice which called to her across darkness, called her name — but had that been a kind of dream? — was not in Brian Halder's voice as he spoke now. He was insistent, now; his voice was almost harsh.

"What is it, Brian?" she said. "I don't understand. I — I got to thinking about the animals, wondering if anyone had fed them. I came down to see." She looked into his face, into the dark intensity of his eyes. But she could not see Brian in his eyes. "Nobody had," she said.

He shook his head. "Why did you come here?" he asked, as if she had not spoken.

"Didn't you realize — didn't you think what might happen?"

She shook her head, and pain surged through it.

"You got hit," Brian said. "Don't you understand that? You might have been killed."

"I don't know," she said. "I was bringing out the food. I thought I fainted." But then she remembered the pain which had preceded the blackness. "Of course I know now," she said.

"You didn't see anyone?" he asked, and she said, "No, Brian."

"At any time?"

She remembered, then. She told him she had thought she saw a man standing on the sidewalk, leaning down to look into the shop; told him that the man was not there when she was nearer the shop.

"A man?" Brian said.

"I don't know. I supposed it was a man. I supposed it was a policeman."

He shook his head; she thought he seemed puzzled. But she felt that she did not, any longer, realize how he seemed, how he felt. In the drawn harshness of his face, of his voice, she could not find Brian.

"There wasn't anybody here when I came," he said. "The front door was open. The light was out. You were just — lying here. I could just make you out. I thought — " He broke off.

"What did Felix Sneddiger tell you, Liza?" he asked.

"Nothing," she said. "I told you — no, I told the others. He didn't tell me anything."

He merely looked at her, his eyes deep in shadow.

"Nothing," she said. "He told me nothing."

"And you came to feed the animals?" Brian said, and his tone did not believe she had come to feed the animals.

His arm had still been supporting her; now she moved, freeing herself, moving away from him.

"Why were you here?" she said, and heard suspicion in her own voice. "If that's so important, why were *you* here?"

He shook his head again, as if that were of no importance.

"We've got to get you out of this," he said. "Can't you see that? Before you get hurt." He paused. "In one way or another," he said, trying to make her eyes meet his. But now she avoided looking into his eyes.

"Why didn't you see anyone?" she asked. "There was — " She stopped. Now she looked at him. "There *was* somebody else?" It was strange to hear her own voice asking this of Brian.

"Of course," he said. "You — apparently you surprised someone. Here for — I don't know why he was here."

"He — this somebody — seemed to be just looking in," Liza said. "As if he wanted to find out what — what could be seen from outside."

He seemed to consider this for a moment; then he shook his head.

"How did you get in?" he asked. She told him. "The place was locked up," he said. "Whoever it was had been in, gone out again, set the catch so he could return. Don't you see that?"

She said she didn't see anything.

"Why wouldn't you have seen this — this man?" she asked him again. "If there was light enough to see me? Or do you think he just knocked me out and went away, leaving me here? Why would he do that?"

"To keep you from recognizing him," Brian said. But now his voice was puzzled.

"Why would he come here?"

Brian shook his head. Then he stood up.

"Will you get out of this, Liza?" he said. She got to her feet, too; got to her feet unsteadily, but moved away when he would

have helped her. "Your people live in Schen-
ectady, you said? Why don't you go there?
For a while. Until — "

"No," she said. "What's the good of that?"

"Something can happen to you," he said.
Momentarily, there was faintly a smile on his
lips, but it was not a pleasant smile. "Something did," he told her. "Next time — "

"No," she said.

"Now," he said. "Tonight. We'll put you
on a train." He was urgent; now, she thought,
he was trying to re-establish contact between
them. But now that was impossible.

"No," she said. "I'm not — " Then she
looked down at the floor. The pans she had
been carrying had slid to some distance from
where she had fallen. The one containing food
for the dogs had overturned; that which held
the meat had not. And she realized the light
was on again.

"I was going to feed them," she said, and
she pointed. "See, I was going to feed them."

He looked at the pans, then at her.

"I've already given them water," she said.
"Look and see."

He merely shook his head. But then he
went to the pans and picked them up. He left
the dried dog food where it lay and went back
into the other room. When he emerged, it was

with both pans, the dog-food pan refilled. He handed both pans to her. "All right," he said. "Feed them."

She did feed the animals, while he stood watching her. It was, she thought, a strange thing to be doing; an absurd, inappropriate thing to be doing. "The kittens?" he said. She stopped and looked around at him. "I did," she said. "I — " Then, suddenly, unexpectedly, she was angry; her head hurt, her world was falling apart, and she was merely brightly, furiously angry. "Look for yourself, why don't you?" she demanded, and the anger was in her voice. But he merely shook his head; he said there was no point to this.

"The point is to get you out of it," he said. "Clear out of it. Before something else happens."

"I'll take care of myself," she said. "You hear that? I'll take care of myself." She paused. "Anyway," she said, "how do I know it wasn't — wasn't *you?* Who else was here? *Was* there anybody else here?"

"Oh, for God's sake!" Brian said.

"*Was* there?" she repeated, standing facing him, ludicrously holding a sauce-pan in each hand, absurdly angry; desperately wishing she could make herself stop feeling as she did, saying what she did.

And then she saw that Brian Halder was flushing; thought, *why, he's angry too.*

"All right," he said. "Do what you want to. Go where you want to."

"You're damned right," she heard herself say. "You don't need to tell me."

She put the pans down on the floor. Then she turned, began to run toward the shop entrance.

"Liza!" he said. "Wait."

"Not for you," she said. "Not for you!"

Then she was at the door, tugging at it, heard his footsteps behind her, had the door open and was running through West Kepp Street, each step jarring horribly in her head, making a pain leap in her head. She had run to the end of the little street before she realized he was not following; that he had let her go. She stopped, then; then anger ebbed out of her mind; *why, he let me go,* she thought. *I didn't think —*

She began to walk on, then; she walked slowly, now; walked through a kind of dull pain, which was only partly the real pain of her aching head. For some time she did not think where she was going and, when she did, it was only to think where she could go, and how, because she had left her purse back in the shop, left it somewhere in the rear room. I put it on the chair, she thought. I put it on a chair. I put it on a chair. The words had the rhythm of her steady walk. I put it on a chair. Six steps more. I put it on a chair.

The Norths were looking at blueprints.

"Far as I can see," Pam said, "even when you take something off, it adds something on."

Jerry North looked at a carbon sheet headed "Contractor's Lump Sum Proposal."

"Maybe," Pam said, "we ought to give up the roof."

Jerry said, with gloom, that he doubted that would do it. The roof and the interior plumbing would be more likely.

"Of course," Pam said, "we could just let the car sit out. That would take care of the garage." She considered. "Probably the car too," she said, thoughtfully. "Which would be better, maybe, because we'd be going up Seven to get there."

Jerry put down the carbon sheet, and looked at Pam North.

"Seven?" he said. "You mean Route Seven."

"Naturally," Pam said. "The dangerous one. Because it hasn't any elbows."

Jerry North shook his head slightly, as if to clear it. He thrust the fingers of his right hand through his hair.

"Listen, Pam," he said. "Elbows?"

"On the sides," Pam said. "Where did you think?" Then she, in turn, looked puzzled. "Elbows?" she said, as if she had heard the word for the first time.

"Oh!" Jerry said. He suddenly beamed at her. "Shoulders," he said. "Shoulders!"

Then Pam North said "Oh." She looked again at the blueprints.

"My parents," she said, "had a house twice this big. And they had hardly any money at all. What's happened to things?"

"The unions," Jerry said, "and I quote."

"I don't believe it," Pam said. "Do you?"

"No."

"Then what *is* it?" Pam asked, and asked as if she, trustingly, expected to be told. "Last year it was too much. So we cut it down. So it costs more. And what was that funny one about square feet?"

Jerry thought a moment. He said she must mean the funny one about cubic yards.

"Earth excavation, unit cost of," Jerry said, remembering. "One bid, eighty-five cents per cubic yard. Another bid five dollars per cubic yard." He looked at Pam blankly, and she looked back, as blankly as her face permitted.

"Look," Pam said, "are these people in

business? Or what? I mean — "

"I know," Jerry said. "I know what you mean."

Pam folded the blueprints up. "Well," she said, "it's nice here, too." She looked around the apartment. "How many cubic feet, would you say?"

Jerry merely shook his head.

"I'll never see the inside of anything again without thinking of cubic feet," Pam said. "At five dollars a cubic foot."

Jerry started to correct that, but did not. It occurred to him that Pam's error was, this time, so minor, if existent at all, that correction would be foolish. He said they might as well go to bed, while they still had beds. And then the door buzzer sounded; sounded briefly, somewhat hesitantly. Jerry said, "What the hell?" and went to the door.

Liza O'Brien was very small, very pale; dust seemed to have been ground into the fabric of her woolen dress. She stood in the doorway and seemed to be trying to smile, but she swayed a little as she stood.

"Brian hit me," she said, in a strange, faraway voice, almost as if she were repeating words she had learned. "I think Brian hit me. I — "

Her small body began to sag, and Jerry

North caught her. But she did not faint, this time. Her eyes were wide open when he laid her on a sofa. They were wide open and looked up toward the ceiling, but seemed to see nothing.

VII

Wednesday, 10:20 A.M.
to 12:45 P.M.

Liza woke up in a strange room, a room hardly larger than her own, yet not her own; a room into which sunlight sifted through venetian blinds. She was puzzled, for a moment; for a moment obscurely disturbed. Then she remembered; then she moved her head to see whether it ached still. It ached only a little, now.

She was at the Norths' apartment; she had walked there from the shop and for a moment as she remembered this she remembered, too, the recurrent beat of her steps, the recurrent "I-put-it-on-a-chair." She remembered Brian, bending over her in the dim light; remembered that he had started to come after her, and in the end had not. It should seem clearer today, she thought. But it didn't seem clearer. It seemed just as it had — muddled, obscure, frightening.

She was at the Norths' because she could

walk to their apartment from the shop, because she had no money for a cab; no — she
was at the Norths' really, honestly, because
she had had to find somebody and had remembered Pam North's face. She had stood
in the doorway and swayed, thought she was
going to fall, had been lifted and carried to a
sofa. Then there had been a doctor — hadn't
there? — a large man with gentle hands; a
man who had said, "Quite a bump, young
lady. Quite a headache?" and then had said,
"You'll be all right; you're at the tough age,"
and had shaken two yellow capsules out of a
bottle and told her to take them. And now she
was here, in a room sifted with sunlight, waking up. She was wearing a very frail nightgown. Somebody knocked at the door and she
sat up and said, "Yes," and started to pull the
sheet about her. But Pam North came in, with
a tray, and smiled at her, and she let the sheet
fall.

"Breakfast," Pam North said, and looked
at Liza with care. "You look fine," she said.
She looked again. "It's very nice on you,
so far as it is," Pam said. "I thought it would
be, although I hadn't realized quite so much
of it wasn't there. Jerry will love it." She
smiled, suddenly. "On me," she said. "Anyway, I hope so. Orange juice, toast, coffee and

a boiled egg. Bacon?"

"I don't know how — " Liza began.

"Nonsense," Pam North said. "Bacon?" Liza shook her head. She drank cold orange juice, hot coffee. She found she was hungry; that the egg, the toast, tasted much better than she could have imagined. "You'll do," Pam told her. Liza started to speak and Pam shook her head. "Finish first," she said. Liza finished.

"Did I tell you what happened?" she asked, then. "I can't seem to remember."

"Part of it," Pam said. "What you thought happened, anyway. It sounded to me as if you jumped." Liza raised her eyebrows slightly. "To conclusions," Pam said. "I don't mean about getting hit, of course. You didn't jump to that."

Liza felt her head again. There was quite a bump.

"Look," Pam said. "We've had to tell Bill, you know. Jerry called him this morning, before he went. You realize we had to?"

"Oh," Liza said. "I — " She stopped and looked at Pam North. Then she smiled, faintly. "I suppose you did," she said. "I know you did."

"We never keep anything from Bill," Pam North said, with virtue. Then she listened to herself. "Never anything important, anyway," she said. "Not permanently, anyway."

Liza nodded. It did not hurt to move her head.

"He's coming around," Pam said. "Bill is. In — oh, in about half an hour. If you're up to it?"

"Of course," Liza said, and started to get out of bed. The fragile nightgown fell away from her shoulders.

"You're pretty," Pam said. "Such a nice way to be. And I was so right about the nightie."

Liza showered, borrowed cream and lipstick from Pam's dressing table, put on the sheer-wool dress, which had been brushed, which would require more than brushing. She needed, she found, to be careful as she combed her hair. But she was all right; that way she was all right. She heard the door buzzer as she was finishing, went out to the living room and found Bill Weigand there, drinking coffee; found Pam North there.

"Good morning," Weigand said. "I thought I told you to take care of yourself."

"I'm sorry," Liza said. "It was a fool thing to do. I got to worrying about the animals."

"A foolish thing to do, Miss O'Brien," Bill said. "I'll admit I thought we had things —

well, under control. Apparently, I was wrong."

"I'm sorry," she said, again.

"Not you, particularly," Weigand said. "Other things, other people."

"Really, Bill," Pam said. "Capote."

Bill Weigand shook his head at Pam. He returned to Liza. "Now," he said.

She told him what had happened at the shop; parts of it, under his questioning, she told him more than once. She did not try to hide anything, or to change anything. He was particularly interested in the man she had seen outside the shop, thought she had seen.

"He seemed to be bent down," she said. "As if he were trying to see into the shop, from the sidewalk, without going down the steps. But — I may just have imagined it. Imagined him. At first I thought he was a policeman."

Weigand shook his head. There had been no policeman; it had not seemed necessary. Policemen are not in unlimited supply. And they had not supposed there was anything in the shop to interest anyone.

"We were wrong," he said. "Apparently it interested — several people. Unless — "

"Two people," Liza said, saying it herself, making her voice steady. But Weigand shook his head, quickly.

They didn't, he pointed out, know that. She might be making it worse than it was.

Liza tried to believe him; tried to be convinced that he believed himself.

"He does," Pam North said, as if she were answering something Liza O'Brien had said aloud.

"Put it this way," Weigand said. "There's nothing in what you tell me, Miss O'Brien, to suggest there wasn't a third man — a third person — there." He smiled at her. "Nothing but your own fears," he told her. "But tell me again — about coming to, finding Mr. Halder there."

She told him again.

"Nothing," he said. "It might very well have been as he told you. Most likely was."

Again Liza tried to believe him.

"I'm having him come down here," Bill Weigand said, then. "I didn't know, from what Jerry said, how you'd be feeling, whether you'd be up to leaving here. I'll have — "

"No!" Liza said. "Please no!"

But Weigand shook his head, and said he was sorry. It was already arranged, already started. Brian Halder might be there at any time.

"You see," Bill Weigand said, "it isn't just

between you and Mr. Halder, Miss O'Brien. I appreciate how you feel. But — I can't act on how you feel. You see that? I have to find out what happened. Make one story out of two stories; yours and his. This time, I think I can do it more readily with the two of you together. And — more quickly."

"I can't," Liza said. "Really, I — " She looked at Pamela North.

"Some time or other," Pam said. "And now's better. Before it sets." She paused. "Things get more mixed up when they set," she said.

Liza was not convinced; she realized she had no choice. She raised slim shoulders under the sheer-wool dress, took a cup of coffee Pam offered her. She had drunk half of it before the door buzzer sounded. Brian Halder, very tall, his face set, tightness around his dark eyes, came in first. The thin detective with the sensitive face, Sergeant Stein, was behind him. Brian Halder looked around the room, found Liza. For a moment his face lightened.

"You're all right?" he said.

She nodded.

Then Brian Halder turned to Lieutenant Weigand and, making a point of it, waited.

"Sit down, Mr. Halder," Weigand said.

151

"Perhaps Mrs. North will give you some coffee."

"Of course," Pam said, but Brian Halder said, "No," in a flat voice.

Bill Weigand said, "Sit down anyway."

Brian Halder found a chair, sat facing the detective.

"First," Weigand said, "did you hit Miss O'Brien last night? Knock her out?"

"Does she say I did?" He did not look at Liza, looked only at Weigand.

"She is — was — afraid you did. Did you?"

"For what good it is," Brian Halder said, and there was bitterness in his tone. "No, I didn't. I told her what happened. I — if she wants to think something else, I can't stop her." He still did not look at the girl he was talking about.

"Right," Weigand said. "Tell me, Mr. Halder."

Brian Halder spoke slowly, carefully; the harshness was still in his voice, Liza thought. There was almost truculence in his voice.

"I went to the shop to feed the animals, Dad's animals," Brian Halder said. "As Liza says she did. I had a key. I went in and looked at them. The boxer was worse. A great deal worse, I thought."

He paused.

"The boxer," Weigand said, no comment in his voice. "The sick dog. What is her name, incidentally?"

"Clytemnestra," Brian Halder said.

"Oh, dear!" Pam North said. "Another!"

Halder waited. "Go on," Weigand said.

Brian Halder had called the veterinarian who had been treating the boxer, waking the veterinarian up, telling him the dog seemed much worse. "The dog," he called Clytemnestra, very carefully, each time he spoke of her. He had described the symptoms; said she seemed almost in collapse. The veterinarian had said that, if Brian could arrange to bring the dog to the hospital, he would do what he could. It was, flatly, too late to make a call. Halder had, he said, wrapped the dog in a blanket and, failing to find a taxicab, had carried her half a dozen blocks to the animal hospital.

"How is she now?" Pam asked.

Halder looked at Pam, apparently in surprise. Then he said that the vet thought she would, with luck, make out. It still depended on her reaction to penicillin. To Pam, about this, he spoke like himself, Liza realized.

"When you left, you locked the door?" Bill Weigand asked.

So far as Halder knew, he had. At least, he

had pulled the door to behind him, and it was a snap lock. He did not think that with the dog in his arms, he had bothered to try the knob. He was uncertain.

"Go on," Weigand said.

Halder had been gone, he thought, about forty-five minutes. He had returned, intending to feed the animals.

"The door was partly open," he said. "The light in the shop was out. But there was a light in the rear room, and the door between the rooms was open. Liza was lying just beyond the light, just on the near side of the light. You know? She was — she was a kind of shadow."

Now he looked at Liza: held her eyes for a moment.

"A little shadow," he said; and his voice was suddenly deeper, soft. *Oh Brian,* she thought, *Brian dear!* But she did not say anything in words, and what she thought she was saying with her eyes she could not have been, because he did not seem to understand; he merely turned back to Weigand.

"I didn't think it was Liza," Brian Halder said. "I thought — I didn't know who it was." (But he started to say something different, Liza thought.) He had run into the room, discovered who it was, discovered, after a moment, that she was alive. She had been lying face down, her head turned to one side. He had put her on her back, found a pillow to put under her head. In placing it there, he discovered she had been struck. Before that, he had thought she had merely fainted. He had been about to call for help when he saw that she was regaining consciousness. Then, very quickly, she had seemed to get all right. Brian Halder looked at her, then. "I thought you were," he said. "Otherwise I wouldn't have let you go. Whatever you said."

"I was all right," she said.

"You were — " Pam North began, her voice indignant. But Liza caught Pam's eye, and shook her head slightly. Pam North shrugged.

"And," Bill Weigand said, "thinking she was all right, although you knew she had been knocked out, you let her walk out of the shop by herself? Made no effort to stop her? To overtake her?"

"I was — " Halder began, but Bill Weigand shook his head.

"You don't want me to believe that," Weigand said. "I wouldn't, anyway."

Now Brian Halder hesitated, his eyes losing focus as he thought, considered. Then he looked at Weigand again and said, "All right."

"I started to follow her," he said. "Bring her back. Something came up. But — I can't prove it."

He was told to go on.

"I heard — thought I heard — someone, something, moving in the little area-way next to the shop," he said. "Between it and the building next door. A narrow passage between."

Weigand said, "I saw it."

Halder had, he said, started to go into the area-way to investigate; had taken one or two steps into the darkness and then — well, then stopped. That was they way he told it. He did not see any movement, or hear any sound and — Brian Halder hesitated.

"Actually," he said, "I suppose I wanted to decide there wasn't anyone. Going in got to seeming — well, like not such a hot idea. There was quite a bit of light behind me and — " He paused, seemed embarrassed. "I just decided to give it a miss," he said.

Weigand nodded, agreed. Only a fool, he told Brian Halder, walked into a narrow passage with the light behind him and possibly animosity ahead. Stein looked at Weigand quickly, looked away again. The lieutenant, on that reckoning, had been several times a fool, and when the danger was not so problematical as this time it had been. Stein had done as much himself, and been three months in a hospital as a result. Of course, that sort of thing was their job, as it wasn't Halder's. Still —

"Mr. Halder," Pam North said. "Are you sure it wasn't because you didn't *want* to find out who this other person was? Didn't *want* to know? Or — were afraid you did know?"

Brian Halder flushed. It's so hard for very young people, Pam thought. So little control over the capillaries. But Halder, if he knew his face had reddened, ignored it.

"It was the way I said," he told Pam.

Bill Weigand frowned, momentarily. But when he spoke, his voice betrayed no annoyance.

"When you saw this shadow," he said. "The shadow which turned out to be Miss O'Brien. Didn't you think it was somebody else?"

"I told you," Halder said. "No."

"No guess?"

"No."

"Merely somebody small?"

Not even that, at first, Halder said. Merely somebody, something, lying on the floor. He had not thought of its being Liza, of its being anyone.

157

Brian Halder realized, he agreed in answer to further questions, that whoever had entered the shop between the time he left with the sick dog and the time Liza arrived and found the door unlocked, must have had a key if, as he thought, Brian had left the door locked behind him. "But now I'm not sure I did," he said. So far as Brian knew, there were only three keys; one which hung, out of sight, on a nail inside the shop door; one J. K. Halder had carried in his pocket; and the one he had given Sneddiger. It was his father's that Brian himself had used; he had asked for it and got it from one of Weigand's men.

"Mullins gave it to him," Stein said. "Figured somebody had to be able to get to the animals."

Weigand nodded.

"But," he said, "why not the second key? The one on the nail? Why didn't you take that?"

Halder hesitated momentarily. Then he said it had not been there when he looked; it was after he had been unable to find it that he had asked Mullins for the other key.

"You're certain there were only two?" Weigand asked. Not "certain" Brian Halder said, and now his voice, to Liza, sounded careful, considering. He only knew of two.

158

"For example," Weigand said, then. "Your mother didn't have a key?"

"She did not." Of that Brian was suddenly, emphatically, certain. Weigand did not comment on the certainty, on the emphasis. He went back to events of the night before; was told that, after Halder decided not to go into the dark passage, he started after Liza, walked to the far end of West Kepp Street, realized he had lost her and returned to the shop. He had gone in again, looked around, found Liza's purse — "by the way, here it is," he said, and took it out of his pocket and held it out to her — and found nothing else. He had locked up, making sure this time, and had gone to his rooms. Later he had tried, several times, to reach Liza on the telephone at her apartment.

"You weren't worried when she didn't answer?"

He had been, certainly. But he had decided she was there and, thinking the calls were from him, deliberately not answered. He looked at Liza: she shook her head.

"Right," Bill Weigand said, and suddenly seemed to have all he wanted. He asked for the key to the shop, said he would see that the animals were fed, stood up and held out his hand. Brian gave him the key after a moment's

159

hesitation. Bill nodded to Stein, who stood up.

"Well?" Brian Halder said.

Weigand appeared to be surprised.

"That's all," he said. "Thanks for coming down. And — leave it to us, won't you?"

Halder flushed again. He looked once at Liza and she thought he was trying to tell her something. But she could not understand what it was and merely looked back at him, knowing there was only a question in her eyes.

Then Brian Halder said, "Well," again, but this time inconclusively and turned toward the door. He stopped there; turned, spoke slowly, hesitantly.

"Can I — can I telephone you, Liza?" he asked. And this time his voice was Brian's again, but a younger Brian's than she had ever heard.

"Of course," she said. "I'll — I'll be home this afternoon." She looked at Weigand, who nodded. "This afternoon," she said.

Then Brian Halder went, and Stein went with him. Bill Weigand finished cold coffee. Liza and Pam North waited.

"I'm fairly sure he didn't hit you," Bill said, finally, to Liza, speaking slowly. "I think he knows, or is afraid he knows, who did. I think that was the reason he didn't go into the passage, not the reason he gave. I think he stayed behind to keep you from being followed and perhaps attacked again. In other words — I think he put on a better show, or at least a different show, than he says. But — "

"But you don't know," Liza said. "I — I have to know."

Bill did not reply to that, except with a nod of his head. He looked thoughtfully at his empty coffee cup.

"Who did he think it was?" Pam said. "The shadow on the floor? Who — which — turned out to be Liza?"

"Oh that," Bill said. "Why — I think he was afraid it was his mother. At first."

There was a considerable pause, while both of them looked at him.

"That she was hurt?" Pam said, finally.

"That it was she lying there," Bill said, after a pause. "I don't know what else he may have thought."

Then the telephone rang. Pam answered it, handed it to Bill Weigand, who identified himself and listened. Then he said, "Spell it, will you?" and motioned for a pencil and for paper. Used to the mute appeal, thinking that even detectives were like other men in such matters, Pam North provided. "Faberworth," Bill repeated and wrote the name

161

down; wrote an address down. "Call him back," Bill said. "Tell him I'll be there within half an hour." He replaced the telephone and got up. He seemed pleased and interested.

"Halder's lawyer called in," he said, answering the question Pam did not speak. "Says he has something which he thinks may interest us."

Isaac Faberworth was, it was very evident, a lawyer in a big way, with his name first on a long list of names discreetly lettered on a glass panel. He was a compact man behind a large, clean desk; his face told little about his age, and much about his intelligence. He stood up when Weigand went in, was polite in a soft voice, desired to see Weigand's badge; saw it and nodded over it. He said he had heard of Weigand. "You considered law, once," he told Weigand. "Columbia Law School."

"Right," Bill told him, sitting in the chair at the end of the desk; the very comfortable, disarming chair. "It was a long time ago."

"A friend of mine there remembers you, nevertheless," Isaac Faberworth said. He gave a name, and Bill Weigand said he was flattered. "Thought it a pity," Faberworth said. "However — " He left it there. He opened the center drawer of the big desk and took from it, with no hesitancy at all, the one paper it seemed to contain. It was a sheet of familiar color, familiar size.

"Arrived yesterday morning," Faberworth said, and handed it politely to Bill Weigand.

"Will call your office noon regard will change, J. K. Halder," the telegram read. Bill Weigand read it twice and looked at Faberworth, who was looking at him.

"That's all," Faberworth said. "Characteristic. Doesn't ask if I'll be in; doesn't ask if I'll be free. Gives no more than the minimal information he thinks necessary, so I'll have the will available. Very characteristic." Faberworth shook his head briefly, modifying his ill speech of the dead. "And, of course, very annoying when he failed to show up," he said. "My secretary tried a couple of times to reach him at the shop. Then, since I was tied up all afternoon anyway, I told her to let it go. I didn't learn what had happened until this morning — in the papers. Then I called you people, of course."

"He did this sort of thing often?" Weigand asked. He indicated the telegram.

"This *sort* of thing," Faberworth said. "If you mean specifically about his will, no. The present will has stood for more than five years. But the method is characteristic." He

163

paused. "I feel I can say now, to you, that my client was an odd man." He paused, selecting a word. "Whimsical," he said, with a faint accent of disapproval.

"You have no idea what he planned?" Weigand asked, indicating the telegram. Faberworth shook his head. He said, about that, Weigand knew as much as he, but to that Bill shook his head. He didn't, he suggested, know the terms of the present will.

"Mrs. Halder gets two million," he said. "That's supposed to be net, taxes from the estate. A few minor bequests. The rest to the children, share and share alike." He regarded Weigand. "A very simple will," he said.

"No ifs?" Weigand asked. "No but whereases?"

Faberworth permitted himself a smile, as from one attorney-at-law to a man who might have been.

"No more than usual," he said. "The law must live, naturally." He smiled again. "A point on which we should agree," he said.

"You said about five years," Weigand said. "Was it very different before that?"

"His eldest son got more," the lawyer said. "The others less, appreciably. Except the widow. She got the same." The lawyer narrowed his eyes slightly and regarded Weigand with interest. "Why?" he asked.

It was, Weigand told him, always interesting in his business to know where the money went, especially when there was a great deal of money. He ended on a rising note.

"At a guess," Faberworth said, "thirty million."

Bill Weigand whistled.

"Quite," Faberworth said.

"Five years ago," Bill said, "how did the eldest son fall from favor?"

Faberworth nodded, as if he were pleased with Weigand.

"Junior," he said. "Junior seems to have annoyed his father." He shook his head. "My client annoyed very easily," he said. "Almost — " he paused for a long time, looking at Weigand intently. "Almost irrationally," he said. "I say that without prejudice, you understand. And — without witnesses."

"Right," Bill said. He waited.

"In fact," Faberworth said, "both Junior and the junior Mrs. Halder annoyed my client. It seems they — ah — began to have a child."

Weigand merely looked at Isaac Faberworth, who slowly nodded; who said, "Quite."

"But," Bill said.

"As it turned out," the lawyer said, "their — ah — expectations were not fulfilled. But

that they should have permitted the — ah
— situation to arise, even problematically,
displeased my client. Displeased him — dis-
proportionately."

"Why not fulfilled?" Bill asked.

Isaac Faberworth closed his eyes, allowed
them to remain closed briefly, opened them
again. He did not give further answer. But
then he smiled at Weigand.

"You must understand," he said, "that Mr.
Halder was legally quite rational, entirely
competent. About that there can be no question. That is understood?"

"Right," Bill said.

"Beyond that," Faberworth said, in the
same grave voice, "I should consider him as
peculiar as any man I ever met. Certainly as
peculiar as anyone with thirty million dollars
I ever met. And, some years ago, I knew him
rather well." He stroked the sides of his face
with two fingers of each hand. "He had fre-
quent need of legal services," Mr. Faberworth
said, with detachment. He paused again and
Bill Weigand waited. "When I was a boy,"
Mr. Faberworth said, "a boy in rather a small
town, there was an old man who lived in a
very large house. Quite the largest house on
my route." He looked at Weigand. "I threw
papers," he said. "That was what we called it.

166

He was one of my customers and once every two weeks I had to collect for the papers. The house was full of cats." He shook his head, toying with a strange memory. "I would have said then, a hundred cats. Probably not more than thirty. But —" He shook his head. "Most of them seemed to come to the door with the old man," Mr. Faberworth said. "It was quite disconcerting. I have never cared properly for cats since, I'm afraid."

He ceased abruptly to be the remembered boy; he became the middle-aged man.

"Mr. Halder often made me think of that man," Faberworth said. "Chiefly, I suppose, because of their common addiction to animals. Of course, Halder gratified his addiction in a — a somewhat more reasonable manner. And he lived, in many respects, an entirely normal life, whatever that is. The old man with the cats didn't." Momentarily, memory again unfocussed the attorney's eyes. "He must have washed very infrequently, if at all," he said. "Mr. Halder, of course, was normally scrupulous. But neither of them cared for people."

"In Halder's case, how seriously should that be taken?" Bill asked.

The attorney put the tips of his fingers together and regarded them.

"This side of anything really approaching — ah — mental incapacity, quite seriously," he said, at length. "He said once, publicly, something to the effect that people made him sick. Not a literal statement, of course. But I always felt he meant it much more than people usually do when they say things like that. He used to argue that people — the human animal generally — had proved so completely inadequate, made such a mess of things, that if it had any decency it would — ah — voluntarily withdraw."

"Nevertheless," Bill pointed out, "he had three children himself."

"Quite," Faberworth agreed. "Of course, his — ah — conviction grew stronger as he got older."

The two men sat silently for a moment.

"Do you know of anything — any particular event, or events — which strengthened this conviction?" Bill Weigand asked, then.

Faberworth shook his head. He said he thought that convictions often grew stronger, more rigid, as men grew older.

"Of course," he added to this, "it is perhaps as often the other way around."

There was another pause.

"I imagine he was to some degree fond of Felix Sneddiger," the lawyer said. "At any rate, they played chess together. Now he's dead, too."

"Right," Bill said. He did not amplify.

"He always named the animals fancifully," Faberworth said. "I'm telling you what little I know about him, always without prejudice."

"And," Bill said, "without witnesses."

"Quite," Faberworth said, and smiled. "Without witnesses. Three or four years ago they were all named out of Shakespeare, although I had never supposed Halder had any special literary interests. Then they began to get Greek names. Chiefly out of the Orestes-Electra legend. Did you know?"

Weigand nodded.

"The Scottie named Aegisthus?" Faberworth said. "The one he gave his wife? The black cat, recently, named Electra? And I think there was another cat, a Siamese, named Pylades. Orestes' friend, you remember."

"Yes," Bill said.

"He called the cockers, the ones he kept in the window, The Furies," the lawyer said. "I believe they had other names but, collectively, they were The Furies."

"You seem to have been familiar with the shop," Weigand said.

"I dropped in now and then," Faberworth said. "I live in that part of town."

169

"Did you gather that the names had special significance?" Weigand asked, when the attorney did not continue. "It seems a little confused. The boxer, the one who's sick, is named Clytemnestra, for example. But Electra's a cat."

Faberworth shrugged. He said he did not suppose the analogy, if there was one, was supposed to go quite on all fours. "Except literally," he added. "As a matter of fact, of course, the name is given to a female dog, you notice. And the lady was, one gathers from Aeschylus, something of a — " He paused, with unnecessary delicacy.

"Did he sell the animals?" Weigand said.

Again Faberworth shrugged. Not, he said, when it could conveniently be avoided; avoided without too much appearance of eccentricity. He preferred to give them away.

"Do you know if he planned to give the boxer to anyone?" Weigand asked. "Before she got sick."

"No," Faberworth said. His voice was flat, not encouraging.

"Was there ever an animal named Orestes?"

"He said something about getting the cat, Electra, an — ah — companion," the lawyer said. "I don't know whether it would have been — ah — "

"A brother?" Weigand asked.

"Really, Lieutenant," Faberworth said. "Aren't we — ah — carrying this a little far?"

"Probably we are," Weigand said. He paused. "You have no idea what he planned about his will?"

"As I said," Faberworth said. "Nothing. Except that he planned to change it, as you see."

"So anyone might have gained?"

"Quite. But someone else would have had to lose."

"And you've no idea whether one of the family had annoyed him? Or, rather, which one had, if any?"

"No idea at all," Faberworth said, and moved his chair back from the desk. Weigand pushed his own back and stood up.

"But some trivial thing might have annoyed him?"

"Oh yes," Faberworth said. "Some quite trivial thing. Again, I speak without prejudice."

"And you have no idea at all, Mr. Faberworth? Not even something that — wouldn't be evidence?"

"None whatever, Lieutenant," the lawyer said, and smiled and held out his hand. "None whatever. Without witnesses. Or not. No idea at all."

VIII

Wednesday, 2:15 P.M. to 6:10 P.M.

After Weigand left, Liza O'Brien had sat for a time looking at nothing. Pam North had poured her fresh coffee and, hardly tasting it, Liza drank. She tried to make the confusion in her mind stand still, tried to make turmoil fall into pattern.

"It's all bits and pieces," Pam said. "I know. It will come right."

But the words were meaningless to Liza, the optimism without substance. Serves me right, Pam thought, looking at the girl, seeing her words rejected. Talking like God's in his heaven. Pollyanna passes. How do I know it will come right? Because, Pam thought — still looking at the girl — her young man isn't what you'd expect; he's so much more everything. And, of course, he hasn't told all of it, particularly not what he thinks. And he's so fond of his mother. As if —

But that was reasonable, Pam North had

172

thought, continuing. A young wife with a young child, a much older husband; step-children older than she. Turning to the child, and he turning to her as he grew, because they were both so young for what they were, she as wife and step-mother, he as half-brother to a man and a woman already grown. Almost another generation, Pam thought; almost as if they were the same generation, somehow. Would he hate his father? — or fear him, resent him? Could that resentment lead — Pam rejected the train of thought. She felt somehow that it might leak from her mind into that of Liza, herself so young, trying so hard to make things fit as she wanted them to fit. The poor baby, Pam North thought.

Martini resented Pam's preoccupation; people were made to think of cats. Martini, sitting in front of Pam, looking up at her, spoke in a voice of anger. Pam did not notice and Martini spoke again. When, still, human attention was improperly directed toward merely human concerns, Martini reached up a dark brown paw and touched Pam's knee. Then, slowly, Martini permitted her claws to emerge. "Ouch!" Pam said. That was better. Martini spoke again, with command.

"Well, come up," Pam said.

Martini went up. She looked into Pam's

face, still with insistence, still with something like anger in her round blue eyes. "Good girl," Pam said. "Nice Martini. Martini is the major cat."

The Siamese, mollified, turned, arranged herself on the roundness of Pam's leg, hooked gently just at the knee to stabilize herself. She then, from a point of safety, regarded Liza O'Brien, who now was looking at her.

"All Monday night I tried to get her out," Liza said. "You know. Practically the whole night. Does she know that now I haven't anything to draw with?"

"Probably," Pam said. "It's a way they are. One of the ways."

The girl and the cat regarded each other.

"Mrs. North," Liza said, "I ought to know. I almost do know. But, precisely — the Greek tragedies? Clytemnestra was killed by her children. I know that. But — "

"Agamemnon came home," Pam said. "He was a king of — of I've forgotten where. He'd been to wars, oh for years. His wife was Clytemnestra and she had been ruling. But it was one of those things — there was Aegisthus." Pam paused. "It happened to a lot of GI's," she said. "We don't seem to get better, do we — more honest, more loyal? Aegisthus and Clytemnestra killed Agamemnon. Then they abused Electra, Clytemnestra's daughter — and Agamemnon's, of course. Then Orestes, Electra's brother, came home from somewhere and the two of them killed Clytemnestra and Aegisthus in revenge. Then they were pursued by Furies." Pam paused, considering this. "Aeschylus gives rather more detail," Pam said, "but that's the gist of it. Somebody's pointed out that it's a police court story at bottom — maybe a lot of people have pointed it out."

"I remember, now," Liza said. "A horrible story."

"Yes," Pam said. "But actually, there isn't any parallelism, except the name of the dog."

But Liza merely looked at her.

"Well," Pam said, "of course Mr. Halder is dead. Only it's probably simpler than we think. Things are, usually." She paused. "Well, *usually*," she said. "Sometimes, of course, they're more complicated."

Liza smiled, faintly. Then she put her coffee cup aside and said it was time she went home. "I can never thank you," she said, and stood up. "And can I come back later — in a few days, maybe — and finish the cats?"

"Don't try," Pam said. "Of course. And don't go unless you want to."

But Liza had gone. She had walked uptown,

crossed through Madison Square, where the benches were filled with people sitting in the sun, collected mail at the desk of her apartment hotel, carried it up to her rooms and then, after riffling through it, tossed it aside unread. She threw open the single window of the living room and leaned out of it, looking down at the strangely distorted people so far below, moving so oddly, seeming to consist so primarily of outflung legs. She got out her drawing pad, then, and went over the sketches, now and then changing a line, deepening or lightening a shadow. But she got no feeling out of the sketches; they might have been by someone else, and after a few minutes she put the drawing pad aside. She showered again, after a time, and changed to a print dress and after that she merely waited for the telephone to ring. She waited a long time, and each new minute was more difficult to endure than the one just lived through.

It was after four when the telephone finally rang, when she finally heard Brian's "Liza?" and said, "Yes, Brian."

"I've got to talk to you," he said. "Shall I come around there?"

"Of course," she said, but then she looked around the apartment. It had grown, during the two hours and more she had been waiting

176

in it, intolerably cramped. "Some place else," she said.

"My place, then?" Brian said and then, oddly, hesitated. "That is," he said, "if you're not — not afraid of me, Liza?"

"Oh, Brian!" she said. "Brian! How awful!"

Then he would meet her there, he told her. Now he was in a telephone booth. He would get there about the time she did, say in twenty minutes? She agreed, replaced the telephone, refreshed lipstick and powder, leaning forward to peer into a mirror over the bedroom chest, indignant, as always, at the lack of light. She carried a light coat over her arm and found a cab quickly and something inside her kept saying over and over, "I'm going to see Brian. I'm going to see Brian, and I'm not afraid." For the moment, that was enough. She could make herself believe it.

Brian Halder lived near Gramercy Park, in an old building converted into "studio" apartments. The "apartment" was almost entirely one room, but the room was large. Liza had been in the apartment only once and then briefly. "Want to see where I live?" Brian had asked, oddly diffident, when they were on their way somewhere and had a few minutes too much time. But they had stayed only a moment or two; he had been careful not to touch her, not even to stand close to her; his awareness of her and the awkwardness which went with it, had communicated itself to her, so that the time had had a strange quality, at once disturbing and exciting. Why, she thought now, as she hesitated before she pressed the bell at Brian's door, it must have been then that we both knew how we felt.

This memory, a sudden nostalgia for those moments (only ten days in the past, two weeks at most) filled her mind and she felt, for an instant, a kind of resentment that things could not be as they were then and, feeling that, realized how far she still was from recapturing the assurance about herself and Brian she had so briefly, as time went, attained. Now that she was here, she did not want to go into Brian's apartment; even shrank from going in. Yet, she told herself, she was not afraid. It was not so simple as that. Finally, she pressed the bell button.

Brian opened the door almost immediately; he must have been very close to it, almost with his hands on the knob. He opened the door and stood, unsmiling, looking down at her, his eyes searching her face.

"You came," he said. "After all."

"I said I would," Liza told him. But that he

seemed to brush aside; that was unimportant.

"I thought you'd be afraid," he said. He continued to search her face.

"No," she said. "I'm not afraid."

But then, only then, she knew that what she said was not entirely true — was not yet true.

"You are a little," Brian said. He spoke slowly, as if, even while he uttered the words, he fought against their truth. "*Liza.*"

She made herself smile up into his set face, then. It was not much of a smile; she knew it was not much of a smile.

"Not now," she said. "Not — not when I see you." And that was true; almost true. "Aren't you going to let me in?" Her tone, then, invited lightness. But Brian, his face unchanged, merely stepped back. "Come in, Liza," he said.

The room was very large; there were two tall windows at the far end, and they were open, curtains moving a little in the breeze. Brian closed the door behind them. Liza walked a few steps into the room and then, because he did not seem to be coming with her, stopped and turned so that, again, she faced him.

"You can turn your back on me," Brian said. "It's safe." And his tone was very bitter.

She merely spoke his name in answer; spoke it incredulously, her shock reflected in her tone.

"You stand there," he said. "I love you very much. You think that last night I tried to kill you."

It was a statement; there was no note of question in his voice. And yet all he said, all at that instant he was, put a question, demanded a decision. Liza stood, her lips just parted, her head back so that she could look up at him across the few feet between them. And now it was she who searched his face. But more than anything, Liza searched herself. Whatever happens afterward depends on now, she thought.

But when she decided, the decision did not seem to come from her mind, did not form itself into words. Her body made its own decision, acted for itself — of itself laid aside (for that moment) whatever remained of fear. Liza stepped toward Brian, her head still back, her eyes still seeking his, but now not searching. As she moved, she lifted her arms, only a little. But it was as if she, with even so small a gesture, abandoned all defense.

For only an instant did Brian hesitate, still seek something in her face. And then his arms were around her, she was held close to him.

And then she was crying.

"I didn't — " he began. But she shook her head against his chest and said, the words muffled, "Be still. Oh Brian, be still." Then he only waited, his arms close around her. After a time she was no longer crying; after rather a long time it was she who moved, stepping back.

"I love you very much," she said then, using the words he had used, the same gravity in her voice there had been in his.

"And you're not — " he began, but she reached a hand up and then he kissed her.

"You do me good," he told her, gravity still in his voice but not, for that instant, in his dark eyes. "You're very good for me. I was a fool."

"How?" she said.

But he told her not to mind for the moment, and took her down the room to chairs and a low table near the windows and then said, "We need a drink on this," and suggested a variety of things they could have. They had Scotch on the rocks. For a moment, the sun came out; for a moment they were merely young, together, at a good hour of the day. But then he put down his drink and, bending forward in his chair, looked at her.

"A fool to try to keep you out of it," he said.

"To think I could just — well, put you to one side, go on with it. Come back afterward and pick you up. But it made sense."

"Not real sense," she said. "Other people's sense."

He hesitated a moment, then nodded.

"I thought you were all right last night," he said. "Better than you were, I guess. And I did try to reach you." He hesitated a moment. "I thought whoever hit you was still around the shop." He looked away, then back at her. "Anyway," he said, "you were pretty damned independent."

She smiled at that, shook her head to dismiss it.

"All right," Brian said, after a moment. "This guy Weigand. Does he think I hit you? Does he think I killed Dad?"

"No," she said. "Of *course* not."

He shook his head. He said there was no "Of course" not about it.

"He doesn't," she said. "He — he thinks you may suspect who did. He — he thinks you may have recognized, or perhaps only thought you recognized, whoever was at the shop last night. Whoever went into the area-way."

"No," Brian Halder said. "That's out. I'm not sure there was anybody, anyway. I thought I saw — perhaps felt is a better word — some sort of movement. I don't know who it was."

"Didn't you guess who it — might have been?"

He shook his head, but he seemed to be only half attending to what she said.

She waited.

"Listen," he said. "Listen, Liza. I'll tell you what's got me — got me going in circles. Do you want me to?"

"Of course," she said. She sipped her drink, finding assurance in the tiny physical action.

But still he hesitated, still looked at her. When he spoke it was to ask her a question.

"We're together, aren't we?" he said. "I'm right?"

Men want things in words.

"Whatever happens," she said, although the words added nothing.

Then he nodded, as if satisfied, and said, rather unexpectedly, that he should have known. Then he smiled and said that, of course, he had known, that it was a question of realizing what he knew, of applying it.

"To the situation," he said. "I didn't. That's why I thought you could be kept out of it. That — well, that I could take it over, without you; that until it was worked out it needn't be a concern of yours. Do you see what I mean?"

He looked at her and shook his head. He said she didn't. She started to protest, but he shook his head again.

"Maybe you do," he said. "It's taken me — well, quite a while. Maybe I merely don't want to admit you're — quicker." He looked at her again, intently. "You see," he said, and spoke slowly, picking words. "I thought this — whatever it is — this community wouldn't begin until we — well, until we were actually married. That you were still just a girl I was in love with. That until then you didn't have to get involved in things that involved me. Only — it isn't that way. Not for me."

It's going to be complicated being married to Brian, Liza thought. So complicated. Such fun. When —

"Not for me," she said, her voice was grave as when she had said, "Yes."

"It's going to be all right," he told her. "Isn't it?"

"It's going to be fine," she said.

He continued to look at her and now, she thought, he's finding what he wants. As he ought to, she thought. *Oh, as he ought to.* But how *much* he wants!

Then Brian Halder picked up his glass and seemed surprised to find it empty and looked at hers. She finished what remained and smiled up at him and nodded. He refilled the glasses. "Water in mine this time," she told him. "I didn't have any lunch that I can remember."

He said, "My God," and looked around the room helplessly, as if expecting manna. She laughed; said it didn't matter; that after a bit he could take her to dinner. "If you can?" she added. He said, "Of course," to that, as if it had all along been arranged between them. But then he looked pleased, went to a cupboard across the room and came back with a box of saltines. They had, she found on biting into one, been there for some time. He looked at her anxiously. "Fine," she told him. "Wonderful."

If it could only stay this way, Liza thought. If only we could go on eating soggy crackers and talking about us!

But they couldn't. After a few minutes it came back to them, but now, although it was still serious — still, when she picked it up again, frightening — there was not the tension there had been. They had what mattered cleared away; it would stay cleared away. *Oh, please*, Liza thought, praying to the optimistic gods of youth and at the same time knowing, because she needed to say a prayer, that she was beginning to be not quite so young.

But Brian appeared to have no doubts. He appeared to regard that as settled. Men *believe* in words, Liza thought, and looked at Brian and said, without forming the words. "I love you very much."

"The point is," Brian said, and spoke suddenly, as if he were going head first into cold water, "the point is — *I'm* afraid. That's the whole point. That's why I didn't go into that passage by the shop. But not the way I told Weigand, let him believe, anyway. Not of getting hurt."

"He knew that," Liza said.

"Did he? I suppose he did. And probably he knew what I was afraid of. You know?"

"I can guess, Brian."

"Of finding the — the wrong person," he said. "Damn it all, Liza. What are we going to do? I was afraid it was — Pine." He looked at her and shook his head. "It's a hell of a thing to be saying," he said. "That's why I had to be sure about us. Because — " He broke off and shook his head. Then he started again. "You see what it means if it was Pine?" he asked.

She saw, clearly enough. She nodded slowly to show she saw.

"You know Dad was at dinner Monday night?" he said, then. "The night he was killed? That he — that for some reason he left early? Or didn't you know?"

She said she had heard Weigand say something about it.

Again Brian Halder hesitated for words. When he spoke it was, seemingly, to go off on another tack.

"My mother's a young woman," he said. "Comparatively. It's hard to realize." For a moment the two in their early twenties tried to imagine that anyone of forty could still be, even by the most favorable of comparisons, young. "She looks it, doesn't she?" Brian asked, and Liza nodded. "She's lovely," Liza said.

"It's partly because she seems young I call her Mary," Brian said. "More often that than Mother. You know she's more than thirty years younger than Dad — was? Younger than either Jas or Barbara?" He looked at her, asking her to share the surprise of this. "Sometimes," he said, "she didn't seem any older than I was. I mean, when I was much younger." He broke off again, began again. "Damn it," he said. "I *like* her, whether she's my mother or not."

Liza nodded.

"What's she supposed to do?" Brian asked, then. "Quit living? Quit seeing anybody? With Dad living downtown? Just sit in that house and what? Crochet?"

He seemed to expect an answer; there wasn't any good one Liza could think of. Maybe Mary Halder had been, by those who supposed for others, supposed to crochet. It was clear she hadn't; it was clear that, to Brian, what else she might have done instead required extenuation, even defense. Then — she smiled, answered.

"Of course not, Brian," she said.

"Dad didn't expect her not to see people," Brian said, and still seemed to be arguing with himself. "Only — well, about six months ago, this Pine comes along. He's an actor, you know. Younger than Mother, although maybe not much. She used to be on the stage, before she married Dad. She's always liked people like that. I guess some of them are fun."

He's so serious, Liza thought. Was that why I used to think him more mature than I?

"Lots of people are fun," Liza said.

Brian said he supposed so. He did not speak as if the matter were one to which he had given much thought. After a moment he continued, speaking carefully; trying, Liza thought, to tell what he so clearly felt the need to tell, yet to avoid implications.

Pine was not the first man with whom Mary Halder, with her husband unavailable, apparently so indifferent, had gone to dinner, to the theater, had "gone around." For years, for most of the years Brian had been growing up in the tall, narrow house, seeing his father rarely, he could remember men calling for his mother, taking her out. But there had been, he thought, no man who had come for her with any regularity; no man who had not seemed, somehow, his father's friend, or at any rate acquaintance, almost as much as hers. Some of the men had, actually, been his father's contemporaries; had, Brian thought — thought now, with perspective of his own greater age — "gone around" with Mary Halder partly, at least, because they felt that her husband had behaved badly toward her and that his generation, which they could represent by proxy, owed an obligation to hers. "Dad's lawyer, for one," Brian said. "One or two other men Dad's age who used to be associated with him, who knew Mother and him before he — moved downtown, used to come to the house."

There had, naturally, been fewer of his father's contemporaries as time passed; more younger men whose acquaintance Mary Halder had herself made. But there had never been any suggestion that these associations were, or needed to be, surreptitious. Frequently, indeed, one of the men would make a fourth with Mary, Jasper Halder and Jennifer. "Jennifer and Mother have always been sort of pals," Brian said. "Jenn would say, 'Get one of your boy friends and come along' to Mary. It was like that." His father, Brian was sure, knew of all these casual friends and did not disapprove.

"No reason he should," Brian told Liza and his eyes demanded her belief.

"Of course not," she said, finding it easy to give the assurance he sought.

But Pine had been, from quite early, different. "Not really different," Brian had said, and flushed slowly. "Don't think I think —" Again Liza assured him, again said, "Of course not, Brian." The difference, Brian explained — explained so carefully — was in his father's attitude more than in anything else. J. K. Halder had not accepted Pine as he had the others. Brian explained that. His father was getting more odd as he grew older. "Harder to get along with." He had always seemed aloof to Brian; seemed to view all of them with detachment, to a degree with irony. But lately he had found fault more often; very lately, Brian felt, he had seemed increasingly annoyed with all of them — with his wife, his older son and Jennifer, Barbara and her "Colonel." Brian himself had got along with his father better than the others, but even he had not known when something he said or did, meant innocently, would antagonize the older man. His attitude toward Sherman Pine, Brian told Liza — and, she could see, told himself — was only part of this increasing irritability. And then there had been the matter of the dog.

"Mostly we kept animals of some kind," Brian said. "Junior's got a couple of cockers; Barb and the colonel used to have a big yellow cat, but something happened to it, I guess. And Mother had a little dachshund for years. Nice little pooch. I suppose — oh, well, I suppose as far as Junior and Barb were concerned, it was partly a matter of keeping in good with Dad. He feels — felt — damn funny about dogs and cats. Thought they were better than people. One of his quirks."

The little dachshund had died. That was about the time Brian's mother met Pine. Two months or so later, when she was seeing a good deal of Pine, J. K. Halder gave her the black Scottie; gave her the dog, told her its name was Aegisthus and, as he told her the name, looked at her in a peculiar manner. Brian remembered it; he had been there. "What a funny name," his mother had said, and Halder had said, "Greek, my dear" and left it at that. Brian did not think the name had any special meaning to his mother; at the time it had none to him. But he had looked the name up in the unabridged dictionary and found out enough to want to make him find out more. "You know who he was?" Brian asked Liza, who nodded. "Sure," Brian said. "Everybody does, I guess. I don't actually know whether Mother looked it up, but I suppose she did. She never said anything to me, of course."

Brian stopped, shook his head slowly. He said it was obviously a hint; might even have been a warning to Mary. "A funny, nasty sort of thing for the old man to do, wasn't it?" he asked. "I always meant to — well, take it up with him. Tell him to lay off. But I never did. He — well, he wasn't an easy man to take things up with and, anyhow, I was fond of him."

But if the little dog's unusual name had been intended as a warning to Mary Halder, it had had no result; at least, no visible result. She went on seeing Sherman Pine as before. "More often, if anything," Brian said, and made the words an admission. He heard the admission in his tone and stopped speaking and looked at Liza.

"All right," he said, as if in answer to something she had said, "maybe they fell for each other. I guess Dad thought so. Well — people do. Even people as old as Mother, I guess. It's — " He broke off.

"Things happen," Liza told him, feeling for the moment as if *she* were old enough to be his mother, wanting to touch him, pat him gently, as if he were a child. He was so troubled, so intensely troubled; the trouble was so dark in his eyes.

"Now that Dad's dead, they may get married, you know," he said. "She'll have the money, and — " Again he stopped. He seemed to be avoiding an idea which he found it difficult to avoid. But then he went on more quickly, as if anxious to get something said. And now he came back to the dinner at the Sutton Place house on the night J. K. Halder died; the dinner which Halder had left so abruptly, without explanation. Brian thought he knew why; was afraid he knew why.

They had had dinner in the dining room on the second floor and afterward had come back downstairs for coffee and brandy. They had been sitting in the rear of the room; Barbara Whiteside, Halder remembered, had stayed upstairs for some reason. Then the doorbell had sounded faintly and Brian had thought that his mother had looked, momentarily, startled and confused. One of the servants had opened the door and they had all looked up the room toward the foyer which opened into it. There had been the faint sound of voices and then Mary, saying something hardly articulate as an apology to the others, had got up and gone toward the foyer. She had joined someone there.

"All right," Brian said. "I think it was Pine. I think before she could stop him, he — well, kissed her. Put his arms around her and kissed her, I guess. Hell — people do."

He was not, Brian said, sure of this. He had looked and then looked away. Then the Scottie yelped upstairs and came tumbling down the circular staircase in a great hurry, yipping and apparently very put out about something, and Brian had been distracted and watched the dog as, he thought, the others had. By the time he looked back toward the foyer, partly because the Scottie was trotting in that direction to tell his mistress what had happened, the front door was closing. And, almost at once, Mary had come back carrying the little dog, and talking to it.

It was almost immediately after that, however, that J. K. Halder had stood up, had said, abruptly, "Good night," and had walked to the door, with no more explanation to anyone, and with no apologies. He had, Brian thought, looked intently at Mary Halder, still holding the little dog in her arms, but he had not said anything to her. After he had gone, those who remained had looked at one another, expressed surprise and bewilderment. "I did, too," Brian said. After that, the party had broken up; Brian had himself left within half an hour or so. Brian had been worried, upset, and wanted to get out of there.

"Because," he said, "well — if I saw them probably he did. Probably that's what made him walk out. And — I suppose Mother knew it. I don't think she expected Pine, or anyway not so early. I — I guess they had an engagement for later. Those family dinners never lasted very long. They did meet afterward. I found that out. So — you see how it would look to — to people. Including this Weigand guy. As if they'd been found out and were afraid Dad would do something about it and so — " He looked at Liza. "Damn it all," he said. "Don't you see?"

She saw; there was no way to escape seeing. And she had to make it more difficult, not easier.

"After you left the Norths'," she said, and her voice reflected her reluctance to say what

he had to know about "somebody called Lieutenant Weigand. From his office, I think.
Apparently — well, Brian, apparently your
father's lawyer had called the police and —
said he had something important to tell them.
I suppose it could be — "

"You don't know what?" Brian said, interrupting her.

She shook her head. If Weigand had heard
on the telephone, he had not revealed what he
heard. Perhaps it was nothing.

But Brian shook his head and now, unexpectedly, he seemed to have gained confidence, decision.

"Probably Dad got in touch with him,"
Brian said. "We may as well face that, Liza.
Got in touch to — well, maybe he planned to
divorce Mother. Or — he could have been
going to change his will, I suppose. So that —
that Pine wouldn't get the money, too. And if
Pine found that out — found it was either
one, because he'd miss the money either way
— Pine might have — " He paused. "You can
see what Pine might have done," he said.
"And how Mother would be — involved."
But then he spoke quickly. "Not in what Pine
might have done," he said. "Not in — in the
thing itself. But how she'd be dragged into it;
get all — fouled up by it." He looked at Liza

intently. "Nothing more than that," he told her. "But that's bad enough."

Oh Brian, she thought. *Dear Brian. You can't make it go away that easily. Not when you're afraid of so much more!*

Brian stood up suddenly; now all the brooding uncertainty, the unhappiness, seemed to have hardened into something else. His eyes had changed most; had hardened most. *Why, he could be dangerous,* the girl thought.

But all Brian did, at the moment, was to look at his watch, as if it were an enemy, and shake his head. Then he looked at her, not as an enemy, since his eyes softened and he half smiled.

"I'm going to get hold of Pine," he said. "Try to — well, shake it out of him, if necessary. But it's after six, and he's probably eating dinner. He's got a part in some show, you know. We'll — I'll catch him at the theater, later."

But that was wrong; that was puzzling.

"Listen," Liza said, "didn't you say he came around the other evening? Monday evening? After you'd all finished dinner? Why wasn't he at the theater then?"

"He — " Brian began, but then he stopped and his brows drew together. He said, after a pause, that it was funny.

197

"You said," Liza told him, "that you only *thought* it was Pine."

To that, however, he shook his head, slowly. Whatever he'd said before, he told her, he was sure it had been Pine.

"Do the police know he was there?" Liza asked.

Again the heavy brows above the dark eyes drew together. After a moment's thought, Brian Halder said he didn't know. He had not told them, naturally. He didn't know whether the others had or whether, except for his mother, they had even known who had come to the door. The incident had been lost sight of Monday evening, forgotten in the greater interest of J. K. Halder's abrupt departure.

"Brian," she said then. "You've asked your mother about this? About all of it. Haven't you?"

Again he hesitated a moment; then he nodded. That was how he knew it had been Pine. His mother admitted it had been Pine. She also said that, from about eleven-thirty that night, she had been with Pine until about one-thirty. "So," Brian said, "if it was Pine, Dad must have been killed some time yesterday morning. Around two or three. Something like that. You see that?" He looked at her. "It *had* to be that way," he told her.

There was one thing more she had to ask; that Brian had to take her asking.

"Brian," she said, "has your mother told the police about this?"

He shook his head; he said, "No, Liza." Then he looked at her almost with challenge. "But she will if they ask."

IX

Wednesday, 6:35 P.M.
to 10:33 P.M.

Jerry North put cracked ice into cocktail glasses; and two of the cats, one sitting on either side of the operation, watched intently, one might almost have thought with comprehension. He finished and both of them looked up at him and waited. "That's all," Jerry told them. He explained the matter to the two cats, who listened gravely. A human put cracked ice into glasses in advance, so that the glasses would be cold. Then when very cold liquid was poured in, it did not lose its chill to the glass. "See?" Jerry asked. Gin said, "Yah?" and tried to rub against Jerry North's arm, her tail wavering over the glasses. "Ice," Jerry explained, with patience. "Ice, not tails." He put Gin down on the floor, and Sherry fell instantly into her role of an abandoned cat, loved by no one, and cried out longingly. Jerry rubbed her ears and put her down by Gin. She immediately began to lick

200

behind Gin's ears. Gin flicked her ears with impatience and the door buzzer sounded. The three cats, Martini appearing out of nowhere, went to assist.

Martini was wary until she discovered that the door opened to Bill and Dorian Weigand. Then she jumped to the radio and made a small sound of welcome. Dorian Weigand, moving almost as gracefully as Martini — but not jumping on the radio — held a slim hand down for the cat to smell. Martini obliged and, very faintly, purred. Bill also was greeted by the cats, returned their greetings. Gin crouched to jump to Bill's shoulders, but Jerry picked her up and put her on his own, whereupon she steadied herself with claws and Pam North said, "Jerry, she's shedding. And that isn't your Siamese-colored suit."

After that, humans could greet and be greeted; after that Jerry, still wearing Gin — to Martini's audible, jealous disapproval — could mix drinks. After that Dorian, slim, green-eyed, looking now rather tired but still moving with her special grace, could find a chair and lean back in it and tuck one foot under the other leg and say, with satisfaction, "Ah." Sherry at once joined her, saying plaintive things, perhaps complaining of Gin's attitude about ear licking.

"It's funny about animals," Pam North said, and the other three looked at her and waited. She looked from one to the other, and seemed puzzled. "I don't know why I said that," she said. "Except something reminded me of something about animals." She looked at each of the cats in turn. "But now I don't know what it was," she said.

Jerry resumed mixing drinks and distributed them.

"Oh," Pam said, "I remember part of it. The way they like people or don't. The way Sherry likes Dorian and tells her her troubles. And some people they just avoid." But the last was said in a rather puzzled tone. "What started me?" Pam asked Jerry. Jerry sipped and gave the matter thought.

"Martini and Miss O'Brien?" he said. "As far as that goes, Martini and almost anybody she doesn't know."

But Pam shook her head. That, she explained, was merely because Martini was by nature shy and skeptical. It was a general attitude.

"Anyway," she said, "what started me wasn't a cat. More like a dog — oh! Aegisthus." She listened. "I lisped it again," she said. Her tone dismissed it. "By the way, Dorian, before Bill tells us about the lawyer,

Jerry's very pleased with Liza O'Brien's cats. Aren't you, Jerry?"

Jerry North said he was. He said there was a nice feeling.

"She's going to be good, I think," Dorian Weigand said. "She's a nice child. She'll break her neck to do a job on the book." Dorian paused to drink. "I hope — " she said, and looked at her husband. Bill smiled at her, lifted his shoulders momentarily. He said it was early days, yet, and was asked by Pam how early. He did not answer directly. Instead he told Pam he hoped she would be pleased to find out there was a will in it after all; a will which was to have been changed. They waited.

He told them, briefly, partially, of his interview with J. K. Halder's lawyer; of the cryptic telegram. With the new information, Weigand had done, and caused to be done, several things. With it, the Monday night dinner, Halder's abrupt departure from it, assumed enhanced importance. Already, the police had been seeking to establish Halder's exact movements on the night he died; with the information from Isaac Faberworth, they went harder to work on it.

They found that Halder had left the Sutton Place house about nine-thirty, perhaps a few minutes earlier — perhaps as early as nine-twenty. He had apparently walked for several blocks; he had got a cab, bound downtown, on Third Avenue at about nine-forty. It had taken much combing by many men to discover this, to find a hacker whose time sheet showed the right pickup, the right discharge of passenger near West Kepp Street. But, once found, the driver remembered; remembered because he got few calls to that part of town, and was helpless there, and had to be guided by Halder. "Brooklyn I know," the hacker said. "But this Green Witch Village — boy!" He remembered that his fare had stopped on the way at a Western Union office in West Fourth Street. It was a small office and they had luck again; Halder was remembered. He had filed his message to his attorney at nine-fifty-eight.

He had gone back to the waiting cab and, according to the cab driver's schedule, had been let out at West Kepp Street at ten minutes after ten. The trail ended there.

"Except that he got to the shop," Bill said, "and was there undisturbed for some time. He was there long enough to feed the animals and to handle the black cat, unless he had spent the evening with black cat hairs on one leg of his dinner trousers."

"He might have," Pam pointed out. "Same color. Like Jerry's Siamese-colored suit. The one he always says he's going to get, anyway."

It was possible, Bill agreed. It was probably not important. Certainly he had been there long enough to feed the animals. There had been traces of chopped meat under the finger-nails of one hand. That, Bill said, he had certainly not worn all evening. At a guess, he had been unmolested for an hour or more. Because, at a guess again, he had been alive at midnight and dead by three o'clock the next morning.

"No closer than that?" Jerry asked.

Bill shook his head and said that, unfortunately, the Medical Examiner's office wanted that much leeway. Pinned down, as hard as the police could pin them, they had consented to prefer one o'clock to say, two-forty-five. It was not, Bill admitted, as helpful as it might be.

Then, at whatever hour was chosen — it might have been as early as midnight, even a little before that — J. K. Halder had been held, or in some other fashion briefly immobilized, and a grain or more of strych-nine had been injected into him, hypodermi-cally. Within fifteen minutes, probably, he had begun to feel an unaccountable uneasiness and the beginning of convulsive movements. Within an hour or so — an hour of agony — he was dead.

"But," Bill said, "until somebody — somebody at the Sutton Place house — panicked and killed Miss O'Brien's little old man, we'd have had a hard time proving this, whatever we thought. The injection was made in his left arm, where he could conveniently have made it himself; the hypodermic was in a cupboard, where he might have placed it after using it; it had only his prints on it. Only one set of his prints, which would have taken explaining. His dying doubled up as he did in the pen, in spite of the convulsions of strychnine poison and your point, Pam, that he would never have used strychnine to destroy animals he was fond of, would both have taken more explaining. But — a good lawyer might have got around them somehow; have convinced a jury that it wasn't proved Halder didn't kill himself. Sneddiger's death was — simpler."

Detectives looking through files and asking questions, technicians looking into a seventy-odd-year-old body, had discovered this much of what had happened after Halder had left the Sutton Place house Monday night. Bill Weigand, assisted by Sergeant Mullins, had been less successful in finding out what had happened before he left the house.

Weigand had talked, at the house, with the Whitesides, Mary Halder and the servants; at her apartment, he had talked to Mrs. J. K. Halder, Jr. He had not as yet talked to "Junior" himself or, further, to Brian Halder. Weigand had questioned on the assumption that something had happened at the dinner which led Halder to decide to change his will and that that decision might have led to his murder. "Then all the rest of it," Bill said, "is trimming." He did not mean, he said, that it was extraneous, necessarily; that in the pattern of these lives, the name given the little black Scottie, the ailing boxer bitch, the small long-haired cat, did not somehow fit. But it was simpler, for the time being at any rate, to assume that it was not because a Scottie was named Aegisthus that J. K. Halder was killed in his pet shop.

"But," Pam North said.

He did not, Weigand said, mean to say that the Scottie's name was an incident, without meaning; that Halder had not, when he gave the little dog to his younger wife and told her it was already named, meant obliquely to imply something, and most probably that he was not being kept in ignorance.

"So obviously subtle," Pam said, with disapproval.

The others agreed to that. But they were
not, Jerry pointed out, sitting in judgment on
J. K. Halder's style, which might well have
been too elaborately indirect. He had not been
killed because he had a habit of going around
Robin Hood's barn. He had been killed
because — But there Jerry North paused,
handed it back to Bill Weigand.

Bill did not immediately pick it up. He said
that, at first, none of the family remembered
that anything of importance had happened at
the dinner. All — Mrs. Halder herself, her
step-daughter and the lieutenant colonel, the
junior Mrs. Halder — had agreed that Halder
had left abruptly. They had agreed in saying
they did not know why. Jennifer Halder, to
whom Weigand had gone first, had thought,
or said she thought, that her father-in-law had
merely decided to be eccentric. This, she told
Weigand, did not surprise her; she could not
see why it should surprise anyone. He had
been, she had said, "a funny old duck"; he
had also, she thought, known it; enjoyed
being a funny old duck, and had been especially "funny" when the notion took him,
needing no actual reason. She suggested the
dinner itself, Halder's arranging of it, had

been only an example of J. K. Halder's "funniness." She had assumed, she told Bill Weigand, that the old man, after calling the family together, had merely become bored with all of them. "As heaven knows — " she had begun, and then stopped in mock discretion. She had been tolerant and detached; had said that she was rather fond of the funny old duck but could not pretend deep grief. "After all," she said, "I very seldom saw him. He was Jas's father, that was all." To her he had been, she indicated, no more than a rather odd abstraction.

But when Bill had told her of her father-in-law's decision to change his will, her detachment had markedly lessened. She had wanted to know whether his intention to do this, expressed in a telegram to his attorney, was in any way legally binding and, when told it was not, had not tried to hide her relief. Nor, except for a moment or two, had she tried to hide her evident conviction that, if the will had been changed, she and her husband would have been losers. This had, apparently, been so much an inevitable conclusion in her own mind that she had taken it for granted that it would be as inevitable in Weigand's, and only when he raised the point that Halder's specific intentions had been entirely undisclosed realized she was being needlessly revealing. Then she admitted, by her manner as well as her words, that she had trapped herself.

But she assumed, she then insisted, that she and her husband would lose again only because they had been the ones to lose before. She told him of the earlier will change, in which they had lost drastically, and of what they assumed to be the reason for it — that they were going to have a child. Bill amplified for his wife and the Norths, explaining that Jennifer Halder's version accorded with that of Halder's lawyer.

"For heaven's sake!" Pam said. "Why — the *awful* old man! The — genocidist!" She considered. "As far as I'm concerned," she said, "it can be suicide any time, after that. Serves him right."

Jerry smiled at her, and shook his head at her.

"Because," Pam said, "he must have been crazy. But go ahead, Bill."

Bill had, he said, questioned along the obvious lines, and Jennifer Halder had denied that, since the time five years before, there had been any new cause for Halder to become annoyed at his older son. Specifically, she had said — and then had smiled, seemed amused

— they were not again going to have a child.

"But of course — " Pam North said.

"Right," Bill said. "I'll agree we have to take her word for it."

"For the time being," Pam amplified, and again Bill said "Right."

Under continued questioning, Jennifer Halder had continued not to remember any incident at the dinner which might have incensed the old man; continued to insist that no incident would be necessary to make him behave oddly. Then Bill had gone on to the Sutton Place house, and questioned the Whitesides, separately, and Mary Halder. Mullins, meanwhile, talked to the servants.

The Whitesides and Mrs. Halder were all, they had assured Weigand, surprised that Halder had decided to change his will; they all, he thought, appeared to be relieved that the cryptic telegram would do nothing to invalidate the present will. But each of them denied that he would expect to lose if the will were changed, all being clear of conscience, sure they had done nothing to offend the old man. This might prove that they lacked the motive Jennifer and her husband might have had; it might also prove they were more reticent than Jennifer had been.

It was Dorian, who had seemed to be almost

211

asleep, except that her fingers gently stroked the blond cat in her lap, who pointed out that Jennifer Halder's apparent frankness might be actual calculation — and that she had after all told Bill nothing he had not learned elsewhere. Bill nodded to this.

Both the Whitesides had, like Jennifer, denied that anything out of the way had happened at the dinner; both seemed to share her belief that Halder had needed no incentive to behave oddly. (The colonel had added, "Particularly during the last few weeks, poor old chap.") And, at first, Mary Halder had taken the same line. But by then Mullins had talked to Burns, and reported what Burns remembered, so that, to Mary Halder, Bill had shaken his head slowly. She had at first seemed puzzled; then she had appeared to understand and had said, "Oh, that!"

"I suppose," she had said, then, "you mean Sherman's coming? But that wasn't anything."

She had been told to go on. She had gone on. At a little after nine on Monday evening, she said, Sherman Pine had showed up at the house. She had not expected him; Burns had let him into the foyer and, recognizing him down the length of the living room, she had at once gone to the foyer. She had been surprised and, after a moment, he had been apologetic.

"He got mixed up on the time," Mary Halder said. "The day. We had an engagement for last evening, not Monday. But he got mixed up somehow and when I didn't meet him, he came around to get me. When he saw how things were, he went away, of course."

She stopped, then, and looked at Bill Weigand, seemed to study him. She said she hoped he wasn't going to make a mistake about this.

"Sherman and I are friends," she said. "Everybody knows it. My husband knew it. Merely friends. There would have been no reason for Sherman not to come in, except that — well, we thought it was going to be a family discussion of some kind; that J. K. had arranged for it to be. Having Sherman drop around wouldn't have upset my husband. Wouldn't have annoyed him." She paused, deliberately. "There was no concealment," she said. "There was no reason for concealment. It will be simpler, Lieutenant, if you decide to believe that."

Bill did not indicate what he had decided to believe. He took her over the incident several times, getting always the same details. She had recognized Sherman Pine, she had gone

213

down the room to the foyer, she had held out her hand to him and he had taken it; she had said something like, "Sherman, what on earth?" and he had asked why she had not met him as they had planned. It had taken only a moment to straighten the matter out; he apologized and left. Could her husband have seen this? He could have; she believed he had sat facing toward the foyer. He had not mentioned the incident. Nor, she agreed, had she; it concerned nobody but Sherman Pine and herself. And, in any case, her husband had almost at once announced that he was leaving. No, she had not thought there was any connection between the two things; she did not think so now. They went over it again; Weigand was patient, she was not impatient. On the second or third repetition, she remembered that, while she was talking to Pine, she had heard Aegisthus yelp and that, a little later, the dog had trotted down the room toward her, and that she had picked him up.

"Incidentally," Bill told Pam North, "she doesn't lisp when she mentions the pooch."

"Neither would I if somebody thought I had done a murder," Pam said. They all looked at her. "Too important," she said. "Every word counts."

There was a pause for verbal digestion.

214

Then Jerry said that Mary Halder's did not seem to him a particularly substantial story. Pam did not agree; it was not, she said, necessarily insubstantial. "Because, Jerry," she said, "we went to a party once a week before it was, or a week after. A day would be easy."

"Who, precisely, is Sherman Pine?" Dorian asked.

Precisely, Bill told her, he was an actor; not a star, now and then featured, rather generally employed. Employed now.

Dorian looked puzzled; Jerry expressed puzzlement. Pine had gone to the Sutton Place house some time after nine on Monday. On Tuesday, until later than that, he had been at the house again — had been there when Sneddiger's body was found. A question arose.

Bill Weigand agreed that it did. But it was not difficult to answer.

"He's in a play which has performances Sunday and none Monday," he said. "Which takes care of Monday. And — he doesn't come on until the last act; doesn't have to be at the theater until around ten or even, in a pinch, a little after. Gives him a short day. He's free, of course, a little after eleven."

"My," Pam said, "it doesn't even cut into his evenings much, does it? What kind of part does he play?"

"A murderer," Bill said, without inflection. They all looked at him. "The play's a melo-drama of some sort. Pine comes on in the last act and kills people."

"And then wipes his hands and goes out to supper?" Pam suggested.

Apparently, Bill said, it was something like that. Pam said it was very interesting. She said she wondered if he always stepped out of character. "After the play's over, I mean," she said, and was told by Jerry that they knew what she meant. But Pam's face remained thoughtful as Bill went on with the little more he had to tell them.

They had, Bill said, not much more infor-mation about the relationship between Pine and Mary Halder than Mary Halder had given them. It could be merely friendship; it could be much more. They would find out.

"Meanwhile, thinking the worst," Dorian pointed out.

"That's the way it is," Bill said.

(Did she still hate it? Bill wondered. She said so little about it nowadays; seemed so completely to accept his profession, which required that he so frequently think the worst of people — of pretty young things like Liza O'Brien, of women like Mary Halder; which made him the pursuer of fearful people running. Once, Dorian had hated all that; because of all that, she had once almost not married him.)

He roused himself; said that that was about where things stood. It could be any of them.

"You keep it in the family?" Jerry said and Bill said that, tentatively, he did.

"But not including the boy?" Dorian said. "Liza's boy?"

Bill shrugged at that. He said that, tentatively, they knew too little to exclude anyone. There were, he pointed out, ar least two possible patterns; the simple pattern of murder for gain or, more specifically, to prevent loss; the more complex pattern to which the name of the little black dog might give a clue. Until they knew more — He broke off. He finished his drink. A little later they walked toward Charles.

There's something I almost remember, Pam North kept thinking as they walked. Something I almost thought of a while ago, something that was on the edge of my mind. But she could not remember what it was, or even decide whether it was important that she should remember. It was very annoying, particularly as (Pam thought) Bill was yet a long way from knowing what came next, and when that was true, it was always so possible that

217

what came next might be unpleasant.

But actually, Charles' bar came next, and it was not unpleasant at all. Pam forgot, after a few minutes, that there was something she had forgotten.

After all their discussion, after what had been almost a struggle between them, it was ludicrous to have the elderly, bald man merely shake his head, merely say, in a bored voice, "Ain't here yet." It was a relief, of course, but it was at the same time disconcerting. You prepared yourself emotionally to meet a problem, you thought what might happen and what you would do, your imagination built a confrontation on the grand scale, and a bored, elderly man, sitting in a kind of window, said, "Nope, ain't here yet," and it was all nothing — all thin air. She looked up at Brian, who was scowling.

"What d'you mean?" Brian demanded and now the elderly man looked at him. But he was still, obviously, not much interested. He had met, one could imagine, a good many forceful people. He merely absorbed force.

"What I said," the man told Brian Halder mildly. "He ain't here."

"He's playing here, isn't he?" Brian asked. The theater doorman appeared to give this consideration; it was as if he decided to skip a point he might have raised. Then he nodded. He did not amplify, nor appear to think amplification indicated. It was apparent he considered the conversation closed.

"Will you listen to me a minute?" Brian asked, and his voice was harsh again, and strained. "I want to see Mr. Pine. He's playing here, you say. The curtain is supposed to go up in fifteen minutes. And you say he isn't here."

The doorman at the Wrayburn Theater took his time. Then he looked up. Then he said, "That's right, mister." But then he relented. "Goes on in the last act, Mr. Pine does," he said. "Before that he's just another guy whistling in the wings. Get it?"

"No," Brian said. He looked down at Liza. "Do you get what he's talking about?" Brian asked her, as if the man were not there.

"An off-stage sound," the doorman said. "That's Mr. Pine, acts one and two. Another guy whistling. In the old days, he'd of done his own whistling. Nobody cares any more. No responsibility. Your Mr. Pine'll roll in about quarter of ten. Ten, maybe. Slap some makeup on. Go on. Come off. Go wherever he goes. Calls himself an actor."

"Maybe he can't whistle," Liza heard herself say. She could feel, as much as see, that Brian made an impatient movement. But the doorman regarded her seriously.

"Sure he can whistle," the doorman told her. "He has to. They just let him get away with it."

"A quarter of ten, you say?" Brian said. "When does he go on?"

"About a quarter after. Twenty after, maybe. There's some laughs in the first act. Nearer four-thirty matinees, but you got to take it slower matinees. You know why? Women."

But Brian Halder was already turning away; turning away abruptly. He, too, had been keyed up to it, Liza realized; he was angered, disturbed, by anti-climax. And my being here doesn't help, Liza thought. It would have been better if I hadn't come.

She did not put in words, in her own mind, precisely why she had been determined to come, to take part in this interview — this confrontation. It was true that she thought it would do little good; it was also true that they might read much in the way denial was spoken; it was true one could not tell what might come of it. And she had not argued with Brian after she had told him that he should tell the police, tell Lieutenant Weigand, what he suspected, feared, and let the police talk to Pine, and Brian had said, only, "No." That, she had realized, would be a futile argument to press, however sound — however obviously sound — it was. It would be futile until Brian was assured that his mother was not involved, and of that there was no way to assure him.

But, since there was to be this meeting, she felt she must be part of it, because that way it would be better for Brian. She shied away from the word "safer" although something like it was in her mind. Since this had happened, there had been a kind of violence in Brian, now seeming to recede, now showing itself plainly. If she were not present when he met Pine, not there to temper the violence by her presence, by Brian's consciousness of his words hitting her mind (as well as Pine's) that violence might — She did not finish that thought, either; indeed, she rather felt than thought it all. But she would not be moved from her determination to go with him, and after a time Brian gave up his attempt to persuade her. And then they had gone to the Wrayburn Theater, found the passageway to the stage door, found an elderly bald man, found frustration.

Now they went back down the passageway by the side of the theater building and, on the sidewalk, stopped irresolute. (A man who, in full sight, remained inconspicuous, leaned against the iron fence, lighted a cigarette, looked at them vaguely, looked beyond them vaguely.) It was Liza who suggested they might try to get tickets, see the play, at least through the first two acts. Rather to her surprise, Brian agreed to this; rather more to her surprise, he managed to get two tickets. They had been turned in late and were not together; one was two rows behind the other and both were on the right side; the seat nearer the stage being also the one nearer the center — and the one to which, after they waited together until the house lights began to dim, Liza was shown by the usher.

The play was one of those carefully casual, cheerfully British, studies of sadistic depravity, although little to indicate this appeared during the first act, which occupied itself with a tea party at the vicar's. There was the brusque, but dear, old lady who was, Liza suspected, destined for no long life; there was a comic servant, also — under her pleasing oddity — clearly marked by doom; there was a pair of young Londoners, correctly assorted as to sex, who were (or professed to be) on a walking trip and had been driven to the vicarage by a sudden rain; there was a pretty girl (a niece of the brusque old lady) and a man in middle life who remained — but whether by intention or auctorial carelessness was not entirely clear — suspiciously unclarified. Save for the vicar, the brusque one and, of course, the servant, who were on-stage when the curtain went up, these characters arrived at suitable intervals during the first act and, gradually, had tea, meanwhile making characteristic and socially identifying remarks. During the latter part of the first act, there was some discussion, still casual, of the shocking occurrence of the night before and the act was almost over before it was revealed that poor dear and neighboring Mrs. Mumble had been found dead in her own sitting room and found, moreover, in two pieces, one of which was her head.

To the perpetrator of this bisection there were no clues or, at any rate, none which seemed of much help to good old Superintendent Brunk, who had the case in hand, if the other characters could call it that, which they could only with humorous reluctance. The old boy was, they felt, a bit out of his depth in the matter, not getting much forrader nor likely to. All the dear old boy had definitely established, indeed, was that someone had heard, or thought he had heard (having had several pints of bitter at the time, and being notoriously tone deaf in any case), a man or woman whistling a phrase from an old madrigal which went like this — The man in middle life, and of undefined status, thereupon whistled a phrase which, for all Liza could tell, might well be from an old madrigal.

There was a pause of several beats after the man had finished the phrase and then, from off-stage, there came a repetition of the little tune and the brusque old lady dropped her teacup, which broke. The curtain thereupon came down.

Liza looked back at Brian when the house lights went up and he gestured with his head toward the rear of the house and pantomimed the smoking of a cigarette. She nodded and stood up and worked her way toward the aisle, past plump, reluctant knees. It took her a little time to reach the head of the aisle and Brian was already waiting for her. When she came up he made a facial comment, wordlessly, on the play. They went out to the sidewalk, with a good many others, and lighted cigarettes. They looked at posters, which bore selected quotations from reviewers. "Where," Brian asked to be told, "is the 'creeping violence' Mr. Barnes wrote about?"

"I — " Liza began, and then smiled and

nodded to Pam and Jerry North, who were standing a little distance off. "Hel*lo*" Pam said, across several people. The four joined and there was talk only of the mimic murder, still attenuatedly potential, and none of the thing they were thinking about. But that was fine, Liza thought, looking quickly up at Brian, seeing that, for the moment, the strain was no longer in his face. Then the lobby lights went down and up again in signal, and cigarettes spurted from fingers, dusted the sidewalk with momentary sparks. They went into the theater.

(The inconspicuous man who, forty-five minutes earlier, had leaned against the iron fence and looked at nothing in particular, lingered after most had gone back into the theater; continued, absently, to smoke a cigarette. Another man, larger, ruddy of face, lingered too. Then, without preliminary, he spoke to the inconspicuous man. "Yours too?" he asked. The inconspicuous man said, "Yeah." "Mine," the larger man said, "are K for Kentucky eight and ten. You want I should call in for both of us?" The inconspicuous man gave it thought; then he nodded. The larger man went off up the street toward Broadway; the other drifted into the theater. He stood in the rear of the house, leaning against the barrier, looking toward the stage.)

The second act was chiefly Inspector Brunk's. He appeared early — large, a little cockney (he had played in the original London production) and steadily affable. He pointed out that the matter of Mrs. Mumble's head constituted a nasty piece of work and agreed with the vicar that it was difficult to tell what things were coming to. (There was a momentary pause in plot development at that point while the inspector and the vicar commented on the Labor Government, their remarks proving unilluminating to all but half a dozen in the audience, who laughed in high, well-bred tones.) It then became, as the inspector himself pointed out, time to get down to cases, and down to cases they got.

Movements became more intricate thereafter, with much coming and going by the couple from London, the anomalous man of middle age and the brusque old lady. The last left the stage, indeed, toward the middle of the act and did not return, which led the more adventuresome thinkers in the audience to put two and two together. From time to time, under unexpected circumstances, someone whistled the phrase from the madrigal, but each of these musical interludes was more or less satisfactorily explained. (The young man of the couple from London, for example, was showing the young woman of the couple how it went. He was warned by the inspector who, in a rather groping way, felt that scale practice was adding a confusing note to an already confused situation.)

In one fashion or another, all the characters save the servant were got out of the vicar's humble — sixty-five by thirty foot — living room toward the end of the act, and the servant went around lighting lamps, while dusk deepened rapidly, watt by watt. She still had a lamp to go when the whistling was heard again, this time much louder and clearer than before. Almost at once, someone knocked on an off-stage door and the servant, who previously had been established as unable to tell "Roll Out the Barrel" from "God Save the King," went briskly and obediently off-stage. The audience sighed audibly, expecting never to see her again.

But in this they were wrong, since she reappeared almost at once and was carrying a hatbox. This she put down on a table downstage center and left there. She returned to lamp lighting, now and then pausing to look doubtfully at the hatbox. Darkness continued to deepen. The servant circled toward the hatbox, moved away from it, reached out and touched it, withdrew her hand, started to leave the room, was drawn back to the box. Finally, she began to loosen the strap which held the top of the box. (And one susceptible member of the audience said, in a shaking voice, "O-o-oh!" The voice was to Liza O'Brien, although she was caught as others in the audience were by the carefully nurtured suspense, faintly familiar. But, watching the woman on the stage, she did not try to identify it.)

The strap was loosened, there was a moment's hesitancy, the top of the box was lifted off. The actress's scream was worth the waiting for. It brought the vicar first, but the others — all the others — were on his heels. The serving woman fainted by that time, leaving clear the vicar's way to the hatbox. He looked into it, shuddered, swayed and then got control of himself by an effort easily visible to the last row balcony.

"Poor dear Agatha," the vicar said, the madrigal was whistled off-stage and the curtain came down.

This time Brian Halder was already standing when Liza twisted in her seat and looked back at him; this time he did not catch her eye, or did not seem to. He began to move, sidling toward the aisle on his right.

Liza herself moved quickly, then, but she had four obstructing, and rather petulant, seat occupants to pass. And, once in the aisle, her progress was again impeded by slowly moving people. Brian, not waiting for her, as it had been clear from the first he did not mean to do, already was through the lobby when she reached the head of the aisle; by the time she reached the open gate in the iron fence across the passage to the stage door, Brian was out of sight. She went down the passage after him.

Brian merely looked at her, merely shook his head, when she found him, talking again to the doorman. Already there was defeat in his eyes, in the tone of his voice.

"That's my orders," the doorman said. "Nobody goes in. Mr. Pine don't want to see you, I guess."

"But he's here," Brian said. "I only want to see him a minute. It's important." He reached toward his hip pocket. But the doorman shook his head.

"Won't do no good," the doorman told him. "That's my orders. See him after the show; see him somewhere else." He looked at Brian's tallness, his evident strength. "And," he said, "don't try to crash, mister. See why?" He motioned with his head down the dimly lit passage beyond his cubby-hole. Liza looked and, more slowly, Brian turned to look also. A uniformed policeman was standing there, regarding them. His regard was detached, but without sympathy. Liza saw Brian's face, Brian's body, recognize and admit defeat.

The group in front of the theater already was dissolving into it when Brian Halder and Liza O'Brien again reached the sidewalk. Three men, one of them inconspicuous yet, to Liza, vaguely familiar, were standing together, smoking, as if reluctant to return to the reticent carnage going on within. They did not look at Brian and Liza; were still talking after the tall, dark-eyed young man and the slight girl had gone into the lobby. They continued to talk for several minutes longer. Then two of the men, one the markedly inconspicuous one, went into the theater and the third went down the passage toward the stage door. The two who had entered the theater were late for the start of the last act, but they did not seem to mind, nor did they seek to find seats. They stood, at some distance from each other, leaning lightly on the barrier, looking toward the stage.

Sherman Pine was already on-stage when the last act curtain rose. He was kneeling beside the collapsed maid servant, with a black bag on the floor near him. It was clear at once that he was a physician, summoned to the vicarage to give succor, although not to the contents of the hatbox. The hatbox, its purpose served, had been removed. After the audience had rustled to its seats, Sherman Pine arose and announced, with gravity and a British intonation, that he thought she'd do. "Shock, y'know," he said to the vicar. "A peculiarly nasty business."

Shortly thereafter the vicar left the room, announcedly to wash his hands; the inspector, after looking protractedly at the door through which the vicar had departed, appeared to reach a decision and went after him and the physician was left alone with the inert body of the maid servant. He looked around, including the audience in his survey, and then puckered his lips to whistle. No sound came, however, and he reached toward his black bag. But at that moment the pretty girl, whose activities during the second act had been so intermittent that the audience had almost forgotten her, came in through another door and began to whistle. She did not seem to see the again kneeling physician at once; then did so with a start of surprise, and with the surprise ceased to whistle the phrase from the madrigal.

Sherman Pine arose again, greeted the girl

(whom he had, it now appeared, known all the time) and was moving toward her, perhaps to take her hand, when the inspector appeared at his door and beckoned with emphasis, his manner indicating that, elsewhere in the vicarage, something — not hell, perhaps, but purgatory — had broken loose. Pine, expressing bewilderment with his back, went to the door and, with the inspector, through it.

Somewhat later, after several other characters had, absently as it seemed, whistled the madrigal phrase, the vicar, the inspector, and the couple from London were in the room, wondering about things, when there came a scream off-stage right. They were frozen for a moment, turning toward that side of the stage. Then a door there opened, rather convulsively, and Sherman Pine fell in, headlong.

Since the available actors were already expressing alarm and horror to the tops of their respective bents, there was nothing immediately in their attitudes to indicate that this was not an expected method of entrance on the part of Mr. Pine. But then the vicar, not at all in the voice he had used before, said, "My God!" and ran toward the fallen man. And then, more or less stepping over Pine, a man in the unmistakable uniform of the New

232

York police force entered, looked at the audience in horrified surprise, and turned back to call, in a loud, uncultivated voice, "Hey! Sergeant!" into the backstage area. And that, as the author of the play might well have said had he been present, tore it. That really tore it.

Realization that this was a variation on the theme of violence, was something not written in advance and acted out with calculation, spread slowly through the audience. (Some of its members, indeed, only dimly realized that things had not gone according to plan until they read, the next morning, the continuing story of the Halder case in the *Daily News*.) A wave of sound, which became conversation, which was punctuated by sharp demi-screams, rolled through the theater and then people began to stand up, and to point, as if this no longer merely mimicked violence demanded some special gesture of attention.

Liza O'Brien turned in her seat and then, to see better, she too stood up. But she did not look at the stage, where now there were several men around the fallen actor. She looked back, searching anxiously, desperately, for sight of Brian Halder. But Brian was not in his seat, or standing in front of it. Brian was not anywhere she could see.

233

X

*Wednesday, 10:33 P.M.
to Thursday, 12:25 A.M.*

Liza looked around, looked every place, but
still she could not see Brian's tall figure.
Where he had been there was now no one; still
only the stage lights illuminated the auditorium of the Wrayburn Theater, and the people in it were shadows. Only those behind
her, touched by the light which emanated
from the stage, had faces. Looking down
toward the stage, she could see only the backs
of shadows.

The uniformed policeman who had come
onto the stage a moment after Sherman Pine
had pitched forward through the door, was
standing now, having moved farther on-stage.
He was looking, still with an expression of
unhappy surprise, at the people who almost
filled the orchestra section. Then, curiously,
he looked up at the balcony and his surprise
seemed to be enhanced. It was incongruous, Liza thought, that this policeman, doing

nothing, had somehow managed to become the dominating figure on the stage.

The actors who had ruled there, had been characters in an intricate mimicry of violence, stood now close together, their faces expressing nothing more marked, more projected, than any ordinary human faces. They looked toward stage right, looked down, ignored the uniformed patrolman who appeared to ignore them in turn. Now there were two men, both in civilian clothes, squatting by Pine and one of them apparently was a doctor. And still the curtain stayed up, as if there were, on the part of someone, an obligation to give the audience all, and more than, it had paid for. Then one of the men squatting beside Pine, the one who was not the physician, stood up and turned toward the off-stage area and called out, loudly, "Somebody put the damned thing down."

Almost at once the curtain went down, was hurried down; it was as if a bedroom shade, left up, forgotten, had suddenly been remembered, almost convulsively pulled against intruding eyes. As the curtain went down, there was a little sigh through the audience. After a moment then a man came out in front of the curtain, pushing it back again and again with his right hand as if he were swimming against it, while he worked in from the wings. He held up his hand. He said, "Please." The audience rustled still, and again he said "please." Then Liza recognized that the man was the actor who had played the part of the vicar.

He got attention, finally. He spoke carefully, projecting his voice, giving each word, each syllable, value.

"The management has asked me to say that there is no cause for alarm," he said. "No cause of any kind. One of the actors, Mr. Sherman Pine, has been slightly injured by — er, by a fall. The management asks your forbearance for a few moments and then, if Mr. Pine is unable to continue, the play will go on with an understudy." He stopped, looked around, smiled with formal informality, spoke in a lighter tone. "Won't you just sit down and wait a few moments?" he said. "I assure you it's nothing serious."

For an instant, Liza could feel doubt and uncertainty in the people around her; could feel a reluctance to accept this minimization of unscheduled drama, a kind of disappointment that what had promised so well had come to so little. But then, here and there, a man or a woman did sit down, accepting what the actor said and then he, knowing his job was done, began to work his way back across the stage to the side from which he had come. And then the house lights, tardily, came up.

With the light, with the gradual subsidence of those around her, Liza, still standing, could look anxiously for Brian, could look with a kind of desperate hopefulness. But she could not see him anywhere. And then a man who, unnoticed, had come down the right center aisle, stopped at the end of her row and, very politely, spoke her name.

"Miss O'Brien?" he said, as if he were in doubt. She turned toward him. "Could I see you a minute, Miss O'Brien?" he asked. He seemed to hesitate. "I have a message for you," he said. He was still polite, his voice very quiet, almost small.

She heard what he said with, at first, relief — relief that Brian had sent her a message — but then with rising fear that the message was about, not from, Brian Halder, and that it would be that something had happened to Brian. She nodded, quickly, anxiously, and at once began to work her way to the man at the end of the row. "Really!" somebody behind a pair of the plump, reluctant knees said, in a tone meant to be audible. "Really!" But Liza paid no attention.

When she reached the man he touched her

arm, kept his hand on it, but without closing his fingers, leaving the touch a friendly suggestion only, and began to walk up the aisle. She went with him, felt herself hurrying. At the end of the aisle he spoke, without stopping, without indicating that she could stop. "They want you back there, Miss O'Brien," he said.

Fear was in her throat, now; her throat was dry and stiff with it. And now she realized that fear had been in her throat, at her throat, since Sherman Pine had pitched forward into the lighted box which was a vicar's living room in Surrey.

She started obediently toward the doors opening from the theater, but the man — and now she thought she had seen him before, recently, but could not remember where — said, "No, this way," and directed her, still with the slight pressure on her arm, toward the aisle which ran down on the extreme right of the auditorium. When they reached the head of the aisle he said again, "This way," and they walked down it, he half a step behind her, but his fingers still on her arm. Those sitting nearest, along the extreme right aisle, looked at them curiously; she could feel question in the way they looked.

The aisle led them behind the boxes, which

were cut off by drawn curtains. At the very end of the aisle there were several steps leading up and, at the top of them, a door. The man reached around her when she stopped on the lowest of the stair treads and pulled the door toward him and said, "Watch your step, miss." She went through and heard the door closed behind them, and was in a narrow passage which was dimly lighted and oddly cluttered. On her right, leaning against a brick wall, were great flats of canvas; on her left were other flats, but these were fixed upright, in a solid wall, and the name of the play and numerals were painted on them in white. She realized that she was outside the vicar's living room; that this was the outside of the box which, to the audience, seemed authentically a room. "Watch it," the man said again, and she realized she had almost stumbled into a platform built against the outside of the box set and then, looking at it, realized that it was like a porch outside a door, and that the door was one of those (one set a little higher than the others, on a low balcony) which opened onto the set, and through which the actors had all evening been coming and going.

To her right, after a moment, the outer wall became a corridor, fairly wide but still cluttered — there were several boxes, and on one of them two men were sitting and now were looking at her. She realized that the corridor was the one leading to the stage door; could see, at the far end, the opening behind which the stage doorman sat. But the man who had been sent for her said, "This way, miss," and led her to the left, along a very narrow passage which took them, she realized, behind the set. After they had traversed this, they came out into a relatively open space, but one which seemed crowded with people.

"Well," one man said, and he was excited, spoke excitedly, kept pulling at his necktie, already pulled far to one side. "Well, do we or don't we?" He jerked his necktie from one side to the other, and used, in a tone inappropriate, words appropriate to prayer.

"Keep your shirt on," the man he was speaking to told him. "The lieutenant will be here any minute."

"But listen," the excited man said. "You o.k.'d the announcement. *Now* you hold us up."

"I told you why," the other man said, and now Liza realized he was the tall, dark detective she had seen with Lieutenant Weigand at the Sutton Place house, and again with Brian at the Norths' apartment. "I told you I wanted to — see who was there. Didn't want them rushing out." He sounded as if he had explained this several times, were tired of explaining it. "Try to get it through your head that the show *doesn't* have to go on," he said. "There's no law it has to. There's a law — " He broke off. He said, to the man behind Liza, "Oh, got her all right?" and then to Liza, "Hello, Miss O'Brien."

She tried to say something, and her throat was too dry for words.

"Take her — " the man began, and then looked again beyond her, and this time also beyond the man who had brought her, and said, in a surprised tone, "Well, hello."

"Hello, Mr. Stein," Pamela North said. "And before you ask, we came to see Mr. Pine act and it was a theater a man Jerry knows had a play in once and he showed us around, so we came." She paused, "I mean, we knew how to come," she said. "Down the right aisle. Where's Bill? And is Mr. Pine — ?" Pam stopped.

"No," Detective Sergeant Stein said, "he isn't. He got slugged, knocked out, apparently concussed. He isn't — " Then he seemed to feel he had already said too much, and looked at Liza O'Brien.

"Listen," the man with the wandering necktie said. "For God's sake listen! Do we or

241

don't we? That's all I want to know. Do we or don't we?"

"What," Bill Weigand said from behind the Norths, "does this man want to do, or not do?"

Stein showed relief.

"Finish the performance with the understudy," Stein said. "I didn't know whether you — ?"

"How long will it take?" Weigand asked the excited man, who threw up both hands in what seemed to be incipient madness and then said, quietly enough, "Twenty minutes."

"Anything on the stage we need?" Bill asked, this time of Stein, and Stein shook his head.

"Hit back here," Stein said. "Standing at the door, waiting for cue. Somebody hit him just as he started to open the door and he fell in." Stein paused. "Very startling," he added. "Quite an entrance."

"Can you finish without using this door?" Weigand asked the excited man, who threw up his hands again, stopped midway and said, mildly, "Yes, Lieutenant."

He was told that, in that case, he might get on with it. His response was to jerk his necktie to the other side of his collar, then throw both hands into the air, then cry out for someone named Tom. "For God's sake," he cried, "where's Tom for God's sake?" A man ten feet from him got up from the box he had been sitting on and said that there he was. "For God's sake where have you been?" the excited man said, but did not wait to be answered. "You'll have to go from the other side," he said. "But work over to this side, so the grouping will be right. It's — " Then he flung his hands into the air again. "For God's sake," he demanded, and now of Bill Weigand, "*why* can't we use this door? Do you realize he'll have to make a complete cross? Without a *line?* While the others just *wait?*"

Bill Weigand smiled faintly. He looked at Stein, who shrugged. "Actually," Stein said, "I don't know what we'll get, Lieutenant. Or even what we'll look for."

"Right," Bill said to the excited man. "Use the door then. But get on with it."

"Get *on!*" the excited man said then. "Get on!"

Four people detached themselves from shadows and Liza saw that they were the vicar, Inspector Brunk and the couple from London. The vicar stepped on a cigarette.

"Take it from the *scream,*" the excited man said. "Di. For God's sake where's Di?"

Nobody seemed to respond to his excitement, but the woman who had been playing poor dear Agatha, and whose head, it was now evident, was not really in the hatbox, spoke from another window and said, "I'm right here, darling."

"Then get on, everybody," the excited man said, and jerked his necktie under his left ear. "Oh, for God's *sake!*"

The vicar, the inspector and the couple from London went through the door, into the box set, out of sight. The excited man went to the door and looked in at them. Now he whispered, carryingly. "Move in, darling," he said. "For God's *sake* move in." What resulted from this was invisible, but apparently satisfactory. The excited man withdrew from the door and the man named Tom took his place. The man named Tom, Liza noticed — was amazed to find herself noticing — licked his lips, then rubbed his hands together as if they were damp and he hoped to dry them. "Di," the excited man said to poor dear Agatha. "Are you ready, darling?"

The woman merely sighed, but she stood up.

"I'll cue you," the excited man said. He looked back into the set. What he saw seemed to content him, since he pulled his head back out, closed the door, took a deep breath and said, suddenly, in the same tense whisper, "Take her up!"

One could hear the curtain going up. But more than that, one could suddenly hear silence. The sound which ended had touched only the subconscious — a dim, multitudinous sound it had been, of some hundreds of people moving restlessly, talking, making the strange, inchoate noise of humanity en masse. But when it stopped, as the curtain rose, the silence rang in the conscious ear.

There was a period during which one might have counted, slowly, up to five. Then the excited man whirled toward the actress who had been poor dear Agatha and gestured violently with both hands. And the actress screamed.

Pam North jumped into the air and almost screamed herself; through Liza O'Brien the scream ran jaggedly, laceratingly. The excited man beamed and then Tom, standing by the door, leaning forward, like a spring runner crouching for a start, whistled the first bar of the passage from the madrigal. He was off pitch; the excited man threw up his hands in pantomime of horror, but he had moved by then to a place where Tom could not see him. Tom finished the phrase, getting back on pitch midway; they could see his shoulders rise with a deep breath. Then he opened the door and walked into the set. The show was going on; the excited man collapsed on a box, spent.

"Goodness," Pam North said to the actress who had been Agatha, "I thought you were dead. I mean — whose head was it, then?"

The actress looked rather relieved and said, "Oh, that. Mine, darling. Of course. But poor dear Lola can't scream, so I give my all darling. But it's supposed to be Lola, being killed."

"Oh," Pam North said. "I — "

"Look," Bill Weigand said, then, and Pam had never heard so much bafflement in his assured voice. (Not even when he's really baffled, Pam thought.) "Look. Do all these people have to be here?" He spoke to the excited man; he waved a hand generally around the shadowy open space, which did seem rather full of people.

"Mine do," the man said. "And for God's sake, Inspector, keep your voice down! They'll hear you out front." He put his hand into his hair; then he put his head down in his hands.

"Now, Doctor," the voice of Inspector Brunk came muffled through canvas, thicker even than it had sounded earlier. "There's a

246

small point on which I'd like your opinion."
Beat. "As a medical man, you'll understand."

"Anything —" a voice which presumably
was that of the substituting Tom said. "—
this nasty business, Inspector —"

It was confused, confusing, even absurd.
And yet, for Liza, the very grotesqueness of
this mingling of what was real and what was
merely pretended, the way the untrue almost
parodied the true, became a babbling comment upon it, enhanced the growing dread
she felt that all that was happening was part of
an irremediable collapse of all that mattered;
of all that had, in Brian's apartment only a little time ago, seemed regained, almost assured.

"Earlier this evening," the inspector was
saying, to someone, his voice rumbling
through the canvas walls of the vicar's living
room in Surrey — "earlier this evening, now,
where would you say you were?"

"Where's Pine?" Bill Weigand asked the
dark detective sergeant. "What does he say?"

"Dressing room," Stein said. "Nothing.
He's still out. He —"

"For God's *sake*," the excitable man said,
becoming excited again, pulling at his tie
again. "They'll *hear* you out front!"

"Now, sir," the rumble came through the
canvas walls. "If you'll just whistle this little

247

tune? Just as an experiment, like?"

"Through here, I guess," a voice said from somewhere in the shadows, and at its clear, unmuted sound the excited man clutched his hair and appeared about to pull it out. Then he leaped up and rushed off into the shadows, going "Sh-h-h-h. Sh-h-h-h!"

A young man in white coat, white trousers, came out of the shadows into which the excited man had gone, and he looked astonished. Two other men in white, carrying a stretcher, came after him. One of them stumbled over something and said "Jeeze!"

The phrase from the madrigal was whistled on-stage. "Thank you, sir," the inspector's grumble said. "Now, miss, if I could trouble . . ."

There was a kind of absurd, cluttered speed about everything, but it was the speed of confusion; it was meaningless.

"This way, Doctor," Sergeant Stein said. "I'm through here. Watch it."

"Lieutenant," Liza said. "Lieutenant. Please — where's Brian? Is he — "

Bill Weigand looked at her. He shook his head.

"I'm sorry," he said. "We found him back here. We're — "

But nothing could be finished. The excited

man came back, pulling at his necktie. He gestured behind him as he came, and his eyes were as wild as his hair.

"More!" he said, advancing to Bill Weigand, looking at him fiercely. "For God's *sake!*"

Then behind him, making their way back of the set as the others had done, Colonel and Mrs. Raymond Whiteside appeared, Mrs. Whiteside in advance and, evidently, in fury.

"Really!" she said, when she saw Weigand. "This man of yours — " Words failed her. "Really," she said, a grande dame confronted by a public nuisance.

"Now Barbara," Colonel Whiteside said. "Now Barbara." He shook his head at Weigand.

"But really, Lieutenant, I must say," he said to Bill Weigand. "To be — summoned, in this fashion."

Bill said, "You were — "

" . . . Then perhaps you will be so good, sir, as to tell me why . . . " That was Inspector Brunk, mumbling from the stage; mumbling on a note of satisfaction, of incipient triumph. . . .

"Voices!" the excited man said. "Oh — please! Voices! They'll *hear* you."

(And still she had not seen Brian; still she

249

did not know; still over all that was important, that was vital, was this idiot babbling,
this meaningless confusion. Oh Brian —
where are you, Brian?)

"How much longer does that last?" Bill
Weigand demanded of the excited man, and
Weigand's voice was drawn thin with irritation. But before the man could answer, the
ambulance surgeon came out of another
shadow, followed by the two men with the
stretcher. The stretcher was still empty.

"A bump on the head," the ambulance surgeon said. "Might have got it walking into a
door. Why it put him out I don't know."

"Is he — " Weigand began, but then the
mumble of the inspector rose; became the tri-
umphant thunder of British justice. "Then,
sir, I must warn you that — " the on-stage
detective said and, as these words came
through the canvas, the excited man stood up,
seemed to be counting desperately although
he made no sound, and raised his hands, fists
clenched. A look of horror began to spread
over his face and then there was the sharp,
reverberating crack of a pistol fired close by.
Everybody jumped; Stein whirled, reaching
inside his coat.

"The wrong *beat!*" the excited man said, to
no one. "Bring her *down,* for God's *sake!*"

And then, as the sound of the descending curtain momentarily dominated, the excited man straightened his necktie, smoothed his hair and, generally, beamed around at Weigand, at Mr. and Mrs. North and at Liza, at Sergeant Stein and Colonel and Mrs. Whiteside and the man who had come with them.

"And there we are," he said, in quiet and cultivated tones. "Went off rather well, I thought? Considering?" His tone patently asked approbation.

"Wonderfully," Pam North said, giving it. "Who got shot?"

"The physician, of course," the no longer excited man told her, as if surprised. "You mean you haven't seen it? But my *dear*. It's running months."

"I'm sorry," Pam said. "I've really been meaning to."

Then it was suddenly much lighter in the area backstage; then the vicar, the couple from London, the inspector and the pretty young woman, whose part in the whole proceedings remained mysterious, came off-stage through the door into which, it seemed hours ago, Sherman Pine had incontinently pitched. The young man named Tom came after them, and everybody gathered around him and began shaking his hand. "Wonderful, my

251

boy," the no longer excited man told him. "I knew you could do it."

"Now!" Bill Weigand said, and, although his voice was not greatly raised, it seemed that he shouted. "Now — all of you. I want . . ."

They were back at the Sutton Place house and Liza O'Brien was beside Brian Halder at last, looking up into his set, unresponsive face.

"Let's have it again, Mr. Halder," Bill said. "Why did you try to kill Pine?"

But Pine was not dead. He was not even badly hurt. There was a white adhesive bandage on the back of his head; now and then he pressed the palm of one hand against his forehead, as if his head ached and he were trying to press the pain away.

"I didn't," Brian said. "But what's the use of telling you?"

His voice was harsh, angry. He seemed unconscious of Liza's fingers, pressing his hand desperately, pressing until her slender fingers ached. *Not this way*, she tried to tell him with her fingers. *Oh, not this way.*

"You wanted to see Mr. Pine," Bill Weigand said, and there was little to be told from his voice; it was a voice stating facts, not for the first time. "You made several efforts to see

252

him, at first with Miss O'Brien. Then, after the curtain went up for the last act, you left your seat — perhaps you had never gone to it — went down the aisle, through the door to the stage area, around behind the set and came upon Mr. Pine just as he was about to make his entrance. You hit him, intending to kill him. Why?"

Brian Halder merely shook his head.

"Or," Bill Weigand said, "didn't you try to kill him? Did you try merely to make it *seem* that you had tried to kill him?"

Again, Brian Halder did not reply; again he merely shook his head. Bill Weigand gave him a chance to amplify, but did not seem surprised, did not seem disturbed, when Halder continued not to speak. Weigand seemed about to continue, but when Lieutenant Colonel Whiteside spoke, turned to him politely, waited politely.

"Isn't it the law, Lieutenant, that a man is entitled to talk to his attorney before he answers questions?" Lieutenant Colonel Whiteside asked. He was as polite as Weigand.

"Right," Bill Weigand told him. "But then, Mr. Halder isn't talking, is he?"

"It seems to me," Whiteside said, "that you are attempting to get him to talk, Lieutenant."

"Really, Raymond," Mrs. Whiteside said. "Brian is a grown man. He can take care of himself." Her voice sounded as if, contemptuously, she did not believe what she said. But her husband said, mildly, "Of course, my dear."

But Brian wasn't taking care of himself, wasn't trying to take care of himself. That was why it was all so frightening. Since they had come to the house, Brian obviously in custody, the others with scarcely more choice, Brian had said almost nothing, had let his face show almost nothing. He had seemed to accept aloneness; it was as if, in some fashion, he had withdrawn himself from all of them, even from Liza. Momentarily, when Liza took his hand, his fingers had responded to the pressure of hers, but then that response ended and, although he did not try to free his hand, the contact remaining between them was meaningless.

"We just wanted to talk to Mr. Pine," Liza heard herself say, and was shocked at her own voice, at the fear palpable in it, at the inadequacy of the words she used. Weigand turned away from the Whitesides and looked at her and waited. She looked up at Brian, trying with a look to arouse him and then Weigand, too, looked at Brian Halder.

"She had nothing to do with it," Brian said.

"What did you want to talk to Mr. Pine about, Miss O'Brien?" Weigand asked, when the tall young man did not go on.

"About —" she began, and stopped. About shaking the truth out of him? About making him admit, or hearing him deny, that, because he was in love with Brian's mother, and with the Halder money, he had killed an aging man with strychnine and folded his slight body, grotesquely, in a pen meant for an animal?

"Go on," Weigand said. "About J. K. Halder's murder, of course. At any rate, that's what he told you?" "He," Weigand's head movement indicated, was Brian.

She looked up at Brian again, desperately, seeking to get some guidance from his fixed face, thinking that, by saying even so little as she had said, she had made matters worse for him. She saw him hesitate, felt his uncertainty.

"Not about the murder," Brian said, and his voice was harsh. "And, I didn't have anything to do with Pine's getting hit."

Bill Weigand did not seem surprised at his answer. He seemed, without comment, merely to hear it.

"Suppose, Mr. Halder," Weigand said, "I

255

give you the possibilities as they occur to me. We found you in Pine's dressing room, ostensibly waiting for him. You seemed to be surprised to hear he had been attacked. One possibility is that you were surprised, that you *were* merely waiting for him. But obviously, you weren't waiting merely to have a little chat about — oh, say, theories of acting?"

Brian Halder looked at Weigand for a moment and then away from him; looked at the others grouped at the end of the long living room, as if from one of them, not from him, the answer should come. He looked, Pam North thought, longest at his mother; at Pine, she thought, Brian Halder did not look at all.

The members of the family, and Pine and Liza O'Brien with them, now joined with them, sat almost in a semi-circle, their backs to the windows which overlooked the East River. The semi-circle was irregular; J. K. Halder's oldest son, "Junior," sat with his wife on the long sofa under the windows, and Barbara Whiteside, erect for all the softness of the sofa, her piled white hair undisturbed in regularity, sat next to her sister-in-law, but seemed detached from her; seemed, by intention, to leave a physical space between them which was meant to emphasize a separation of a different kind. In a chair at the end of the sofa, next to his wife, was Lieutenant Colonel Whiteside — a firm, heavy man with a strong face. Or was it, Pam North thought, that he has adopted an expression of strength; an expression put on a face not quite designed for it? Whiteside looked back at Brian Halder, at Weigand, without change of expression.

Almost, not quite, at right angles to them, opposite the spiral staircase, was another sofa, smaller than the one under the windows. There Pine sat, holding his head, looking up now as they waited for Brian, looking away again as Brian's eyes passed over him unseeingly. And next to Pine, one hand on his arm, sat Mary Halder.

She looked young, Pam North thought; young and fragile and, certainly, very pretty. She was in a black evening dress, her white shoulders bare — a pretty woman, younger than her years. If I were a man, Pam thought, I'd want to protect her. But —

Brian Halder stood across the room from his mother and Pine and Liza O'Brien sat in a chair beside him, her right hand in his left. But she's holding his hand, not the other way around, Pam thought; the poor kid, Pam thought. What's the matter with the man?

Jerry and Pam more or less faced the members of the family. As if we were a jury, Pam thought. And Bill Weigand, with Mullins a little behind him, stood where he could look at all of the Halders, at Pine and Liza, and he was looking at them now. He looked at them slowly, carefully, and then back at Brian Halder.

"Well?" Bill said.

"I had a fool idea," Brian said. "Nothing came of it, so it doesn't make any difference. I didn't see him. I didn't see anyone, except somebody — some man — who told me where the dressing room was. Pine's dressing room. The next person I saw was one of your men." He looked at Mullins, at Stein, at a precinct man, all standing a little in the background, "I don't see him here," Brian said.

"And at that time you didn't know Mr. Pine had been attacked?"

"No." Brian Halder looked at Weigand. His face was still set. "I told you that. You don't believe me. So what?"

Bill Weigand shrugged to that.

"Mr. Pine?" he said. "Did you see Mr. Halder backstage? Talk to him?"

Pine raised his head. He said, "Huh?" with un-actorlike enunciation. Bill repeated it.

"I didn't see him," Pine said. "I was waiting to go on. Somebody stepped up behind me and hit me." For a moment he looked almost amused. "Must have been a hell of an entrance," he said.

"You hadn't planned to see Mr. Halder?" Weigand asked the actor. "Didn't have anything in particular you wanted to talk to him about?"

Pine shook his head. Then he appeared to wish he hadn't and clutched it.

"Poor boy," Mary Halder said.

She had not spoken before, or Pam could not remember she had spoken. She had been in the house, dressed as she was now, when Weigand brought the family home, brought the Norths with the family, and she had gasped when she saw the bandage on Pine's head, and had gone to him. They had spoken briefly, presumably he had told her what had happened. She had greeted the others; smiled at Liza O'Brien; greeted her own son with almost equal detachment. But whether that was of her choice, or because of something in his manner, it had been hard to determine. Pam had felt, obscurely, that in some manner Brian had warned her off. After that, she had merely sat quietly; one might almost have thought numbly.

But now she seemed to have come to a decision, and one which had nothing to do with her almost absently expressed sympathy for Pine. Because she did not look at him as she spoke, but looked instead at Brian and Liza beside him. What she saw in her son's eyes, what she had put into her own, there was no way of knowing, but then she shook her head quickly, as if telling him he was wrong.

"Brian," she said, and in the silence her voice was unexpectedly strong and clear. "Whatever it is dear — everything's got to come out, now."

She looked at him, must have met refusal in his eyes.

"It will be all right, Brinny," she said. "Whatever it is."

It was more the tone than the words which made so oddly touching what Mary Halder said to the tall young man who looked down at her, his face still set. Or perhaps, Pam thought, it was the tone and her use of the diminutive. She must have called him that when he was a baby, Pam thought. And now, all at once, he's — why, to her he's a baby again. That's what it is.

"You must, dear," Mary Halder said, in the same tone.

Then Brian looked down for a moment at Liza O'Brien. She said nothing in words; said with her eyes, with her face, with all the hope and expectancy in her, "Yes, Brian. Please, Brian."

Then Brian turned to Bill Weigand.

"I thought there was a chance Pine knew something about — Father's death," he said. "I wanted to try to find out. But — you knew that."

"Right," Bill said. "I assumed that. You didn't see him, you say. Didn't talk to him."

"No."

"Wait a minute," Pine said, and started up. "What the hell?"

"Not now, Mr. Pine," Bill Weigand said. "Go on, Mr. Halder. You thought Pine might know something? Why? Because you thought he might have a motive?"

Brian's fixed expression changed little, but it changed enough.

"Go on, dear," Mary Halder said, her voice still clear, very gentle. And Liza's fingers tightened on his own; this time his fingers responded for a second.

"Partly that," Brian said, and he spoke slowly, looked only at Weigand. "Partly — I think he was at the shop. I don't mean the night Dad was — was killed. I don't know about that. Last night. When Liza was hurt."

It came out then, slowly, was brought out carefully by Brian Halder, who stood facing

261

Weigand; who qualified much of what he said.

It had been when he was taking the sick dog, the dog named Clytemnestra, to the veterinary hospital. A block or two from the shop he had seen a man going toward West Kepp Street. He had been too far away to be certain, the light had been too dim.

"But for what it's worth," he said, "I thought it was Pine. Or, rather, it occurred to me a minute or two later, that it might have been Pine. And — Liza had seen somebody when she got there. Somebody looking in the window." He looked down at Liza, and Bill Weigand looked at her. She shook her head.

"I don't know," she said. "It could have been — anyone. A shadow."

Weigand turned to the actor, then, and Pine was looking at Mary Halder. Mary nodded.

How careful everybody is of her, Pam thought. But is she that — that breakable? And — does she *want* them to be so careful?

"Well, Mr. Pine?" Bill Weigand asked.

Pine cleared his throat. The sound was unexpected.

"Really," Mrs. Whiteside said.

"He could have seen me, I guess," Pine said. "I was there."

Now everybody looked at him. It was clear that Mary Halder had known what his answer would be; the others seemed surprised. Even Brian Halder seemed surprised.

"Right," Bill said. "Tell us about it, Mr. Pine."

Again Pine looked at the slight, pretty woman beside him.

"We both had the idea," she said. "That is — we talked it over. Because — " now she looked directly at Bill Weigand — "we knew what you might be thinking, Lieutenant. What you could be thinking."

Bill's face had no expression as he looked back at Mary Halder. Then he shifted his eyes to Pine's face, and waited. Brian Halder made a sound, started to speak his mother's name, but she smiled across the room at him and said, in her light, clear voice, "Don't be frightened, Brinny. It's not the way — "

"Go on, Mr. Pine," Bill Weigand said. He looked around at the others. "We'll do one thing at a time," he told them.

"Well," Pine said, "it was this way — "

He needs somebody to write lines for him, Pam North thought, as the actor hesitated and looked once more, as if for guidance, to Mary Halder. She smiled at him, turned to Weigand.

"Mr. Pine and I probably will get married in a few weeks," she said. "We would have some months ago if I had been free." She looked at Weigand, smiled faintly. "Our friendship is a little deeper than I admitted before," she said. She paused a moment and went on. "Mr. Pine has very little money of his own and what I will receive from my husband's estate will make it easier — much easier." She looked again at Pine; then at her son. "Men are so afraid of the obvious," she said. "So — foolish."

"Really, Mary," Barbara Whiteside said. "How — how impetuous of you! How — straightforward."

And she hesitated over the final word, appearing to choose it from many others — from among words which would have meant something quite different and been more apt. And, Pam North thought, Mary Halder flushed a little, and momentarily.

"Dear Barbs," she said. "Always so — "

But Jennifer Halder had got up from her place beside her husband, had crossed to Mary Halder, held out both hands to her.

"It's grand, Mary," she said. "I'm so glad."

Mary Halder took the younger woman's hands, smiled up at her. Then she relinquished Jennifer's hands and looked at her son, who still stood, whose face was still unaltered.

"Poor Brinny," Mary said, and the lightness in her tone was not real. "It'll be all right, Brinny." She shook her head slightly, she was gently tolerant. "Couldn't you see everybody knew, dear?" she asked him. "Sherman and I could."

It was because Mary Halder and Sherman Pine could see the obvious (although I'll bet she had to tell him, Pam North thought) that Pine had gone to the shop, had been there about the time Liza was hit from behind, knocked unconscious. That, at least, was the way Pine finally told it, seeking words, finding them slowly.

They had realized, he said, that a good deal pointed to them. "The damned dog, for one," he said and looked at Bill Weigand and waited.

"Aegisthus," Bill said. "Right. Go on."

"Mary looked it up," Pine said. "Aegisthus was this guy — "

"We know that," Bill told him.

"It was like the old guy had been — pointing at us," Sherman Pine said. He shook his head, as if in wonder. "What kind of a guy — " He shook his head again.

"Even without that," Mary Halder said.

"We've always been the obvious ones. Isn't that so, Lieutenant? Isn't it always the widow — or the man whose wife is killed — you think of first? Suspect first. Particularly when — "

"Mary!" Brian said. His voice was not harsh, now; it was anxious, it held a kind of desperate concern.

"Oh," his mother said, "but we didn't. Brian. Didn't you know?"

"Oh," Brian said. "I — of course I — "

But he hit it too hard, Pam North thought. Even now, he isn't sure. And Liza, gripping Brian's hand, was wordless even in her mind, feeling his fear almost as her own, knowing no words, but only the pressure of her fingers, which might assuage it.

"The damnedest thing," Pine said, and none of this seemed to touch him; he remained in the circle of his own bewilderment at J. K. Halder's oblique insinuations. "He named one of the dogs Clytemnestra, too. All out of this Greek Play. And a black cat — "

"Right," Bill said. He was being patient, Pam thought. He needed to be. "What did you do, Mr. Pine?"

Sherman Pine and Mary Halder had talked it over; had decided that they would have to help themselves.

266

"Because," he said earnestly, "we hadn't done anything. It just looked as though — "

He sought acceptance of this statement from Weigand. "Go on," Weigand said, his voice without comment, his manner neither accepting nor rejecting the assertion. Pine seemed baffled for a moment; he looked down at Mary Halder. She nodded to him, encouraging him.

He and Mrs. Halder, Pine said, had "put their heads together." They had decided that their best chance was to find out what Felix Sneddiger had known and why he had come to the Sutton Place house, and found death there. "Because," Pine said, "neither of us had seen him. That is — "

"He only knows what I told him," Mary Halder said. "They see that, Sherman."

"They'd better — " Pine began, but her head signalled him again, and he went on.

Mary Halder knew that Sneddiger had been in the habit of dropping into the pet shop, almost without regard for time, when he had reason to think J. K. Halder was there, and awake. "Wanted to play chess, for God's sake," Pine said, bafflement again in his voice. So they had thought — "that is, Mrs. Halder did most of the thinking, I guess" — that Sneddiger might have dropped in, or started to drop in, on the night Halder was killed, and that he might have seen something. But they had thought — again Pine indicated Mary Halder, the source of thought — that if he had actually gone in, the murderer would have seen him and, since he had proved himself ready to kill, would then have killed. So they had thought that Sneddiger might have seen something from outside, perhaps through the shop window.

But neither of them had known whether that was possible; whether, precisely, it was possible for Sneddiger to have seen without being seen. So they decided that he would go down to the shop and try to find out. They had been in Pine's apartment when this decision was reached, and Mary had waited there for him.

And then, involuntarily, Brian Halder sighed. It was a revealing sound.

"No, Brinny," Mary said. "I wasn't there." She looked at Liza. "Did you think I — " she began, and Liza said, quickly, "I never did, Mrs. Halder. Really I didn't."

"Did you think you saw your mother, Mr. Halder?" Bill Weigand asked. "Perhaps in that passageway you — didn't enter?"

"I just heard someone. I thought of Pine because — well," Brian said, "I thought I'd

268

seen him nearby. I guess I — "

"Poor Brinny," Mrs. Halder said. Then, unexpectedly, she laughed, her laughter low, amused. "We aren't that — inseparable, dear," she said. Then Brian Halder flushed. "It's all right, Brinny," his mother said. "Only — you mustn't be *too* much like your father."

That's unkind, Liza O'Brien thought. Can't you see, he's not at all like his father, so much he wants not to be like his father? That it was always you? And then she thought, until now. She looked up at Brian and, this time, his gaze met hers, this time the aloofness faded from his deep-set, intent eyes. His eyes were unhappy still, worried, but now she found acceptance in them.

Mary had remained in Sherman Pine's apartment and he had gone to West Kepp Street; this was after the theater, after they had talked it over for some time. That was their story. Pine had found a single light burning in the pet shop and had spent some time peering into it through the window, moving to various positions, trying different angles. If Miss O'Brien had seen somebody looking in, probably it had, Pine said, been he. And — he had satisfied himself that someone going down the steps to the shop, or starting down them, and happening to look through either the door or the window, could see and probably identify anyone within, even with only the single bulb lighted.

Pine could not be at all exact as to the time he had reached the shop, except that it was some time after midnight; perhaps in the neighborhood of twelve-thirty. He had not seen Brian Halder carrying the dog, but he thought he might well not have. He was trying to find West Kepp Street and had begun to think he had missed it. In the end, however, he had found he had been all the time on the right way.

And Brian was no more able to be exact as to the time he had left the shop with the boxer, and, a few minutes later, seen the man he thought — belatedly — might be Pine. Again it was "some time after midnight." But he thought the trip to the hospital and back had taken around three quarters of an hour.

"Miss O'Brien?" Weigand said. "I suppose you didn't look at your watch at all?"

"No," she said. "I wasn't more than — oh, perhaps five minutes — in the shop before — before somebody hit me. But I don't know when I got there. Of course, if it was Mr. Pine I saw, obviously he got there first."

"You saw somebody apparently looking in the window," Weigand said. "But when you got there, there was nobody. You didn't see anybody walk off up the street? Or, pass anybody coming your way?"

She shook her head. She looked at Sherman Pine.

"Of course," she said, "the street isn't well lighted."

Bill Weigand shook his own head at that. "Well?" he said, this time to Sherman Pine.

Pine seemed puzzled.

"I didn't try to hide, if that's what you're getting at." he said. "I didn't go into the shop and hide and wait for Miss O'Brien, so I could hit her."

Bill Weigand listened to him.

"There are plenty of places to hide in the shop," he said. "Plenty of shadows. Of things to get under."

"No," Pine said. "Not me, Lieutenant."

"You looked in the window a few times," Bill said. "Through the door. Satisfied yourself. Then just walked away. Openly. Right?"

"That's the way — " Pine began, and then stopped. "Wait a minute," he said. "There's a passage next to the shop. You know?"

Weigand indicated that he knew.

"I thought for a moment there might be another window, opening off the passage," Pine said. "I stepped in the passage for a moment. But there wasn't anything — just a brick wall."

"At the rear of the building there's a window," Bill told him. "Barred. Opening into the place Mr. Halder slept. Did you find that?"

Pine hadn't. He had gone only perhaps ten feet into the passage, satisfied himself there was no window, gone back.

"But," he said, "while I was in there, Miss O'Brien might have come along. I mean — she might have seen me looking in the window in front and then I might have gone into the passage and seemed — "

"Right," Bill said. He looked at Pine. "You cover things, Mr. Pine," he said. He looked at Liza.

"It could have been that way," she said.

"Right," Weigand said again. "It could have been." He paused a moment. "Then you went out of the passage, without looking into the shop again, and went back to your apartment, Mr. Pine."

"Yes," Pine said.

"And Mrs. Halder was still there?"

"Oh yes," Pine said. "Of course."

"I had been there all along," Mary Halder said. Her voice was light, assured. "Of course, I can't prove it, can I?"

272

"I don't know," Weigand said. "Can't you?"

"No," she said. She smiled at Weigand, but her smile was not warming.

"You want to make it clear," she said, "that I could have gone down to the shop, getting there after Sherman did, struck Miss O'Brien, somehow got back to his apartment and been there when he arrived? Is that it?"

"Couldn't you?" Weigand asked.

She said she didn't know. She would think —

"Did you go by subway, Mr. Pine?" Weigand asked.

Pine had. And — he had waited several minutes for an uptown local at the Sheridan Square station. He lived four blocks — four cross-town blocks — from the subway station nearest his apartment, and he had walked them. He agreed that the whole trip might have taken considerable time. Yes, perhaps as much as half an hour.

"And I could have taken a cab," Mary Halder said. "Only — I didn't." She looked at Weigand intently. "Why should I?" she asked.

Lieutenant William Weigand shrugged to that one. Why, he said, should anyone? Presumably, with the intention of silencing Miss O'Brien, who might be thought to know too much.

"Somebody followed her to the shop. Somebody hit her," Weigand pointed out, his tone level. "Presumably would have killed her if — if not interrupted by Mr. Halder. Presumably because somebody thought she knew too much." He looked at Liza then.

"Do you, Miss O'Brien?" he asked.

"No," she said.

"Whatever Mr. Sneddiger may have known, he didn't tell you?"

"No," she said. "Oh no."

Weigand looked at her for a long moment. Then, he said he hoped that was true.

XI

Thursday, 12:25 A.M. to 2:35 A.M.

"I'd like to believe you, Miss O'Brien," Lieutenant Weigand said. He looked at her very steadily. "For your own sake," he said.

The light fell in a certain way, made Weigand's thin face planes and shadows to Liza, masked its expression. He seemed to be trying to force something into her mind, but she felt only confused, and now very tired, wholly spent. She tried again, so assured did Weigand seem, to seek back into her memory to discover whether he might not be right; whether the little bright-eyed man had said something, before or after they discovered the hideous thing cramped in the animal pen, which, if Weigand knew of it, might end this slow — groping; this nightmare-like search through fog. Almost any assurance would be better than this, Liza O'Brien thought, her mind exhaustedly turning over the past, turning over words which had no meaning.

Almost — but no, that was not true.

"Because," Weigand said, "you are in danger until you tell. If you have something to tell. Someone thinks you have, you know. Someone here." He looked slowly from one to another of those in the room — at Jasper and Jennifer Halder, at the substantial, matter-of-fact Whiteside, and his white-haired wife; at Mary Halder and Pine and at Mary's tall, dark-faced son. "One of you," Weigand said. "Because one of you killed Halder, killed Sneddiger because he knew too much, tried to kill Miss O'Brien and — perhaps — Mr. Pine. One of you here."

He paused. He looked back around the circle, slowly, carefully.

"Something happened in this room Monday evening," he said then. "I think it was in this room. It may have been at dinner. As a result of what happened, Mr. Halder decided to change his will. One of you knew, or at any rate suspected, that he would do that. One of you followed him to the shop. One of you took strychnine and a hypodermic. How those things happened to be available I don't pretend to know. I'd guess that one of you killed an animal that way once, and — didn't use up the supply."

He looked from face to face, and Liza, her

276

mind dull, looked as Lieutenant Weigand did from one to another. To her, none of the faces revealed anything. She looked back at Weigand.

"One of you went to the shop," he said. "You may have given Mr. Halder a chance to change his mind. Perhaps you did not. You injected the poison and watched him die. To make us believe that his eccentricity had finally culminated in suicide, you put the body in the pen, pressed his fingers on the syringe, put the syringe and what was left of the poison in the cupboard in which he kept medicines for the animals.

"But you were seen. I think you were seen. I think Mrs. Halder and Mr. Pine guessed" — he hesitated over the word, his tone enclosed it in quotation marks — " 'guessed' correctly. It was probably just that simple. Probably Mr. Sneddiger looked in the window, saw one of you there. Perhaps he thought it was — oh, say, Mr. Halder." Weigand indicated Brian's tall half-brother. "Perhaps he had heard his friend talk about the family, even describe members of it. At any rate, he came here to be sure he was right. He was right."

Weigand paused again; his voice had grown heavy on the last sentence. He repeated it.

He was making them see it, take it in, Liza

thought. And she saw the little man in the depths of the closet, crumpled as if he had been tossed there, discarded there; saw again his horrible face, the marks of fingers on his throat, and the eyes — oh, she thought, will I ever forget the eyes? Please —

"But Sneddiger had been for a time with Miss O'Brien," Weigand went on. "One of you believes he told her something; believes it whatever Miss O'Brien says. And — you may be right. There is no point in my denying that; in Miss O'Brien's not admitting what it — might mean."

Now he was looking at her; waiting for her. She moved her head slowly, wearily. Why doesn't he leave me alone? she wondered. Why doesn't —

"One of you tried to kill her," Weigand said. "Would have succeeded if, I suppose, Mr. Brian Halder hadn't returned when he did." He looked at Brian. "I suppose that," he said. "I don't know. Mr. Halder may be lying. On one or two points I'm certain he is."

All the heads turned toward Brian. It was strange, frightening, to see the detachment, the speculation, in those alien eyes. Liza pressed his hand, but his fingers did not answer hers.

"But more than one of you is lying," Weigand said. "Perhaps for what seem good reasons. And at least one for — for the obvious reason. Because you did the things I've just told you."

He paused again.

"I'm not expecting anyone to confess," he said. "Obviously, that would be absurd. But we will find out, you know." He shook his head slowly, as if deprecating the stupidity of the one he was talking to. "We'll dig back; we're digging back. We'll find who once bought strychnine to — kill rats, was it? Or to — put to sleep — some pet? We'll find out all about you, you know. All about all of you. Or didn't you know?"

He half smiled, then.

"One of you thinks, 'He's bluffing. He's talking big. Trying to scare me,'" Weigand said. "That is very stupid. But the whole thing has been stupid, of course. It is stupid to kill. Stupid to kill in this — spectacular way. One of you has been stupid that way." He might have been talking to children. "One of you will do something stupid again," he said. "Will do something. Or forget to do something. Take too big a risk, or fail to take a necessary risk."

As if involuntarily, against his will, Weigand looked at Liza; looked away again, almost guiltily.

"I — " Weigand said then, and was interrupted. He was interrupted by Aegisthus, who came into the room gayly, apparently from his lodgings below stairs; who was clearly delighted to see so many people, anticipatory of their varying odors. He began the rounds, but Mary Halder called him and he went to her, put forepaws on her knees, looked up at her with enquiry in his eyes and with his tongue slightly hanging out. He was told he was supposed to be in bed; he wagged his rear end. "Bed," Mary Halder repeated. He stopped wagging but continued to beam, contending that the word had not been spoken, or had been spoken in jest. "Bed!" Mary Halder said, firmly.

The little black dog continued to look at her, hopefully indicating disbelief.

"Bed, Aegisthus," Mary Halder said. "Go to *bed*."

He got down, then. He looked back at her over a shoulder, from the corners of his eyes. She would relent, of course; of course she did not mean it. He moved reluctantly toward the area behind the circular staircase; toward the stairs leading down to darkness, away from the enticing odors, the pleasant sounds, of humans.

"Really, Mary," Barbara Whiteside said.

"That dog! Of all times!"

Aegisthus looked at Barbara Whiteside briefly. He looked away. He looked back at Mary Halder, but she made a negative motion with her head. Aegisthus became smaller; he was a dog abused, crushed by human ingratitude. He went behind the spiral staircase; he thumped down other stairs, not rapidly.

The appearance, the unhappy withdrawal, of Aegisthus relaxed the tension which Weigand had slowly built. Liza could feel the change as now, with the dog gone, the others looked again at the detective. Apparently, Weigand could feel the change too. He did not resume the sentence which had been interrupted. Instead, he said, "Right," with a kind of finality.

"Before I go," he said and smiled faintly at the look of relief on the faces around him. "Oh, yes, I'm going. It's late; you can have some sleep. Tomorrow we'll start again — the slow way, the hard way — unless one of you, or several of you, decide to tell what you know. Tomorrow, anyway, you'll have the chance. But, before I go tonight, I want to get one thing clear."

Briefly, he told them what it was. They had all, he understood, come down to this room Monday night after finishing dinner. Here, presumably, had happened whatever had moved J. K. Halder to his sudden departure, to his eventually fatal decision about the will. Now, Weigand wanted all of them to sit as they had sat that evening, insofar as possible, do what they had done then.

There was a moment of hesitancy, then they began to move. They rearranged themselves, Pine withdrew entirely, the place he had occupied beside Mary Halder was left vacant.

Only Mrs. Whiteside seemed at first not to remember, looked around doubtfully.

"I don't think I — " she began and interrupted herself. "I stayed upstairs for a few moments," she said. "When I came down, Father was already leaving. I — " She looked at the stairs, back at Weigand. "Really, Lieutenant," she said.

It was not necessary for her to go upstairs, Weigand told her. If she would merely come out of the circle? She did so, imposingly. Liza also abandoned her place, moving reluctantly from Brian's side, joining the Norths in a area which seemed for spectators. Or was it for the jury? Pam North patted Liza's arm, smiled but did not speak.

"Mr. Halder?" Weigand said asked, and Mary Halder put her hand on the seat Pine had left. "Here," she said.

"Mullins," Weigand said and then stopped. "No," he said. "Wait. Pam, will you sit there? Where Mr. Halder sat?"

(I wish, Pam thought, I knew what Bill's up to. She had been wishing that for some time. He's not like himself so he's up to something, Pam thought, because he usually doesn't needle people unless —)

"Please, Pam," Bill Weigand said, and she went to sit beside Mary Halder.

"You can see the foyer?" Bill asked, and Pam looked. She could see the foyer.

"Now — Mr. Pine," Bill said, "will you go down to the foyer and stand about where you did Monday night?"

Pine looked at Mary Halder. It was evident that her eyes told him to go. He went.

They watched him walk the length of the room, saw his stature diminish slightly as he went down the steps to the foyer level.

"Now," Weigand said. "You have all come down. Except Mrs. Whiteside. What happened?"

But they looked at one another, and seemed puzzled. It was Lieutenant Colonel Whiteside who spoke, finally.

"Nothing," he said. "At first, anyway. We — somebody had served coffee. I offered brandy around. I think Father Halder took some. I suppose we talked, but I don't remember — "

For how long? Perhaps ten minutes, perhaps a little longer.

"Then?"

"Then," Mary Halder said, "the doorbell rang and Burns answered it. There are stairs directly to the foyer, you know. From the kitchen area. The door opened and — well, Sherman came in. But I — I guess none of us paid any attention." She smiled at Weigand. "This silly house," she said. "No service entrance. The front bell's always ringing."

"You thought it was a delivery of some sort?"

Mary shrugged. She had not, she indicated, thought about it one way or another.

But then Burns had come up the steps into the living room and started down it, and, a little way down, had indicated, without words, that Mary Halder was being asked for.

"I got up, and then I saw it was Sherman," she said. "I went to the foyer. Shall I now?"

"Please," Weigand said.

She got up from beside Pam North and moved, unhurriedly, the length of the room. She joined Pine there. Weigand looked interrogatively at Pam North.

"Yes," she said. "I can see them."

"And recognize Mr. Pine?"

"Of course," Pam said. "But then, I know he's there, don't I? I mean if I didn't — if I thought it was going to be the boy from the cleaner's, only it would have been pretty late for that."

"If you knew Mr. Pine fairly well," Bill said.

Pam looked.

"Yes," she said. "Of course, what one person can see another — "

"Right," Bill said. He addressed the others, generally. Had the elder Halder had normal vision?

"Twenty-twenty," Whiteside said. "Thereabouts, anyway. He was far-sighted."

"Right," Bill said. "Now, at this point, what happened?"

"Aegisthus came down," Jasper Halder said. His voice was oddly harsh. "Came down fast and yelped. Looked around, heard Mary's voice, apparently. Went to tell her his troubles."

"Down the stairs?" Bill asked, nodding at the spiral staircase.

They all agreed.

"He had been lying on one of the beds," Barbara Whiteside said. "He's very badly trained. I put him off, closed the door of the room. I suppose that — annoyed him. He's not supposed to be above this floor at any time."

Mary Halder had come back with Pine.

"He's just a little dog," Mary said. "A puppy, almost. Barbara's very — stern with him."

"Really, Mary," Barbara Whiteside said. "Somebody's got to be."

Mary did not deny this.

"I came back, carrying Aegisthus," Mary Halder said. "And then J. K. stood up. He — he looked at us. That is, at me, of course."

Bill looked at Pam. She stood up.

"Then he said something like, 'I'm going, now. Good night,' " Mary Halder said. "And — well, just went."

Weigand looked around at the others.

"That's the way it was," Whiteside said. "Only, Barbara came down — oh, just as Mary was returning with the dog. I think it was about then, dear?"

The last was to his wife. She returned from her exclusion, joined the others. She had, she said, reached the foot of the stairs almost at the moment her father had stood up.

"He looked hard at Mary," Barbara said. "Of course, dear, I don't mean — " This last was to Mary.

286

"I've already said that," Mary Halder said. "I'm sure the lieutenant heard me, Barbs."

The edge in her voice was faint; it might almost have been the edge of amusement.

But Bill had turned away for the moment, was conferring with Sergeant Mullins. When he turned back, he was almost as abrupt in leave-taking as J. K. Halder had been. They were to stay in town, stay available; they were to see that they could be reached at any time. Weigand gestured with his head to Pam and Jerry North and started toward the door. Then he seemed to remember something.

"Oh, Miss O'Brien," he said. "Will you come here a moment, please?"

She went down the room toward him. He spoke for a moment in a low voice, his words indistinguishable to the others. She answered him, shaking her head.

"Right," Weigand said then, his voice more carrying, an edge of exasperation in it. "I can't force you. I think you should let us — " He broke off; they could see him shrug. He gathered Mullins and the precinct detective; he departed.

Pamela North announced, out of the darkness, that she didn't care what Jerry said.

"Fine," Jerry said. "In that case I'll go back to sleep."

"You!" Pam said, and turned on the light and sat up in bed; then leaned forward so she could look around the light at Jerry in the other bed. She was wearing the nightdress which had looked so attractive partially on Liza O'Brien. It was also partially on Pam North. "What do you say?" Pam demanded.

"Hel*lo*," Jerry said, looking at her.

Pam reassembled the nightdress, insofar as that was possible. She told Jerry to be serious. Why did he think everything would be all right?

"After all," Pam said, "it seldom is."

Jerry sighed; he reached for a cigarette and lighted it; he was told to throw one to Pam and did so, and pushed the lighter to her across the night table between the beds.

"Because," he said, "unless I am very much mistaken, Bill is planning to put something over. Is, specifically, setting a trap."

"With Liza as bait," Pam said. "Would you like me as bait?" She leaned forward again.

"Well," Jerry said, thoughtfully.

"Will you be serious?" Pam asked him.

"Seriously," Jerry said. "Of course not. Which is one of the reasons I think we should leave — "

"Whatever you think, we can't do that," Pam said quickly. "Because we could have insisted. We could have *made* her."

Gerald North drew deeply on his cigarette and sat up in bed.

"Listen, Pam," he said. "We asked Miss O'Brien if she wouldn't feel safer coming here with us. We said — you said — you'd feel much happier about things if she did. We insisted. And she said 'No.' And her hair's too short."

"What?" Pam North said. "*Jerry!*"

"Sauce for the gander," Jerry said. "To drag her by."

Pam looked at her husband with some suspicion. His expression was guileless.

"Some time," Pam said, "I'll take that one up. There's something wrong with it, somewhere. Do you argue we just lie here?"

Jerry didn't, he told her. He argued they should go to sleep.

"Think of something else," Pam said. "If you don't care about that poor child, who's going to do the pictures? Think of that."

"In the morning," Jerry said. But then he shook his head. "Seriously," he said, "what do you want us to do? Bill's at least as conscious of the risk as you are. It's almost certain he's taken precautions."

"Almost," Pam said. "And once when he did, a vase got broken over — oh!"

"Precisely," Jerry said. "He took precautions against a murderer. *You* broke a vase over my head. A heavy one."

"Well," Pam said, "it came out all right. And it was a good vase to get rid of. Aunt Flora would never have thrown it away. We could at least call her up."

"Listen," Jerry said. "It's" — he looked at his watch — "twelve minutes after two. After *two*. In the *morning*. Probably she's been asleep — "

"Don't say for hours," Pam advised. "After all, we came straight here. It hasn't been more than — it hasn't been half an hour."

"In ten minutes, I can go to sleep," Jerry said. "In five. On a bet, I could — " But then he looked into Pam's eyes; saw the real worry in them. "Baby," he said. "Call her, then. You won't sleep till you do."

The telephone was on the table shelf; but Liza's number was in the address book by the living room extension. Jerry got it, read off the number for Pam, watched her fingers twirl the dial. He watched her expressive face as it prepared itself for speech, saw the breath drawn in. But she did not speak. He did not need to hear the tone of ringing, repeated over and over, futilely, to know that the telephone in Liza O'Brien's apartment went unanswered. But Pamela held the telephone toward him, so that he could hear the repeated tone.

Pam replaced the receiver and handed the telephone to Jerry. Sometimes, not often, she made a mistake dialing. He read Liza's number again, dialed it carefully. He gave her plenty of time.

"Of course," he said, "she may have decided to go out again. Been hungry, gone for a sandwich."

Pam looked at him.

"All right," he said. "Let's give her — oh, ten minutes. She could have been under the shower, not heard the bell."

They gave her ten minutes. When again the telephone in Liza's apartment rang unanswered, Pam merely looked at Jerry and waited. He dialed again, this time the number of Bill Weigand's office. There was an answer, this time; no call to the office of Homicide West goes unanswered. But the answerer was not Bill Weigand, nor Mullins, nor Stein. When Jerry identified himself, there was polite elaboration of the earlier "Sorry, not in." But it was merely elaboration; it added nothing. Bill and Mullins and Stein were out;

291

probably together. The lieutenant was not at his home; when he called in, if he called in, he would be told the Norths had called. Was there another message?

"Tell him — " Jerry began, and decided it was fruitless. "Never mind," he said. "Just that I called."

He replaced the receiver. Pam was already out of bed, the nightdress sliding from her. And now Jerry, getting out of his own bed, reaching for clothes, did not protest. He did not even want to protest. They should have brought Liza home with them, should have insisted. Now he no longer believed, as he told himself he believed, that Bill had laid a trap. A trap would necessitate that Liza remain, under guard, available; that she be in an expected place, her apartment almost surely. But if she were in her apartment — free, unhurt — she would have answered her telephone.

It was not until they had found a cab, with unexpected ease, and started uptown that Jerry thought of another possibility. By then, it had been more than an hour since they had left Liza O'Brien to go alone into the apartment hotel in which she lived; had waited until she was safely walking through the big, old-fashioned lobby, about to enter the automatic elevator.

XII

Thursday, 1:45 A.M.
to 3:05 A.M.

I'm not brave, Liza O'Brien thought; I'm terribly afraid. She wanted to turn back, wanted to run through the lobby to the sidewalk, wanted to tell the Norths that it was wrong, all wrong, that she would go with them — be safe with them. Each step away from the entrance, toward the elevator which would carry her to her apartment floor, was possible only with a conscious effort; only by determining that now, once more, she would step away from safety, walk alone toward peril. If only Brian —

But she could not turn to Brian now, could not turn to anyone. That was in the bargain. It was the bargain that she was stubborn and unafraid; incapable of foreseeing danger, or imagining terror. She went into the small elevator and closed the door behind her and was solitary in the moving box, obedient now to the pressure of her finger. (As it will be to any

293

finger, so that anyone may come.) Liza O'Brien, small and young and frightened, wanted to beat on the wall of the box, wanted to scream through it. But there was no danger while she was in the moving box.

What was almost panic passed, had passed when the car stopped at her apartment floor. It was only momentary, Liza told herself; the first plunge was all that was hard. Walking away alone from Pam and Jerry North, from their offer of safety — that had been hard. And really, of course, there was no danger. That was part of the bargain too. She walked down the corridor to her apartment door, fingering in her purse for the key. Party of the first part covenants with party of the second part that — that — that what? It will be stopped in time? That party of the first part is almost sure it can be; will do everything possible to see it is? For — how did it go? — good and valuable consideration? Was that it? If the contract is duly fulfilled, if there are no acts of God, nothing which could not be anticipated, then tomorrow will be like, will be almost like — She had to remember back Monday had been a good day; a fine day. She had made sketches of cats and they had come out well. Tomorrow would be like Monday, if she were good and brave, and there were no act of God,

294

nothing which could not have been allowed for. It would be all over tomorrow.

That was the consideration, good and valuable. Not that it was promised so; nobody had undertaken that tomorrow would be like Monday. That was the interpretation of her own mind; the deep certainty of her own mind. Nothing they found out tonight, if they found out anything, could touch Brian; it would be all right for Brian. (Essentially all right for Brian; it was not to be supposed that any solution would leave any of them, for a long time to come, carefree; murder is no localized infection; murder spreads far. Afterward, even for those on the perimeter of its contagion, there is a time of convalescence.)

Liza opened the door of her apartment and went in, making her movement confident, making her body deny its fright. (It was too soon; far too soon. Nothing could happen for a long time yet; for hours yet. Now she only rehearsed assurance.) She switched on the lights, and closed the door behind her. She put the chain on the door. (It must not look too easy; it must not be impossible. That was the bargain.) The little living room was as she had left it, and she was surprised to find that there was evidence she had left hurriedly. What had she been doing when, so many hours ago, Brian had finally telephoned? Had she been reading the magazine which now sprawled on the floor by the chair and tossed it there, heedlessly, when she went across the little room to the telephone? Or had it been the drawing pad, as carelessly thrown onto the sofa, so that some of the sheets were bent back, she had discarded when she heard the telephone bell?

Liza stood for a moment inside the door and looked at the room and said to herself, you've got it bad, my girl. You've got it very, very bad.

The kitchenette was in a closet at her left and she opened the door and looked into it, hardly realizing that looking into it was a precaution. The inadequate alcove, with everything compacted into something else, was orderly. She went down the living room, toward its window, and around the corner into the bedroom, which paralleled the living room, had full possession of the other window, had the bathroom behind it. She had certainly been in a dither that afternoon while she waited for Brian to call. She had spilled bathpowder and then walked in it, so that tracks led to a chair, on which she apparently had sat to put on stockings. Anyway, she thought, looking at the footprints, the girl had nice arches. They can always say that about her. Liza O'Brien came to a bad end, but she had nice arches.

That's the way to do it, she told herself. Be flippant; you are young and gay. (*Oh, Brian! Oh, darling! I'm so afraid!*)

She straightened the bedroom somewhat, went back to the living room and looked at it irresolutely. What did she do now? Oh, yes — now she was to behave as usual; now she was not to worry. Well, her usual behavior at this hour was to go to bed. That much of it, at any rate, she could do.

She lowered the venetian blinds at the living room and bedroom windows, turning the slats so that air could enter while privacy was assured. She undressed, hanging her clothes up neatly; much more neatly than usual (Liza O'Brien came to a bad end, but she was a neat girl.) She remembered that her grandmother had always stressed the importance of neat underthings, because one never knew when one might be in an accident. Well, Liza thought, that was one way to look at it. Liza stepped into the stall shower and let the water plunge on her; shut out the world and the world's sounds. She left the shower reluctantly. She dried, dusted herself (she might as well smell nice too, while she was about it) and remade her face. Really, she thought, I *ought* to do all these things every night. After this I — She stopped suddenly, holding lipstick to her lips, not moving it. My eyes are so frightened, she thought; so terribly frightened.

She put on a long, close-fitting robe and zipped it up the front; she drew the belt tight about her waist. It had been a long time now since she got home, she thought; perhaps nothing was going to happen after all. She took her watch from the chest and looked at it as she clipped it on her wrist. It had been only about half an hour since she had walked away from the Norths into the lobby of the building. It was twenty minutes after two.

She looked at the bed; she even turned the covers back. But she could not make herself get into it. In bed, one is defenseless. It is easy to die in bed. She went into the living room and, at the moment she entered it, the buzzer of the apartment door sounded. It was raucous, insistent. Involuntarily, Liza lifted both hands to her throat, the fists clenched. She could feel the blood of the neck arteries pulsing against her knuckles. Now —

I am not to seem frightened; I am to seem surprised. I am to deny, but not so I will be believed. I am to manage to leave the door

chain — I must reset the catch on the door —
I must —

She walked to the door and opened it
against the chain, cautiously. With the chain
on it opened a few inches.

"Yes?" Liza O'Brien said. She had the
word ready, the tone ready — the tone of surprise, of slight annoyance; the tone which
would indicate only that she was tired and had
had a day, was on her way to bed, wanted no
callers. The word came out as it had been
formed to come out before her mind caught
up, the identity of the caller became clear.
"*No!*" Liza said then. "Oh — *no!*"

There hadn't been enough time, not nearly
enough for an adequate job. If any profession-
als were involved, they would spot it instantly,
have it out in no time. It might, one could
hope it would, be a different matter with only
amateurs concerned. One could hope that this
would, as the lieutenant was betting, wind it
up quickly, before anyone else got hurt. One
could hope — Sergeant Stein could hope, sitting in a commandeered room, at a strange
desk, earphones clamped over his head —
that the one they were after was as stupid as
the lieutenant assumed; as the lieutenant
insisted he all along had proved himself to be.

That was one of the reasons the lieutenant wanted it wound up quickly, on the theory that stupid murderers are dangerous, are of any the most dangerous.

Stein looked at his notes.

"0151, L.O. in."

"0152 — 0201, moves around apartment, apparently straightens up."

"0201, leaves living room, apparently to bedroom. Bad pickup."

You can't do a decent job without time; can't even cover an apartment as small as that without time. Stein had left the theater before the others; he and the technicians had worked fast. Still there were, there had to be, dead spots. He had been able to hear the girl faintly as she moved in the bedroom; had gone into the bathroom. The sound of the shower had come through better.

"0216 — telephone rings. Not answered. L.O. in shower."

It had been a toss-up whether she would hear the telephone; it was not surprising, not alarming, that she had not. But Detective Sergeant Stein had been relieved when he had again heard movement in the apartment. The whole thing was ticklish, although it was pretty certain they had it covered. Certainly there has been no one in the apartment when the girl had gone in; certainly no one had come in since unseen — and unheard.

"0216 — door buzzer."

"Here," Stein said. "Get on it." He waited until the police stenographer was seated, then pulled the headset off, watched it go, fast, on the other's head. "O.K.," the stenographer said. "Got it." He pulled a pad toward him.

"Taking the chain off the door," he said, at the same time making the hieroglyphics of his craft.

"I hope to God she remembers to leave it off," Stein said. "*And* remembers the catch."

The stenographer held up his hand for silence.

"Sounds surprised as hell," he said. "Said 'Yes?' as if she were just a little put out. Then said 'No — oh, no!' as if she were surprised as hell. Wait a minute."

He twisted one receiver away from his ear, and Stein leaned down to put his own ear to it. He listened a moment. Then he said he'd be damned.

"Get it all," he said, put the receiver back against the stenographer's ear, and reached for a telephone. What, he wondered, was the lieutenant going to make of this?

"I say you've *got* to," Brian Halder told

Liza. He had come in; she had let him in. She shrank back and let him in, and color drained out of her face. He did not seem to notice this at first; he was filled with his own anger, insulated by it. "I don't care what you agreed."

"Nothing," she said, but her voice was thin with fright. "I don't know what you mean, Brian."

He paid no attention. He seemed to Liza even taller than usual; it seemed to her that a kind of violence emanated from him — from his face, his voice.

"Get dressed," he said. "I'll get you out of here. Before — " He stopped. "Whatever you know," he said. "Whatever it would prove. The point's to get you out." He reached forward and took her shoulders. They resisted, her whole body tried to shrink away.

"Don't," she said. "Don't, Brian!"

Still he was oblivious to what she said; still insulated by his seeming anger, by his own determination.

"Get dressed," he repeated, still in the same harsh voice. "I'll take you somewhere. You can't stay here. Wait for — "

"Please," she said. "Please listen, Brian. What is it? What do you mean?"

She was to wait; someone would come. She

was to wait. And Brian came. She tried to pull herself away.

"What do you want?" she said, and now she looked up at him. "Why did you come here?"

"To get you away," he said. "Good God, what do you think?"

"I don't know anything," she said. "I tell you I — I don't know anything."

That was not the way she was supposed to say it; that was what she was supposed to say, but not that way of saying it. She was to hesitate, to sound as if — But this was Brian. *This was Brian!*

"Nobody believes that," he said. "Can't you understand? Nobody. The police don't. Weigand made that clear enough."

"He — " Liza began, and then she stopped. But the bargain — what was the bargain? This was Brian.

"He was pretending," Liza said. "It was the way he planned it."

For an instant, then, Brian Halder seemed to listen. She saw his eyes go quickly around the room, take in the room — its single door, its window far above the street. He laughed, shortly.

"I came here," he said. "Nobody stopped me. If I — if I were the one who needed to, you see what I could do." His hands were still on her shoulders. He shook her, his fingers biting into her. He looked at his hands. "It could be your throat," he said. "What could anybody do?"

The man outside the door, bending to the lock, worked with infinite slowness, infinite care. He looked up at Bill Weigand, standing over him.

"Got it," he said, his lips forming the words almost without sound. "Do we?"

"No," Weigand's moving head told him. Weigand bent, spoke into the man's ear. The man looked doubtful, said, as softly, "I can try."

Patiently, slowly, so that the door made no sound, he pushed it open, only inches open. He could reach a finger in then and press the button which released the catch. He pulled the door closed again. The resetting of the lock had made the slightest of sounds, the closing door made none. "She remembered the chain, anyway," the man said, and stood up. Weigand nodded. There was no use regretting that she had not remembered the latch. She had been surprised. So, Bill Weigand admitted to himself, had he. But he should not have been.

The telephone bell rang. It was shrill, absurdly loud, in the tiny living room. Liza moved, seeking to turn toward the telephone, but the strong fingers on her shoulders only tightened.

"No," Brian said. "Let it ring, Liza."

His hands were heavy, they would not let her move.

"Whoever it is will think you've gone," Brian said. "That's the best way."

The bell continued to ring. It stopped; started again. But now Liza O'Brien did not try to move toward it, did not try to resist the hands which held her. It didn't matter; nothing mattered. Mind and body both went limp. All that mattered was that it had been Brian who came — came filled with anger and violence, trying to get her to go away somewhere, came to put hands heavily on her shoulders, tell her how easily hands could move to a throat. There had been heavy hands, strong hands, on the throat of the little man whose eyes once had been so bright, the little man who had known too much. Well — if it was to be this way, to be Brian, nothing mattered enough to fight. It —

"That's better," Brian Halder said. "You make sense now. You're — " But then something in her attitude, her limpness in his hands, seemed to reach him, and he stopped abruptly and looked down at her. She should not look at him. That she could do; she could avoid looking at him. She could know it was Brian, but she did not have to see it was Brian. The hands could be merely hands, heavy, hurting. In the end it might even seem that they were not Brian's hands.

"Liza!" he said. "You're shaking!"

She would not look at him, would not answer him. The telephone was no longer ringing.

"What the hell's the matter with you?" Brian demanded. There was a strange note in his voice now. One might have thought something about her surprised him. "Liza!" he said again. His voice was not raised, but it seemed as if he were shouting at her. "What the — " He stopped again. "For God's sake!" he said. "You don't — "

He shook her as if she were asleep and must be wakened. Again, insistently, he repeated her name.

"Why," he said, "you thought — !" Suddenly his hands dropped from her shoulders. And then she looked at him.

"My God!" he said, standing in front of her, looking down at her. "My God, Liza!" He moved as if to touch her, but his hands fell back to his sides. "You thought I — " he said, and seemingly could not, still could not, put into words what she had thought.

It was hard to stand alone, to look up at him, to hear the note in his voice of unbelieving surprise, of defeat. For a moment, so complete was the change, so utterly had everything become different, one tension been superseded by another, Liza was only strangely helpless. Even horror can be a bulwark; one can cling even to fear. But then new emotions came, mixed, confused. Relief was one of them, and something beyond that — hope beginning again. And with this there was the beginning of a kind of heat, almost anger. Why you! she thought of Brian. Why — *you!*

"You were afraid of me," Brian told her. "After everything — you were afraid — again!"

She was shaking more than ever now; now she wanted his hands. Now she hated his hands.

"You were the one who came," she said. "It was *you!*"

"Before someone else did," he said, and now his voice was dull.

"What did you think I'd think?" she said. "You were the one who — "

307

"You thought I came to kill you," he said, in the same dull voice. "Or to take you away somewhere and — I don't know." He shook his head slowly. "I'll never know what you think," he said. "You think I killed Dad, Sneddiger — could hurt you. *You.*"

She was not shaking now.

"You come here and grab me," she said. "You — you talk about choking me. You order me around. You ask a lot."

"Too much," he agreed. There was the beginning of bitterness in his voice. "Too damn much. Evidently. You thought I hit you at the — "

"Keep still!" she said. "Keep still! You frighten me. The bottom falls out. And it's *my* fault. My fault."

Her voice was bright with anger. She wanted to put her arms around him, hold him tight. She wanted to hit him in the face — to hold his face between her hands and kiss his lips — to touch his eyelids gently with her fingers — to shake him until his teeth rattled.

"Damn it all," she said, "I love you — you — you!" There was no word. She shook her head. "You enormous fool."

Suddenly she was closer to him.

"*You!*" she said, and began to beat his chest

with her fists. It made her hands hurt. It was fine.

And the buzzer sounded.

The commandeered room was just across the hall. Stein stood at the door, now. The door was inconspicuously open. He turned, held up a hand just as the stenographer with the headset spoke, in a low voice, to Bill Weigand. Weigand had just said, "Right," into a telephone. "She just called him a fool. An 'enormous' fool." The adjective became a quotation, its choice admittedly puzzling.

"Maybe he is," Weigand said. "On the other hand — "

Then Stein's gesture stopped him. He moved quickly to join the tall, dark sergeant.

"0237 — door buzzer," the police stenographer wrote on a pad, in long hand. He poised the pencil over his notebook.

"Damn," Bill Weigand said. "I hope they have sense enough to — " He stopped, because the door across the hall was opening. It opened only a few inches, evidently was stopped by the chain.

"Yes?" Liza O'Brien said. Her tone held just the planned combination of surprise, minor irritation, tentative rejection. She looked through the door's opening at the broad, the substantial, man standing in the corridor. "Why," she said. "Mr. Whiteside."

Whiteside did not seem matter of fact now. There was anxiety on his face and in his voice.

"You're all right?" he said, and then, before she could answer, "Thank God for that."

"What is it?" she said, and kept, carefully kept, the note of surprised enquiry in her voice. "I don't understand."

"I've got to talk to you," Whiteside said. "I came as soon as I could. Before —" He stopped, as if he had almost said too much. "Before anyone else," he said. He looked at her, looked at the door. "You must listen," he told her, and put his hand on the door.

"Well," she said, "it's terribly late." Now there was hesitancy in her voice, uncertainty. But when he looked at her and waited, she slipped the chain from the door and opened it, slowly. Raymond Whiteside looked up and down the hall; he went in quickly. Inside he closed the door, he looked around the room rapidly, as if making sure they were alone.

"No one's come?" he said. "You're sure? Or — or tried to reach you?"

"No," she said. "Why?"

"And the police?" he said. "They're not

watching you? Doing anything to — to take care of you?"

Now there was a note of incredulity in his voice and as she shook her head, he said, slowly, "My God! Don't they realize?"

Again she said she did not know what he meant.

"You know something," he said. "At least, the police are certain you do and so is sh — so is the one who's — responsible for all this. All this — " He stopped and shook his head slowly. "And the lieutenant — this Weigand — does nothing to protect you."

"But I don't know anything," Liza said. "I keep telling everyone that."

She had drawn back into the room, but was still standing, holding the blue robe about her. Yet she was oddly unafraid, and it was not only because Brian was in the bedroom, was near, could come quickly. It was chiefly that there was nothing frightening about Lieutenant Colonel Whiteside, standing in front of her, not trying to move nearer her, a look on his face which was more of concern, of anxiety, than, remotely, of threat.

"Perhaps you don't," he said. "I realize that, Miss O'Brien. Or — perhaps you have already told the police?" He waited for her to answer.

"What?" she said. "What could I? I don't *know* anything. What does everybody think I know?"

"Sneddiger must have known something," Whiteside said. "That was why my — why he was killed. And you were with him. It would be natural for him to tell you what he knew. To hint at it."

She shook her head again. She made the gesture weary.

"You told the police everything you knew?" he insisted. "Or — everything you remembered?"

"Yes," she said, and sighed as if she had said all this too often before.

He looked at her steadily,

"I almost believe you," he said. "I'd — I'd like to, Miss O'Brien. There's been so much of this already. But you see what a chance it would be. How dangerous." He moved his head slowly, doubtfully. "For you, I mean, of course," he said. "Because, whatever I believed, it would never be possible to be sure that — that others would believe you. You see what I mean?"

"No," she said.

"I want to stop all this," Whiteside said. "I've been trying to without — " He broke off again. "It's very difficult," he said. "You

can't understand how difficult, Miss O'Brien.
How much is involved. But I can't let things
go on. I realized that tonight." He seemed to
interrupt himself. "I mean, of course, that
you were in danger as long as you were
thought to know something. And that nothing you said would convince her."

"Her?" Liza said.

"I didn't mean to say that," he said. "The
— the one who killed poor Halder. And then
Sneddiger." He looked at her steadily. "Whatever you guess, Miss O'Brien, I can't — it's
hard enough. Desperately hard." He seemed
to try to smile. "You're very young, my dear,"
he said. "You see things differently. More
simply. But I can't be the one. And I have to
try — " He seemed to find talking very difficult. He was no longer, Liza thought, the substantial man he had been, the assured man.
He was, she thought, very troubled, and now,
slowly, it had become clear why he was so desperately troubled, why he tried to imply so
much and yet avoid the words, and most of all
the name, which would be irretrievable.

"We haven't a right to ask anything," he
said. "Not that you conceal anything. I realize
that. But — " he shook his head sadly — "one
always wants time. Keeps on hoping for
something. That's partly why I came, I sup-

pose. But chiefly it was for your sake. To see that you aren't harmed. You see — the one I'm talking about isn't home now. I don't know where she is. I was afraid — "

Once again he broke off; once again he started over.

"Won't you go away for a time?" he said. "For your own safety? To give me time? Perhaps, later, you'll remember there was something — something Sneddiger said, something you saw. Then, of course, I'd expect you to come back at once, go to the police. I'd — I'd be able to see that nothing happened to you. Will you do that?"

He seemed to be entreating her. She seemed to hesitate.

"Only for a few days," he said. "Until I — can make certain arrangements. Of course, I'll take you wherever you want to go. Put you on a train — a plane. You'll be safe tonight."

Now for the first time he moved toward her. Then he stopped and looked beyond her and, from behind her, Brian Halder spoke. She turned at the sound of his voice.

"It won't be necessary, Raymond," Brian said. His voice was harsh again. "You and I together can — take care of Miss O'Brien."

And then, as if the words were spoken at that instant, not hours before — now, not when she and Brian were in the shop, with Halder's body still twisted in the pen — she heard Brian Halder say, "I'll take care of Sneddiger." No, not quite that. "I'll take care of Felix."

It was at almost the moment their taxicab stopped in front of the Murray Hill apartment house that things fell into place for Pamela North; it was as if, she thought, I dropped something and, instead of breaking, it came together. As if I dropped the pieces and got the whole.

"Jerry!" Pam said. "They don't *yelp!*" There was triumph in her voice, and she turned to look at Jerry. He halted in the movement of pulling his billfold from his hip pocket and looked at her, his face blank. "Don't you see?" Pam demanded. Jerry started to shake his head. But Pam was reaching for the door handle.

"Soon's that other hack pulls out I can — " the driver said, but by that time Pam had the door open and was starting to get out. By that time, Jerry was pushing a bill at the driver.

They were just in time to see Mrs. Raymond Whiteside, bareheaded, her white hair still coifed high, still undisturbed, go into the apartment house door. The cab which had brought her, which momentarily had stopped the Norths' cab, pulled out.

"Jerry," Pam said, and began to walk very rapidly toward the entrance. "Hurry."

But the bill had been a five; the driver was slow with change. Pam, not hearing Jerry's steps, stopped, turned back. "Oh," she said. "Hurry!" Jerry hurried.

But when they were inside the lobby, Mrs. Whiteside was just closing behind her the door of the automatic elevator. As they hurried toward it, it started to ascend, the indicator above it moving slowly, majestically, toward the right of its arc.

There was another elevator. But the door was wedged open, the inner metal gate locked closed.

"We'll have — " Jerry began, but Pam was already hurrying toward the stairs.

"No time," she said. "Come *on!*"

Jerry North went on.

"What floor?" Pam called back, her heels clicking on metal treads of the fire stairs.

Jerry had remembered to look up the suite number before they left. He remembered it now.

"Five J," he said. "My God!"

The stairs turned at a landing. The Norths climbed, Pam still leading. To Jerry, following, she seemed to be clicking as rapidly as ever. They reached another landing, this one with a door marked "2" — free-handedly, in white paint — and Jerry said, "Pam!" It was as much a gasp as speech; the m-sound escaped in a small, helpless puff. Pam North kept on going. At the next landing Jerry gained a little; could almost reach out and touch her. But then the steps began again, and Pam still clicked brightly. What I need, Jerry thought, is — but then he found that even thinking in words winded him.

The third floor landing was crucial, Jerry decided. If he couldn't reach her then, stop this mad clicking ascent, he would merely have to lie down and wait — wait presumably, until Pam, unconscious from her exertions, rolled down on top of him. And on the third floor landing, one hand reached Pam's shoulder. She looked around; she was breathing quickly; her eyes were bright.

"Jerry!" she said. "Are you all right?"

Jerry held on; told her he was not all right; more by pushing than by directions he was able to gasp out, got her through the door into a third floor corridor. It took them a time, then, to find the elevator. But, pressed for, the elevator came almost at once, and almost at once carried them up. Jerry tried to tell

Pam he had tried to tell her. For the most part, he devoted himself to breathing.

The elevator stopped and Pam popped out and said rapidly, "A-B-C-D-E-F-G — " She looked up and down the corridor. "This way," she said, with enthusiasm and confidence, and started off. Jerry tried to ask her to wait a minute, and started after her.

He caught her standing in front of a door, looking at it. The door said "5-M."

"A-B-C-D-E-F-G-H-I-J we've come too far," Pam said, with great rapidity. "What comes before M? A-B-C-D — "

"For heaven's sake," Jerry said. "L."

"What?" Pam said, in surprise. "Oh — I thought you said — "

"I know," Jerry said. "Why do you go all the way through it each time?"

"I always do," Pam said. "I have to get a running start. Otherwise — *Jerry*. We can't just *stand* here! It must be the other way."

She started off the other way. They went rapidly past the automatic elevator, which remained where they had left it. It seemed to Jerry North that, behind its glass-panelled door, the elevator was leering at them.

"A," Pam said, looking at the first door. Now we're — " She started off without finishing. She reached the end of the corridor and

"B" and turned sharply right.

"Pam," Jerry said. "Wait a minute. We were right before. L next and then K and then — "

But Pam was going on, passing doors, saying in a low, hurried voice, "A-B-C-D-E — " After a time it was necessary to turn right again and then there were merely windows on their left and no doors of any kind. Pam stopped.

"They've run out!" Pam said. "This is the maddest thing, Jerry."

"Go on," Jerry said. "It runs around the elevator shafts, probably around a court. Only, if we'd gone *down* the alphabet instead of *up*."

"What on earth?" Pam asked him.

It had sounded clear enough to Jerry when he said it; now he realized that it baffled explanation — that some time, in the quiet future, if they had one, it would continue to baffle explanation, that — in some strange and uncanny fashion — they had now, finally, managed to become hopelessly entangled in the alphabet.

"Go on," Jerry said, and gave Pam a slight push. "It'll be all right. Incidentally — where are we going? I mean, *why* are we going?"

"The dog wouldn't have yelped," Pam

319

said. "It's as clear as anything. Whimpered, maybe; even growled. His name didn't have anything to do with it."

"Oh," Jerry said. But Pam had started on.

"A-B-C-D-E — " Pam North said, came to the end of the corridor and turned sharply to the right. "Oh, good — F. A-B-C-D-E-F — "

"G-H-I — " Jerry said, entering into the spirit of it.

"So of course he was kicked," Pam said, and then, suddenly slowing, suddenly making her voice small, "Here's I."

"Here's — " Jerry began, and then said, "Oh, of course." His voice, also, was lowered. Apartment 5-J was, clearly, next. Pam had stopped. She turned to Jerry, looked up at him. "You see," she said, "Bill *isn't* here. So — come on."

She went on. As she pushed open the door of Apartment 5-J — pushed confidently, as if inevitably it would open — Jerry tried to get ahead of her. He did not succeed. But he went into the living room almost as she did, and stopped as quickly.

Pam North stopped because Mrs. Raymond Whiteside, still a dowager for dignity, her piled white hair still unruffled, was standing a little apart from the others in the room — from her husband, from Liza O'Brien, from Brian Halder, standing tall with his face darkly angry, near the small, frightened girl. Liza's face was white, her eyes enormous; looking at her, one could see her trembling.

The three of them were gazing at Mrs. Whiteside who had in her right hand a rather substantial black automatic. The gun was incongruous in her hand; the lacquered nails ridiculous against its butt. As the Norths came in the two men looked at them quickly, startled, then back at Mrs. Whiteside. Liza did not seem to be looking at anything.

"Well," Mrs. Whiteside said. "Really!" Her tone questioned the propriety, the good breeding, of so abrupt an entrance. She moved the automatic so that they would be sure to see it; would notice that they, too, were in its range.

"Well," Mrs. Whiteside said, making no further comment on the Norths, "are you coming?"

It was difficult to tell which of the three she was addressing. She seemed to speak to all of those who had been in the room when the Norths entered.

"Barbara!" Whiteside said. His voice had risen almost an octave. "Barbara. You mustn't try —"

"Be quiet, Raymond," Mrs. Whiteside said.

321

"There's been enough of this. Are you coming?"

And now it was apparent that she was speaking not to Liza O'Brien, not to the tall young man who had, imperceptibly, moved closer to the girl, but to her husband. And it was apparent that the tension, the attention drawn remorselessly taut, was between the two.

Jerry felt a hand pressing hard against his side, making him move away from the door, and moved in response to the command, without finding it surprising, almost without knowing that he moved. He had eyes — they all had eyes — only for the slowly lifting automatic. And then —

Then Brian Halder moved suddenly, had Liza in his arms, whirled with her there so that his back was to the white-haired woman, his body between the girl and the gun. Liza started to scream as he touched her, then seemed to go limp in his arms. Then Raymond Whiteside, moving more quickly than seemed possible, lunged toward his wife, grabbing for her hand, for the automatic in her hand. He moved so rapidly that Mrs. Whiteside seemed only astonished; the expression on her face was, in the instant before he closed with her, began to struggle with her, one of unutterable surprise.

She did not seem to struggle, to make any great effort to retain the weapon. That Jerry North thought, as he moved again — was moved, this time by a strong hand against his shoulder, heard Bill Weigand's voice say, loudly, "All right, drop it!"

But Whiteside did not seem to hear Weigand. He fought, with a kind of desperation, for the automatic in his wife's hand and then, when it seemed he almost had the gun free, it was discharged and the little room roared with sound. He stepped back as his wife fell, let the automatic fall between them.

Then, almost at the same instant, he was on the floor beside Barbara Whiteside, saying her name over and over, his voice uncertain, anguished. For the first moments he was oblivious to everyone; then he looked up.

"Get someone," he said. "For God's sake — she didn't mean — "

His suffering was terrible to watch, Pam thought. Whatever his wife had done, he had loved her. To have it end thus, so terribly, so differently than he had planned when he had risked his life to keep her from again — oh, Pam thought, we were such fools, so slow.

She touched her cheekbones with her fingertips, in an involuntary gesture, as if she were about to cry. She watched Bill move into the room, put a hand on the shoulder of the broken man. There was little, now, one could do for him, but Bill was doing all —

"Get up, Whiteside," Bill Weigand said, and his voice was cold, without expression. "You can quit that now and get up."

Raymond Whiteside turned, looked up at Bill Weigand.

"Right," Weigand said. "That's the way it is, Colonel. You're all washed up. You can save this sort of thing for the jury."

Raymond Whiteside's face seemed slowly to gape open. *And mine must be,* Pam North thought, and the fingers of her left hand moved, of themselves, to touch her lips.

"Right," Bill Weigand said again, and now he seemed to be lifting the substantial lieutenant colonel to his feet. "Halder — Sneddiger — perhaps your wife, Colonel. The attack on Miss O'Brien. It's quite a list, Colonel." Weigand put both hands on Whiteside's shoulders and completed lifting him with a sudden jerk. "Get the hell out of the way," Weigand said. "Let them get to her."

But Mullins was already kneeling beside Mrs. Whiteside, working quickly, deftly. He looked up after a moment. "Maybe," he said.

"I wonder if she'll want to," Bill Weigand

said, slowly. "Come on, Whiteside. Let's get going."

"Oh!" said Pamela North.

XIII

Even now, sitting in the Norths' living room, sketching the Norths' major cat, Liza O'Brien found memories difficult to sort out, felt as if she had, as nearly as anything she could think of, fallen over a cliff. It had all been that sudden, that meaningless. If she had fallen she had been caught; evidently she had been caught. But not even about that was there real assurance.

She had not quite fainted when Brian seized her; she could hardly tell, even now, looking back, whether she had come so near to fainting because of terror or relief or — when you came down to it — mere surprise. She thought Brian had touched her face gently, tenderly, as he held her, after the gun had gone off; she thought she could remember, as from a long way distant, the voices of Weigand and the others, of Raymond Whiteside. (His voice, at the very last, had gone suddenly high and

326

shrill.) And she had been there — surely she had been there still? — when men with a stretcher came and lifted Mrs. Whiteside onto it and carried her out. But all of it was misty, as if the air had fogged against both sight and hearing.

Strangely enough, the thing clearest in her memory was Pam North's voice, and Pam was speaking in the taxicab which brought them to the Norths' apartment, where nowadays she seemed always, somewhat inexplicably, to be coming.

"But he *wouldn't* have yelped," Pam was saying, in this clearest of Liza's memories. "Don't you *see?* So it *had* to be her."

She remembered the tone of Pam North's voice, which was one of entire astonishment.

The next thing Liza — now putting in the delicate tracery of a whisker — could remember clearly was Pam North's again bringing her breakfast in the small guest room and telling her, surprisingly, that it was almost two o'clock; saying, in answer to what must have been a look of disbelief in Liza's eyes, that nevertheless, that was the time it was.

"They're doing something about the colonel," Pam had said, putting down the breakfast. "Indicting him, I think. It seems they were sitting, so it was a good time."

The few hours since then were clear enough, if uneventful. "They" had promised to come back as soon as they could. "Yes," Pam said, "Brian too. He's with them." She had smiled quickly then. "He's all right, you know," she said. "He was trying to keep you from getting shot, because at the moment nobody knew quite what was happening and, anyway, you can't tell about guns."

And Mrs. Whiteside, still alive, likely to live — "if she wants to," Pam interpolated — was in a hospital and her husband was in jail, and a good deal more than likely to remain there. But beyond that, Pam North had not seemed a great deal clearer than Liza was herself.

"Apparently," Pam said, after Liza had breakfasted and showered, come into the living room, begun to watch the cats, "apparently he was the one who killed everybody. But I must say it's confused as far as I'm concerned. Because I thought it had to be *Mrs.* Whiteside. Oh — "

Pam stopped then and, after a pause, said, "Of course. He saw him see it. I knew it had to be the dog."

But she had not gone on from there; had said it was still confused, and they might as well get it straight from Bill, who would be there any minute. But a good many minutes had passed without Bill Weigand, and after a time, because Martini seemed today entirely agreeable to sit within view, Liza had begun to sketch, using typewriter paper and a stub of a soft pencil.

Then — just as Liza realized there was something wrong with the tracery of whisker; that you didn't really *see* a cat's whiskers that way — they came. Bill Weigand and Jerry North came and Liza O'Brien knew this vaguely, and saw Brian. And Brian saw her, because he walked across to where she was sitting and looked down at her, his face, his eyes, strangely questioning. For a second she looked up at him, her own eyes dark (for that instant her mind, too, shadowed) with uncertainty, and then all that vanished and she stood up and was holding herself tight against him in the fragment of an instant before his arms closed about her, and held her tighter still. And then Liza O'Brien sighed deeply — so deeply, so revealingly, that for a moment she felt her face flushing, and pressed it even more anxiously against Brian's chest. But nobody seemed to be paying any attention to them, and after the first second Liza realized it did not matter at all who paid attention, or how much.

Jerry was mixing drinks, then, and Bill Weigand was on the telephone, saying "at Pam and Jerry's, come on" in a voice which meant, to a now partially disengaged Liza, that he was talking to somebody he loved. That was fine, she thought; that was beautiful, and smiled up at Brian and pressed his hands, asking him to know how beautiful it was — everything was. She thought he did. Then suddenly he grinned at her and said, in a voice only for her, "I ought to slap your funny little face."

"Of course," Liza said. "Any time. Always." Then she decided she must be getting a little hysterical, and further disengaged herself, although without letting go of Brian. Then they found a part of a sofa which was the right size for two people who wanted to sit as closely as possible together.

"All right," Pamela North said, when the drinks were distributed. "Why was I wrong, Bill? Because I thought it was Mrs. Whiteside. Because she must have been the one who kicked the dog."

Bill Weigand looked incredibly tired; so, Liza saw now, did Brian and, almost equally, Jerry North. Apparently none of them had slept until two in the afternoon. Probably Weigand had not slept at all.

"He was always more likely," Bill said. "The thing which set it off worked for both. And Sneddiger was strangled." He paused. "By hand," he said. "Her hands might have done it — but her nails would have cut the skin. The skin wasn't broken. Also, if there's an alternative, I'm inclined to doubt children murdering parents. By premeditation. It happens, of course. It doesn't often happen. But it *was* the dog, of course."

"It yelped," Pam said. "And from where he sat he could see the top of the stairs. I realized that when I sat there. You could see the people in the foyer. But you could also see up the stairs."

"Right," Bill said.

"Would it be all right," Jerry North asked, starting around with a shaker, "if we lapsed into English? Temporarily? For Miss O'Brien's sake?"

Pam looked momentarily surprised, but the others laughed, and they were still smiling when the door buzzer sounded and Jerry let Dorian Weigand in. She told them it all seemed very jolly, and asked where her drink was, and then said hello to the cats, who remained, in spite of what they evidently regarded as a throng of humans. Dorian got her drink and found a place to sit — a place beside Liza, whose shoulder she patted gently, as if in approval.

Then everyone looked at Weigand.

"The grand jury returned a true bill," he said. "Charge, attempted murder of Mrs. Whiteside. That will hold him; that will be superseded, of course. Murder first on Halder; same on Sneddiger. As I told him, there's plenty. If necessary, we can add assault with intent on Miss O'Brien. Even simple assault on Pine, where there wasn't any intent, I imagine. He's not admitting anything; he's got a lawyer." He shook his head. "As a matter of fact," he said, "the D.A. doesn't think it's going to be easy. Neither do I. It'll be all bits and pieces, a little here, a little there. And if he hadn't, in the end, tried too hard to do just that, he might have been able to hang it on his wife. But then, all along he tried too hard."

"From the beginning," Dorian Weigand said. "Please, Bill."

But Bill looked at Pam North.

"The beginning was the dog who yelped," Pam said. "Mrs. Whiteside said she merely lifted it off a bed, put it out of a room. But it yelped, and they do when they're kicked. Or stepped on, of course. And as soon as he yelped, he came down the stairs. *And*, from where he was sitting, Mr. Halder could look up the stairs and see — well, whose foot it was."

"Anyway," Bill said, "the others were all there. Mrs. Whiteside had stayed behind for something."

"Right," Pam North said. "And — wait a minute. She couldn't have seen that he had seen, because she would have been too high up." She looked at Bill Weigand. "I could make that clearer," she said. "I guess. I should have thought of that."

"She admits she — pushed Aegisthus with her foot," Bill said. "She's conscious now; ready to talk. I — I rather think she will. She was trying to rescue her husband there at the end; get him out of it, give him a chance to run. He tried to kill her for her pains, while pretending to struggle for a gun she was ready enough to give up — to him. She seems — well, a little annoyed about it all."

Bill Weigand paused. Unurged, he continued.

"Whiteside saw what happened, saw his father-in-law's face," Weigand said. "He knew the old man pretty well; they all did. I suppose to the old man anybody who kicked a dog was — well, peculiarly depraved. Certainly asking for punishment. Whiteside realized that; realized they were in for trouble when Halder got up abruptly and left probably looking like — " He hesitated.

"A thunderhead," Pam said.

Bill Weigand accepted it.

"Listen," Dorian said. "Is a jury supposed to understand this? Was Mr. Halder *that* eccentric?"

It was one of the problems, Bill agreed. But he thought so. The whole pattern of Halder's life had been so eccentric that any jury, almost the lowest common denominator of any jury, ought to be able to extend eccentricity to cover Halder's rage at witnessing what he no doubt considered the abuse of an animal.

"Whiteside tried to do something to fix things up," Bill said, then. "He went down to the pet shop; probably tried to calm the old man down, first. But — he went prepared. The old man was stubborn; probably told Whiteside that he was changing his will, cutting his daughter down — perhaps throwing her out entirely. Probably told Whiteside, to prove it was settled, that he had wired his lawyer. So — "

"But," Pam said, "didn't he take an awful risk? Suppose Mr. Halder had wired — oh — 'Planning to cut daughter Barbara out of will because she tried to kick dog downstairs stop will come office tomorrow stop'?"

It would. Bill agreed, appear so. But — Halder had not wired in detail, and this Whiteside had somehow found out. Presumably, Halder had repeated to him the actual content of the wire; perhaps even shown him a copy. In any event, Whiteside had had reason to feel the risk wasn't great; that it was of no importance against the certainty that his wife would be disinherited the next day.

"And — " Bill started to go on, but Pam North stopped him. Pam said, "Wait a minute," and, when Bill waited, said, "What was the hurry? Was the colonel terribly broke or — ?"

"Oh," Bill Weigand said. "No — not more than usual. He'd lived for years on his wife, who lived on her father, but he wasn't particularly broke. The hurry was that Halder would have died in a few months. The income from him would stop and, if the will change went through, the Whitesides wouldn't inherit. Halder might, actually, have died the next day — or the next week. And, somehow, Whiteside had found out about it. Probably the old man told him. We found out, of course, from the autopsy."

Pam said, "Oh."

"Quite possibly," Bill said, "Halder had summoned the family to tell them that — perhaps even to say he had decided to come home for his last few months. We'll never know. And it doesn't matter. He never got around to telling them at dinner; he may have told Whiteside that night — something like 'Don't think I'll change the will back; I won't live long enough.' So — the colonel hurried."

He had killed his father-in-law and, to make it appear suicide — "while insane, presumably" — he had put the body in the pen; put the poison left over in Halder's medicine cabinet; pressed Halder's fingers on his own hypodermic.

"The strychnine?" Jerry asked, and Bill shrugged. He said they were trying to trace it; expected to, in the end.

"At a guess," he said, "Whiteside got it a couple of years ago to kill a cat they had. At least, they had a cat and — " He looked at Brian Halder.

"A yellow cat," Brian said. "They said it died. I don't know. Come to think of it, the cat disappeared very suddenly."

"Right," Bill said. "That's hypothesis. We'll find out more. Anyway, he had it. And used it. And, at some stage in this, Felix Sneddiger looked in the window and saw him. Here again we have to assume — Sneddiger's dead, Whiteside doesn't talk. But I assume that Halder had described the members of his family, that from the description Sneddiger thought the man he had seen was Whiteside and — well, went up to be sure." Bill paused. "He found out," he said.

Sneddiger might, before he died, have insisted he had told what he knew to someone else, Bill Weigand went on. That in an effort to save his own life by making his murder useless. He didn't save his life, but he alarmed Whiteside. Later, when Whiteside found out that Sneddiger and Liza had been together when the body was found, he jumped to the conclusion that Sneddiger had talked to her.

"He didn't," Liza heard herself say. "I've kept saying he didn't."

"Right," Bill said. "Early on, I decided he hadn't. But — Whiteside couldn't take the chance. He followed you to the shop, Miss O'Brien, tried to kill you; would have if Mr. Halder" — he indicated Brian — "hadn't come back at a fortunate time. I presume he hid in the shop momentarily, ducked out when Mr. Halder went for a pillow, and hid in the passageway. I presume he was the person Mr. Halder heard — and was afraid was Pine or his mother. Or both of them." He smiled faintly as he looked at Brian Halder. "You did think that?" he said, but then said, "Never mind," before Brian had time to answer. If, Liza thought, he needed to answer. Poor Brian. Dear Brian. Again she pressed his hands. He smiled down at her.

Again Jerry North made the rounds with a cocktail shaker; Liza smiled and shook her head. The others let their glasses be filled, and Bill Weigand drank from his and went on.

"Incidentally," he said, still to Brian Halder, "you didn't drop into a bar after you found your father's body and telephoned us. You tried to find your mother. Right?" Brian merely looked at him, but failure to deny was affirmation. "Called the house, probably," Bill said. "Found she wasn't there. Tried Pine's apartment. Not there either?"

"Nobody was," Brian said. "They'd — they'd stopped by the theater to pick up Pine's mail. Fan mail." The last was ironic; Brian was not, Liza realized, likely ever to achieve enthusiastic regard for the man who was evidently to become his step-father. Poor Brian. She would have to explain to him — somehow, as time went on — that neutrality in such matters was possible; that things were not always, not necessarily, so desperate. His hands were strong, she thought then, with profound irrelevancy. . . .

Whiteside, finding that Liza had remained alive, must have been at first frightened and afterward puzzled, Bill Weigand said. He spoke slowly, formulating it in his own mind; speaking as much to clarify things for himself as to explain them to the others. No doubt, Whiteside expected Liza to tell, at once, what she knew. But when there was no evidence she had told anything, when the police did not show by action that they had new information, he was left to guess whether she really knew nothing or, knowing something, was keeping quiet for purposes of her own. Liza herself had come back by then, was listening again.

"What purposes?" she asked. "Why wouldn't I have told what I knew? Since, that is, it was about Mr. Whiteside and not — " She broke off, and flushed slightly.

"Because," Pamela North said, "he could have thought you were going to blackmail him. Because what we think about other people is because of what we know about ourselves and he would have." She paused a moment, and looked slightly worried. "Only," she said, "how do I know that about *him?* I mean if — "

"We know, Pam," Jerry told her. "It's all right. We like you anyway." He went to mix another round; the sound of ice against glass was, for a few moments, a pleasant obbligato to Bill Weigand's low voice. Then Jerry passed drinks again, and this time Liza did not refuse.

" — uncertainty," Weigand was saying. "It showed all through the last few hours. Not knowing which way to turn. The absurd attack on Pine, for example. It was supposed to complicate matters for us; gives us something difficult to fit into a logical case against Whiteside himself. Why would he try, apparently, to kill Pine? No reason. Why should Mr. Halder here?" Bill indicated Brian. "We had a choice of reasons. Mr. Halder thought Pine had killed his father and was trying to get revenge. We'd been directed to Greek tragedy — which was more or less extraneous incidentally — by Mr. Halder's father. We could think of Pine as Aegisthus — the character, not the pooch — and Mr. Halder as Orestes. Or — Pine knew something which would involve Mr. Halder, and had to be silenced. Whiteside evidently saw you two" — now he indicated both Brian and Liza — "coming from the stage door, guessed accurately you were trying to see Pine. Guessed, again

rightly, we would — find out about it. Or — "
He paused.

"Ever so many others," Pam North said.
"Brian was trying to make it appear he
thought Pine was guilty, although he was
guilty himself, which would make you think
— where was I?" she looked at her empty
glass, with something like reproach.

Most of the glasses were empty, then. And
most of it, Bill Weigand's attitude revealed,
was told. He seemed abstracted, now; he
would be, Liza thought, thinking of the next
steps, of the things which, for him, for other
detectives, for the district attorney's men,
would go on and on, far beyond this, more
intricately than this, more —

"He didn't try to kill Pine, then?" That was
Jerry North, as if from a distance.

"Right," Bill said. "No use to him dead. He
and his wife were at the theater, you know.
He left his seat after the lights were out — our
man missed that — went down the aisle to the
door Mr. Halder used later and — "

But for us it's over, Liza thought. All that
matters is over. For us it's just beginning and
there ought to be lots of time. Please, make it
lots of time for Brian and me — oh please. . . .
And then she thought, he takes things so
hard, so desperately, and there will be so

many things to understand . . . and it was such an odd way to start but now I know so much more and . . .

Why, Liza O'Brien thought, I'm going to sleep. Brian put his arm around me and I'm going to sleep. What . . . a . . . nice . . . place . . . to . . . Liza O'Brien thought.

"The nice thing about an evening with the Norths," Pam said, her voice very low, for Jerry's ear, "is that it's so stimulating."